Hospital in Sudan

ANNE VINTON

Hospital in Sudan

Originally published as Harlequin Romance #439

CRAIG

Harlequin Books

TORONTO • LONDON • NEW YORK • AMSTERDAM • SYDNEY • WINNIPEG

First published by Mills & Boon Limited
under the title *Doctor Immacula*

ISBN 0-373-00439-7

Harlequin edition published October, 1958
Reprinted 1959
1959
1962
1972

This **Harlequin's Collection** edition printed 1976

Printed in Canada

CHAPTER ONE

MAC TURNED, her blue eyes full of fun, her honey-colored hair riotous in the cool wind.

"Race you up the scree!" she challenged, and charged laughingly towards the grey slope ahead. She heard Barney's feet crunching and slithering behind her, and Rogue's excited barking, fore, aft and all around.

"You're cheating!" she shouted, as Barney forged ahead, and then as he turned to argue she whipped his stick from under his arm and yelped like Rogue as it was quickly retrieved and playfully threatened her rear.

"Oh, Barney!"

She was falling now, but without fear, for she knew Barney would be sure to catch her. He was as dependable as the rock of Gibraltar.

"Mac!"

There was something in his voice as he held her tightly, but she was heedless, gazing instead at her ankle where a slate chip had pierced.

"Blood!" she announced dramatically. "Oh, doctor, will I live?"

He helped her up the rest of the scree, dumped her on the wind-swept grass by the cairn and patiently removed her shoe while she peeled down the fine nylon of the now-ruined stocking.

Barney had a large pocket in his old tweed jacket which always yielded bandages and whatever else was needed in an emergency.

"Iodine?" she queried hopefully.

"No. Let it run freely. Bleed to death!" he told her, his eyes twinkling. Then more seriously, "It has gone rather too deeply for iodine, Mac. I think a clean dressing is the answer and let it resolve itself." Again that warmth had crept into his brown eyes.

"You know"—she was studying him with interest—"when you gaze at me like that you look just like Rogue."

"Er-ruff!" barked the clumber spaniel, hearing his name.

"We're both just a couple of old faithfuls, I expect," said Barney.

Mac glanced at him quickly, but he deftly finished the dressing and turned to look across Silverdell Valley below, a paradise in the lee of the Westmorland mountains, sea to one side, rolling, crag-dotted country to the other. It was territory to which she had introduced Barney two years ago when he had come, freshly fledged from a big city hospital, to be her father's partner. Doctor Hayes' health had been failing through overstrain, but Barney was now well established and could do the heavy work of the practice, while the older man pandered to the elderly, who resented change, and expectant mothers who had a preference for the "Old Doctor", as they affectionately called him. Barney, however, had made a niche for himself in the valley and was now accepted as an inhabitant.

Mac now took him for granted as part of Redcroft when she was home. Of a long line of physicians herself, she had not allowed her sex to turn her away from medicine, and had not only taken an M.D. in her stride during her sojourn in Edinburgh, but had added another diploma to her name after a further year of work under a Professor of Pathology, and recently had included six months spent in the study of tropical diseases and their causes before heeding her father's injunction to "Come home for some leave before you begin to look like something under a microscope yourself!"

Mac found her appetite for her job insatiable.

"Why are you content with just pottering about here, Barney?" she asked as he lit his pipe successfully with the sixth match. "I want to go on all the time learning something new. There's always a new book out or a new theory or a new drug . . . I feel I'll never know it all. Yet you practise and——" she hesitated in some embarrassment.

"And I don't know half as much as you, eh?" he finished the sentence for her.

"You know I don't mean that!"

"But you *do*, Mac. I don't mind it coming from you. Maybe I'm not so ambitious as you are—for titles. I would rather make my knowledge work. You see I was the hack student of the class in my set, and I was hopeless at exams. But the patients got to asking for me by name on the wards and that sort of inspired me. I felt a tremendous reaching

8

in myself towards humanity, and I knew I was a born G.P. with comfort more than skill in my fingers. That thought, a sort of modest dedication, helped me through my finals and here I am. Pottering about, I think you said?"

"Sorry, Barney!" Mac put her small, skilled hand on his large, comfortable one. "You have made me feel very small. I haven't thought much about humanity yet—only the filthy scourges which attack it. Of course it's all wrong. I could go on studying until I was ninety, but what a useless individual I would be with all my knowledge! I must get a job soon, I suppose, and see if I'm any good in practice!"

"Enjoy some leave first," Barney suggested.

Mac had arrived the previous evening. It was a glorious time of year to be home. The valley was bursting into spring in seventeen different shades of green: seventeen—she had counted them with Barney.

"I believe old Mrs. Jolley has a varicose ulcer?" she asked as they rose and swung into step down the long, winding track serving Silver Crag on its lee side.

"Yes," Barney agreed, puffing away at his pipe. "Would you rather hear about Mrs. Jolley's ulcer or the way I feel about you?"

Mac stopped, flushed, looked uncertain and then walked on.

"Whichever you like, Barney," she told him frankly.

"You know, don't you, Mac?"

"I know you're fond of me, Barney, and I"—she hastened on as he would have spoken—"of you. I like to think there's nothing more than fondness at the moment. I'm not prepared to let it be more"—Barney's hands hesitated in their grip of the slim shoulders and fell lamely back to his sides—"because I don't want to be distracted, Barney, dear. *Do* try to understand."

"All right, Mac. I was out of step for a moment. I'm with you again, now." He smiled broadly and offered a companionable hand-grip. "Do you know what loving is, my girl?"

"Loving is what I feel for my father. Being in love is a hopeless pain I once felt for someone in an equally hopeless situation. I don't think I could go through the hell of that again. This friendly happiness I share with you, Barney, dear, is all I want at the moment. May I have it?"

"With or without kisses?"

"Oh, I think without," she said in sudden alarm. "Kisses can bring on the other thing or—or ruin a friendship. At the moment I want emotional security."

9

"My lady's wishes are my commands. May I say my lady is looking very fetching with her wind-swept hairdo?"

"Thank you. I would curtsey, but that might disturb the clot which will by now have formed over my wound."

"I would not allow you to make such an obeisance to me."

"Oh?" her eyes twinkled up at him. "You'll have to learn to be masterful with women, Barney. The arrogant lords and masters always win in the end, you know!"

"They do?" Barney was a chunky six foot, he weighed all of fifteen and a half stone. This concentration of muscle and brawn now swept the slight girl completely off her feet, disregarded her howls of nervousness and anguish and hungrily sought her lips in an equally muscular kiss.

Almost weeping she wanted to thud with her fists against his chest as he set her own on her feet again, but desisted as she saw his face, his eyes troubled and questioning.

"I told you not to do it!" she blazed at him. "Now look what you've done!"

"What I've done, Mac?" he asked dazedly.

He didn't know. She realized as she impatiently turned away that Barney simply didn't know he had cut her completely off from him in that stolen embrace. When they had started out on the walk Barney had been a pleasant, unknown masculine quantity. Now he had revealed himself to her and she knew beyond any shadow of a doubt that he could never mean any more to her than an emotional irritation. The valued friendship was over.

"I only hope he feels the same way!" Mac thought as they strode across the valley with its grey and white boulders lying as they had lain for centuries, spewed up from the earth in some far-off volcanic eruption. Rogue was happily chasing imaginary rabbits, flushing unwary plovers and retrieving the sticks Barney occasionally flung for him.

Mac's little coupé was where they had parked it beside the narrow road. As she felt for the ignition keys in her pocket Barney's arms again claimed her, but gently this time.

"You mustn't!" she told him firmly. "Barney, have sense! I could soon *hate* you for this sort of thing!"

"Sorry, Mac!" he looked unhappy. "I ought to know it's no good giving a second dose of the medicine which has upset somebody the first time. It won't happen again. Say you forgive me."

"I do, Barney. Now let me go."

10

Rogue was after a willow-warbler swooping in flight as Barney's soft brown eyes still dwelt in Mac's, which were speed-well-blue, when the big car came silent and lethal round the bend.

Rogue's howl was drowned in Mac's scream of anguish as she tore herself from Barney's arms. The big, hateful, foreign car slithered to a standstill and a black-haired, dark-eyed individual strode back to the spot.

"Any harm done?" he inquired, bending down to investigate the ominously still liver and white body by the roadside.

"He's dead!" Mac accused, her tears streaming.

"But it wasn't anybody's fault," Barney felt bound to add in all fairness, "he was always dashing into the road like that."

"You can say that at a time like this?" Mac demanded, feeling doubly bereft of her friend and her dog.

"It's true, Mac," Barney said gently.

The stranger raised dispassionate eyes from the dog to Mac.

"I should pull yourself together," he advised. "I can't find anything wrong with this fellow and his heart's going like a hammer. I certainly didn't go over him. It's my opinion I caught him broadside and hurled him into that boulder. He is probably suffering from concussion. May I transport him to the nearest vet for you?"

"We are quite capable of looking after our own dog, thank you," Mac said coldly and politely.

"I had my doubts about that a moment ago," the stranger smiled. "However, if I can do no more to help you I'll get along."

"You could at least say you're sorry!" Mac blazed at him.

"It goes without saying I am sorry to have caused suffering to a dumb animal," the man said, still smiling patiently as though Mac was ever so slightly unreasonable. "He looks a nice old fellow and deserves to be looked after and properly trained. In future while you're—er—otherwise engaged you must remember to leash him. Good-day!" With a slight bow and another smile in Barney's direction the fellow climbed back into his car and purred away.

"Hog!" Mac decided.

"It's a Mercedes," Barney said admiringly. "They have an 'oomph' our cars haven't got."

"It nearly 'oomphed' poor old Rogue," Mac decided. "Ah, he's opening his eyes, the darling, and there's no blood anywhere. Maybe that creature was right about its being concussion." She looked up at Barney suddenly. "Who does *he* think he is, telling a couple of doctors what was wrong with Rogue, anyway?"

Barney's shoulders were shaking with silent laughter.

"The couple of doctors didn't show up in too good a light, did they?" he teased. "Do you sign death certificates for all your patients if they've got their eyes shut, Mac?"

Rogue struggled rather dizzily to his feet and shook himself.

"Er-ruff!" he decided tipsily.

"I suppose I was rather rude," Mac said thoughtfully. "Now that's the kind of man I . . ." she stopped and gulped.

"Yes?" Barney prompted.

". . . I should hate to work with," Mac finished rather lamely. "Arrogant, efficient and—and always right."

"One of God's deputies?" Barney queried.

"Sort of."

During the short drive home Mac was pointedly uncommunicative.

CHAPTER TWO

MRS. TUNNEY, the housekeeper, raised her eyes from the potatoes she was hollowing out to stuff with onions as Mac entered by the kitchen door, encouraging the stiff, bruised spaniel after her.

"What in the world's up with him?" the woman asked sharply. "Have you and Doctor Combe walked him off his poor feet, then?"

"He has been knocked down by a fiend in a big car, Tunney dear, but escaped with his life, thank goodness! I'm going to ask Daddy to look him over, but in the meantime will you let him lie on the rug in front of the fire and pet him a little? Some brandy in warm milk might be a help, too."

"I'll get that," the housekeeper promised, leaving the job she was doing and bending down over the dog, now acting the invalid to the best of his considerable ability. "Is it a sore paw, then? Poor old chap! He shall have a nice drink."

12

Mac went through the kitchen and met her father in the hall.

"Oh, there you are, dear! There's a Doctor Kingsland to see you. I've been chatting to him in the study but I can't wait much longer. I'm expecting Mrs. Binns' baby this evening. Do hurry and tidy up, Mac."

"But I don't know a Doctor Kingsland, Daddy. Who is he?"

"How should I know?" Doctor Hayes raised his brows expressively. "He asked for you. *Miss* Hayes, he said, and he knows you're a pathologist."

"My fame must have spread," Mac decided. "Very well, Daddy, I'll be right down. Rogue's just had a bad bump with a car. Will you run your fingers over him for me? He's in the kitchen."

"Where's Barney?"

"He stopped by to see Mrs. Jolley for you. He knew you might be tied up with your confinement."

"Thoughtful of him. I'll have a quick look at old Rogue before I go out. He never had much traffic sense, and a bruise or two may have taught him to watch out in future."

Mac ran lightly downstairs a few minutes later, her hair smooth and shining in the late afternoon sun: she wore a plain blue linen dress the color of her eyes and her small waist was nipped into a broad, shiny black belt. She had put a plaster over the cut on her ankle which showed faintly beneath the fine nylon of her fresh stockings. It was Immacula who descended on three-inch heels and once again went into the kitchen.

"Daddy," she said accusingly, "where are my spectacles?"

"You don't need spectacles to see Doctor Kingsland," her parent assured her. "There's six foot three of him, I should think."

"Daddy, you've hidden them again!" Mac chided him. "I left them on the hall table and won't see Doctor Kingsland without them, so there!"

Doctor Hayes reluctantly produced a pair of horn-rims from his pocket.

"Of all the ridiculous affectations!" he decided. "A girl with eyes like yours commits a crime each time she hides them behind such monstrosities! You don't need glasses— you never have needed glasses—and what you imagine they do for you I can't think!"

As Mac minced frowningly out of the kitchen Doctor Hayes turned to his housekeeper.

13

"Mrs. Tunney, you've known Mac a long time. . . ."

"Nigh on twelve years, Doctor. Watched her grow up, I have, and as pretty as a picture she is."

"I wish she would be more normal, have boy-friends and get married—things like that. Do you realize, Mrs. Tunney, she knows more about doctoring than *I* do, in theory? She frightens me."

"Go on, now, Doctor! There's nothing wrong with a girl being clever, and Miss Mac will marry as soon as she's worked off some steam in other ways, so to speak. I have thought she and Doctor Combe might. . . ."

"Good lord!" the old doctor looked startled. "I never thought of Barney as a possible suitor. I wonder if Mac does?"

"They've been up the valley together all afternoon."

"She didn't look particularly starry-eyed to me just now when she was in here. You're an old gossip, Mrs. Tunney."

"You're not such a bad one yourself, Doctor, and what'll it be for pudding tonight?"

"Oh—ask Mac. I don't suppose I'll be in until late. You know first babies, *and* their mums. . . . There's the phone and it's sure to be Mrs. Binns! Tell Mac I. . . ."

"Rush—rush," the housekeeper philosophised, "and hardly ever a meal in peace. If it isn't babies coming it's the old ones going or little Johnny pulling a pan off the stove to see what's in it. I sometimes think I'd like a place where breakfast was regular at eight and dinner twelve hours later, and *no telephone*. That'd be heaven. But I won't leave Doctor Hayes as long as he needs me, nor Miss Mac neither. I promised the mistress I'd stick by 'em, and Ethel Tunney's as good as her word."

*   *   *

The study was empty when Mac entered. She looked round in some consternation, noting the initials on the briefcase standing by the open french windows. R.V.K. An imposing little cluster, she decided, and again felt an uneasy niggle at the back of her mind that she had seen them before. Had she studied anywhere with a Kingsland, she wondered, puckering her brow and gazing out over the long, green velvet lawns—for which Silverdell Valley was famous—bordered profusely by tossing banks of daffodils and Easter lilies. Kingsland wasn't a name to forget easily, and she boasted an excellent memory. Why, she could still clearly identify the six Smiths of her Edinburgh career, and all the Joneses of her more recent sojourn in Liverpool.

14

One Kingsland was child's play compared. Still she felt that the correct jog would confirm her suspicions that she ought to know an R. V. Kingsland, and the most obvious way of administering a jog to her recalcitrant memory was to see the individual in question.

"Here goes the mountain to Mahomet!" Mac shrugged, stepping out into the cool air and following her nose round the side of the house in the direction of voices coming from the sunken garden, where the roses would shortly show a reward of beauty for all the winter care lavished upon them by Willis, the jobbing gardener. Willis' voice was now holding forth professionally.

"Some roses do like it 'ot, sir, but not Lady Barnum. Not 'er. She flowers early and goes off by July when it's gettin' yumid. Now what you want, sir, is Blushin' Bess; she'll settle anywhere an' likes a bit o' sand. She'll give you a nice flower an' a nicer scent. Some folk call 'er a cactus-rose, owin' to 'er prolific tendency to thorns"—Willis' horticultural vocabulary always exceeded his social chatter in brilliance—"but I like my roses to 'ave names, then I can think of 'em like yuman bein's."

"How very delightful!"

The voice struck a chord in Mac's memory, but from the rear she still didn't recognize her visitor. He turned as Willis indicated her presence at the top of a flight of mossy steps, and then with a chilling of eyes she recognized the fellow who had almost accounted for Rogue.

"Good afternoon!" she greeted coldly. "You must be Doctor Kingsland?"

"Yes, I am, Miss Hayes," he ran lightly up the steps and half proffered his hand, then the recognition was mutual and he gave a rather rueful smile instead. "How is the old fellow now?"

"Bruised and sore," she told him shortly, "as one would expect after such an experience."

"But still unquestionably with us, I hope?"

Was he daring to laugh?

Looking up Mac could read nothing in the deep, dark eyes. They were eyes to keep secrets in, revealing no more than they intended.

"He'll recover if that's what you mean, Doctor Kingsland."

The name again jogged at her memory. His face had meant no more to her than the recollection of an irritating incident during the day when she had not known who he was, so obviously they hadn't met at the university.

15

"Was there anything else you wanted with me?" Mac asked with frigid politeness as they reached the study windows together.

"No"—he hesitated only a moment—"nothing else. I'm glad I didn't kill your dog. You would be surprised if you knew how it would have spoilt my evening had I done so." He picked up his brief case. "Good evening to you, Miss Hayes. I may leave this way?"

"Er—just a moment, Doctor Kingsland," Mac said hastily, "my father wouldn't wish you to leave without a drink at least, or would you prefer coffee?"

"Your estimable father looks like a man who knows his wines. I shall be happy to drink his health before I go."

Mac poured from the decanter.

"This is rather good," she recommended, passing the glass across the table. "It has just occurred to me that it is rather odd you should know my name and that I am a pathologist, Doctor Kingsland."

The visitor finished the drink rather quickly and saluted her briefly as he set down the glass.

"Not so odd really, Miss Hayes," he smiled. "A young and pretty pathologist must rate as the eighth wonder of the world. Everyone must know about you."

"I feel *you* regard me as a somewhat amusing phenomenon," Mac said somewhat irritably, "but *I* am quite serious about my work."

"Excellent!" applauded the other. "I beg of you not to be too serious, though Medicine needs brightening up a bit. A few lapis lazuli eyes glued to microscopes might well fill the depleted ranks of the lab boys."

"Good-bye, Doctor Kingsland," Mac said, breathing hard.

"Good-bye, *Doctor* Hayes."

There was a fuming little silence and then he left by the french windows. She didn't watch his tall figure striding down the long drive; instead she listened tensely for the noise of the great car purring away from behind the screening laurels. When it had done so she relaxed visibly, sinking into her father's chair and feeling even her toes uncurl. It was in that moment it came to her suddenly why the name of Roy Victor Kingsland, M.R.C.P., had struck a chord within her. Only yesterday she had seen his name written up on the notice-board of the Hospital for Tropical Diseases where she had completed her training: he was to give a lecture that day to the students and all interested staff.

"What a pity you'll miss it, Mac," her chief had

declared. "Kingsland and you are two of a kind, always on the ferret for something under a microscope. I'm sure you'd want to work with him if you could hear him!"

"And where does this wonderful person work, sir?" Mac had asked lightly, keen to get off home to Silverdell and to rid herself of city sights and smells.

"In Hades, poor devil!" Doctor Wynford had declared wryly. "Somewhere in the Lower Sudan. But"— he had shrugged—"that's how he gets to know his tropical medicine!"

Just then Barney's bland, uncomplicated face peeped round the door, interrupting her thoughts.

"Hallo!" he smiled. "I wondered if I had to take evening surgery."

"I expect so," Mac said rather impatiently. "Daddy's gone out to a confinement. Goodness knows when he'll be back."

"Are you doing anything just now?" Barney asked hopefully.

"Obviously not," Mac told him, then added contritely, "Come in, Barney, and have a drink. I'm sorry to be so snappy, but ever since Rogue's accident I've been on edge."

"Understandable," soothed Barney, and took pleasure in surveying her as slowly as he sipped his sherry.

"Barney, is it a good thing or a bad thing when somebody makes a tremendous impact on you, to slide out of danger and try to forget it?"

Barney looked thoughtful, even ponderous.

"That would depend . . ." was all he vouchsafed.

"I wanted to strike somebody a little while back," Mac went on. "I felt primitive and—and"—she thought for a word—"betrayed, almost. But I had the strangest feeling deep down inside me that if I once allowed myself to open fire I would be hopelessly involved in no time the other way."

Barney tried to look intelligent.

"Put it in plainer words, Mac," he pleaded.

"Oh"—her gesture was one of utter impatience—"it's a good thing you're not in psycho-analysis, my lad! Very well, in plain words, I felt if I started by kicking, I'd finish up—maybe—wanting kisses. There! Even you can understand that, I think?"

A slow dawning light spread over Barney's large, pink face.

"Oh, Mac, you *should* have kicked me, darling, if it'd have relieved your feelings this afternoon! I wouldn't have

17

minded. And if you mean you might feel fonder of me if you did it, kick me any old time. Kick me now!" he invited.

Mac had suddenly crumpled back into her chair.

"No, Barney," she sighed. "I shall never be tempted to hit out at you. It would be like hitting Rogue. Someone who doesn't hit back. And take no notice of my foolish chatterings. I've had my head in textbooks so long I'm ever so slightly inhibited, I expect. After dinner I shall drive into Westington and see a purely romantic film without any doctors in it!"

CHAPTER THREE

DOCTOR HAYES was sitting up reading when Mac returned home that evening, feeling rather flat after a large dose of Hollywood's celluloid sentimentality.

"Hallo, darling!" she greeted her parent. "Got your baby yet?"

"Oh, yes. It was rather a difficult birth. The stupid grandmother had told the girl to eat enough for two and the baby was positively flabby with fat. Nine pounds two ounces to deliver at a first go! Some feat!"

"I must try and see this big laddie."

"Yes, do. The mother is tremendously proud of his size. Oh—there was a phone call for you, Mac, from Doctor Wynford."

"What did he want?"

"He asked that you ring him back, dear. He said it didn't matter how late it was because he was on call for the night. I think I'll turn in now, if you don't mind."

"*Do* go off to bed, Daddy darling. You must be tired." She kissed the top of his head.

He seemed to sense her depression.

"Mac. . . ."

"Yes, Daddy?"

"Aren't you happy?"

"Enormously. Why do you ask?"

18

"I don't know. I wondered. . . . You do realize the whole of this practice will be Barney's one day? I mean it *could* be half yours if you wanted it, but I think you aim to specialize, perhaps? This is a big house. Maybe you could turn it into a private clinic with Barney doing the general work?"

"I refuse to consider any eventuality which doesn't include you, darling. No—I shall work where there's a little more scope for my peculiar talents."

"Then you and Barney aren't. . . ?"

"Aren't what, Daddy?"

". . . In love?"

"Gracious, no!"

Doctor Hayes rose a little creakily and stretched his limbs separately.

"Don't think I'm prying, Mac, but wasn't there somebody during last year who meant a great deal to you? I couldn't help observing your great, inward happiness and then—your pain." Mac lowered her eyes suddenly. "What happened, dear?"

The blue eyes regarded him frankly.

"He was married, Daddy."

"Oh! I'm sorry. Mac, did he . . . I mean did you. . . ? I don't know what I mean!"

"I do, Daddy, and we didn't. We were never lovers, if that is what you were going to ask me. In fact as soon as I knew how things stood it all finished and I went to Liverpool. I haven't forgotten, but I think I'm over the worst now. I couldn't bear to be so much in love again!"

Doctor Hayes smiled gently.

"The heart heals, Mac, like anything else, but there's nothing like another love to cast out the old once and for all. Now if you and Barney. . . ."

"Daddy"—Mac put gentle fingers over his lips—"now you go off to bed and stop being an old match-maker. It could never be Barney with me."

"Very well, my dear, I'll stop. I would like to see you married, though, before I. . . ."

Again she shut his lips before the fateful word could leave them, and with a final ruffling of her hair he left the room.

She put the telephone call through to Dr. Wynford from the study, wondering what he could want with her at this hour and fearing she had been found out in something unforgivable like a wrong blood grouping, or had left unstopped a tube of deadly bacillus. These things she knew she could never be guilty of, however, her training was too

19

thorough, her mind too disciplined and clear. Still it was strange that the "chief" should want her to call him back like this ... obviously it was a matter of some importance to both of them.

Doctor Wynford's voice came at last quite cheerfully, however.

"Hallo, Mac! Sorry to keep you waiting but we have just finished transfusing a rhesus-negative baby, a black one. You would love him. He's just like a piccaninny doll now that his lips are pink again! How are you, girl? How's leave?"

"I haven't had much time to find out yet, sir. You had me thinking I was being missed for a moment there. ..." She realized her voice sounded almost hopeful. "As a matter of fact, I think I'm rather bored. Home's wonderful from a distance, but I miss my work. I must get a job."

"Well, how about Kingsland? What'd he have to say to you?"

"Kingsland? Doctor *Roy* Kingsland? Did you know he was calling here, sir?"

"Of course. I gave him your address. He was most interested in your career and wanted to see you. Don't tell me you missed him, Mac?"

"Er—no. Not exactly. But as he almost killed my dog with that mechanized bomb of his we didn't talk of anything else. What did he want with me, sir?"

Doctor Wynford was chuckling at the other end of the line.

"I say, Mac, we're over three minutes and this'll be charged to you, you know. Do you want me to go on?"

"Please do, sir."

"I'm sorry about your dog. I can't help but laugh at old Kingsland, though, rushing north to secure you for his hospital before anybody else got the chance, and then turning you completely against him at the outset by doing a fool thing like that. .. !"

"Rogue *did* rush across the road without looking, though," Mac felt bound to explain, "and he isn't much worse for the experience now. Doctor Kingsland didn't mention any job to me, and he struck me as being a person who would be extremely difficult to please. Not like you, sir."

"Roy Kingsland is just about tops in his own field, Mac. He would expect perfection, no less, in his assistants. Can you blame him for that? He has given himself completely to his job. We have just offered him a Fellowship, and an unheard-of salary, to stay and lecture for us, but he never hesitated in turning us down. He said there were far too many people talking in medicine nowadays and exactly three doctors on the staff of El Belada, where he works, which is one man per thousand sick people. An impossible state of affairs. He said he had come recruiting, not to act Judas on those left behind. I'm surprised he didn't try to enlist your services, Mac."

"From our brief encounter his single intention appeared to be to poke fun at me," Mac protested. "He seemed to think a young—and as he said, pretty—pathologist was one huge joke."

"Maybe *you* were a bit high-hat with him, Mac. You are sometimes, you know."

"Doctor Wynford!"

"Now don't hang up on me, I'm only teasing. I do honestly think you'd have liked working with Kingsland, though, Mac, and he's about the only person I can think of who could satisfy your professional voracity. But—look, I have to go now. Can I do anything for you?"

"You can give me Doctor Kingsland's address, sir. I would like to know why I wasn't considered for recruitment to El Belada, at least."

"Kingsland lives in the Lake District. Coningwater will find him. That shouldn't be far away from you."

"No, it isn't."

"Let me know how you go on, Kingsland or not. We can always find you a job here, you know."

"Thank you, sir, and good night."

She felt angrily stirred as she replace d the receiver and lit a cigarette from the box on her father's desk. Why should Roy Kingsland change his mind about trying to recruit her for a job for which she knew herself to be so eminently suited? It couldn't have been the Rogue episode only, though this certainly had not endeared them to one another in the first place. Doctors were above petty personal dislikes when it came to the serious business of their work. Why, she had known a Resident Medical Officer who was in a state of daggers drawn with a certain Senior Surgeon out of duty hours, yet who wouldn't trust his patients to anyone else when they needed surgery, though there were three other fully qualified surgeons always available. Doctor Kingsland hadn't seemed to believe in her, somehow, but hadn't Doctor Wynford assured her he was impressed by her qualifications and had actually rushed off to find her before she could have had time to study the various appointments columns in the *British Medical Journal* during the leisure hours of her leave? If the situation remained static she would always be conscious of a sense of personal and professional affront, and would much prefer to "have it out" with Doctor Kingsland for her own peace of mind. Of course she could never consider working with him in El Belada now, but there is more satisfaction in renouncing than in being renounced. No one was going to renounce Immacula Hayes and get clean away with it!

* * *

Roy Kingsland threw a pebble idly into the lily-pool and as he watched the ever-widening circles ruffling the clear water, his mother gazed at him over her crocheting and observed in her unemotional voice:

"I think Fiona is ready to marry you now, Roy, if you still want her."

Her son stiffened slightly but threw another pebble before he spoke.

"Very interesting, dearest," he decided. "Is that your way of trying to find out if Fiona and I made love last evening?"

Mrs. Kingsland trebled ten stitches with exaggerated calm.

"Did you?" she asked brightly, scratching her nose with her crochet-hook.

"No, you old vixen. We didn't. Fiona was on duty and showed me round the clinic. You can't imagine Fiona doing anything so unethical, can you?"

"But she will be off duty today," Mrs. Kingsland decided, "and she's coming over to tea so that you'll have time to go for a walk round the lake before dinner. You *have* been in love with Fiona for a long time, haven't you, Roy? Don't imagine a mother misses these things."

"I hope I was decent about the whole thing," Roy said rather shortly. "While she was Adrian's fiancée I couldn't have been more formal with her."

"But Adrian was killed," sighed Mrs. Kingsland, sparing a thought for her handsome first-born, a man and flying aeroplanes while Roy was still an undergraduate. "Do you think she really loved Adrian, or liked being engaged to the best-looking pilot in the R.A.F.?"

"Mother!" exclaimed Roy sharply.

"Well, my sons are noted for good looks," the woman insisted coyly. "I thought Fiona would naturally have turned to you after a decent interval, but perhaps she thought you too young for a husband, being the same age as herself. Anyway, she is at the moment unstrung. . . ."

"Good gracious! She seemed all right to me last evening."

"I mean she has no strings to her bow just now, dear. The Director of the clinic got married eight weeks ago. Wasn't that about the time she wrote and suggested she might come out and take charge of El Belada?"

"That's right," Roy agreed.

"Well, there you are, then! Fiona is unattached, attractive and thirty-two. She has to do something about it quickly or she'll be forty-two before she knows where she is. You are home on leave and there are daffodils by the lake."

"And you are a conspiring little match-maker!" Roy said fondly. "Do you want me to marry Fiona?"

"Do you want to is more to the point, my son! I don't like to see unmarried men. They get to an age when they need looking after properly, and a wife does it so much better than anyone else. But there are more girls than Fiona, Roy. You don't have to take your brother's—and goodness knows who else's—leavings."

"That's a feline thing to say, Mother, of your neighbor's adored only child. I believe you're trying to warn me off Fiona."

"I'm wondering what they all found wrong with her. When she was promised to Adrian she was always here, being nice to me. But I've hardly seen her since until eight weeks ago when she called to tell me she had jokingly suggested she go out to run El Belada for you. 'Run it', mind you, her very words. Then I knew if she was even considering such a thing she had finally come around to considering you as a husband. In casual conversation"— Mrs. Kingsland glanced obliquely at her son—"I then learned that Doctor Ferryman—or Mister, as these surgeons call themselves nowadays—was marrying some Irish girl he'd known for ages, and that seemed to me to be very revealing."

"I don't like you talking so about Fiona, Mother," Roy said uncomfortably. "After all, we were kids together, and I would always feel defensive about her if nothing else. You have given me the gipsy's warning, if that was your intention, and now remember that I, also, am thirty-two and not your baby son any longer. If Fiona was the most utterly designing minx in creation she would still have to be in love with me before I would consider marriage with her. Love is a difficult emotion to fake, and I am old-fashioned enough in my ideas to want it to be the keytone in my relationship with a woman. After all, I've waited so

23

long, and I'm afraid I shouldn't be content with the second best of anything. I find it deuced cold out here on the terrace, Mother. I'm going inside."

Mrs. Kingsland knew that she had given her son something to think about, and that he had left her deliberately to do his thinking in private. Wisely she remained where she was, tucking her silk shawl more firmly round her knees and gazing with a tight little smile across the waters of the shallow lake ahead, where fat kine straddle among the bulrushes to drink, and the banks were starred with the bright corollas of the Easter lilies for which the district was renowned. From this terrace she would be the first to see Fiona's approach from the big, yellow house at the head of the lake, and seeing her, noting the way she was dressed and the hair-style she favored, assess her designs upon Roy. Not everyone knew, as she did, that Adrian had died knowing that his fiancée's affections had a habit of straying when he was not around, and even in "peace-time" young fighter pilots were not around home very often. In fact Mrs. Kingsland knew that there had been a flaming row between the sweethearts during that all too brief last forty-eight hours' leave before Adrian went off to help quell a flare-up in the Middle East. Perhaps if Adrian had not been so emotionally upset he might have survived that last sortie, but there is nothing gained by living in a world of might-have-been. No one wept more tears at Adrian's funeral than the fair Fiona, and she had feverishly gone into nursing with the solemn dedication of a blighted young life given in service, and triumphantly announced her engagement to a doctor nine months later.

Mrs. Kingsland didn't know what had happened to the doctor, but he had gone abroad quite suddenly, and then there had been a barrister who squired Fiona for a while, followed by a motor-racing enthusiast. Fiona's mother had confided that her daughter had "too much choice" in the matrimonial stakes, but that could not be so for ever, and the field was rapidly narrowing down. Now Roy was the single and final objective, Mrs. Kingsland was sure, and she did not feel at all happy about the situation. There might be no evil in Fiona Bardale, but Roy deserved more than was in her to give. She would always be a lover and preserver of herself above all, and when such a creature has the calm, cool beauty of a Madonna and the statuesque perfections of a Venus, how can a mere mother protect her beloved child who has grown into that most vulnerable of all God's creatures, a handsome, talented, and unattached man?

24

CHAPTER FOUR

MAC HAD HAD time to indulge in second and third thoughts about her proposed visit to Doctor Kingsland during her waking hours that morning. Mrs. Tunney had brought her breakfast to bed, which was a very spoiling thing and for which she had gently chided the housekeeper, only to have that worthy silence her with, "There, now, Miss Mac, it's not to spoil you I do it but to save myself. I know you like a good old-fashioned bacon-and-egg in the morning, and if you'd come down wanting it at ten o'clock, right in the middle of my surgery cleaning, I wouldn't half have blessed you, my girl! As it is, you can enjoy your breakfast and go back to sleep again, if you want to. After all, it *is* your holidays."

Mac was young and healthy enough to enjoy her food, and Mrs. Tunney could always be counted on to coax an appetite, so she set to with a will and thought about the day ahead.

Was it permissible to beard a medical lion in his den while he was on well-earned leave? It might not be an ethical thing to do, but then, Doctor Kingsland had hardly been ethical himself in asking George Wynford for *her* address. A visit to him at Coningwater would only be tit for tat, and she was very curious to know the opinion he had formed of her as a person—even as a female—if not as a doctor wishing to practise pathology. He had called her pretty, and likened her eyes to lapis lazuli. Somehow, today, her irritation settled like sediment at the bottom of a cup, she found pleasure in remembering these things, and in recalling the laughing brown eyes and the dynamic personality, which had seemed to hit her like a wall at the same time. She had looked him up in the *Medical Directory*, surprised to find him a recognized authority on tropical diseases, medicine and bacteriology. He lectured at Khartoum University and was a visiting examiner: he had opened the hospital at El Belada and established a self-supporting leper colony near by. Mac was most amazed to realize that such a man, who had achieved so much, was still, to judge from the date on which he had qualified, not much over thirty. He couldn't have had much time for women in his crowded career, and Mac had no illusions that the Lower Sudan was anything but the "Hades" Doctor Wynford had described. Obviously Roy Kingsland had taken one look at her and thought, "Ah, fragile! Too fragile for El Belada. I can forget about Miss Immacula Hayes from this moment on!"

"But he doesn't know how tough I am," Mac defended herself aloud. "And anyway, I would like to be consulted, at least. I will go up to Coningwater and see him. If I weaken at the last moment I can always fish in the lake!"

*　　　*　　　*

Combing her long, dark hair in front of her dressing-table mirror, Fiona Bardale decided upon a loose knot tied with a yellow ribbon. She remembered Roy once saying he "liked girls with ribbons", and deliberately overlooked the fact that this was a preference dated by at least twelve years. It wasn't as if she looked any older, her skin was flawless, like ivory, and the puce of her lipstick flattered it, emphasising her natural pallor. She wore a yellow dress—she wanted Roy to think she went well with the daffodils—and a lacy white cardigan. There was no need to wear more for the short walk by the lake to Kingsmount. Her heart fluttered as she pondered on the love scene which would take place before the evening was over. Roy had always blindly adored her, she knew, but not until last evening had she really seen him as a mature male with Adrian's devastating good looks and a quiet, apologetic charm peculiarly his own. Last evening he had called unannounced at the clinic—that spoke volumes in itself—but she had remembered he was a doctor and would, perhaps, be watching her behavior with a detached, professional eye. So she had played Miss Nightingale to perfection, her behavior as impeccable as her uniform, and only in the last moments unbent to announce that she was free on the morrow, and was rewarded with the sudden anticipatory warmth in the deep, dark eyes.

"All day, Fiona?"

Better not appear too eager so early in their reacquaintance, Sister Bardale decided.

"Not all day, Roy. Sorry. . . ." Her eyes were liquid, her

26

smile the pity of a goddess. "I'll phone your mother and ask her if I may come to tea. Like the old days, eh, Roy?"

Roy didn't particularly want to be reminded of the "old days" when he had been invariably the odd one out in a threesome, but he had told her his mother would look forward to her coming as much as he would, which Fiona doubted very much in her secret heart but didn't venture to express in words. Giving a final twirl in front of the mirror she pondered on the price she would probably have to pay to become Roy's wife.

It was El Belada.

She had seen pictures of the place and it even looked hot on a photograph, a glaringly white, veranda'd hospital casting opaque black shadows on the white, sandy dust of the compound. The patients would all be Sudanis with unpleasant diseases—Fiona made a face—and there was always the thought of the leper colony two miles distant, to and from which Roy journeyed all in the day's work.

Fiona positively shuddered and almost weakened. Her nursing—since her training period which she thought of nowadays as years of hard labor—had been of a refined character: she had worked for specialists chiefly, young and unattached specialists in particular. Mr. Ferryman was an orthopaedic surgeon, a consultant at the big lakeland hospital but with his own private clinic where Fiona could be said to reign decoratively. There wasn't much actual work, the Sister-in-Charge saw to it that the four nurses and two orderlies did most of that, but she toured the private rooms at least twice a day, turning her smile on and off automatically, for most of the patients were wealthy and prepared to pay for a little extra cosseting, and she had always imagined herself as being "very close" to Mr. Ferryman, whom her mother entertained to dinner quite regularly on her behalf, until he suddenly brought that Irish baggage out of the hat and married her—just like that!

Ferryman's defection still rankled in Fiona's breast. She only wanted to be quite, quite sure of Roy before telling the surgeon he could find himself another Sister-in-Charge as she was leaving to be married.

". . . And serves him right!" was Fiona's final comment before leaving for Kingsmount.

She had no eyes for the lake, no eyes for the purple pikes beyond: she saw the diminutive figure of Mrs. Kingsland looking towards her from the terrace of the house, and even from a distance sensed the older woman's hostility.

"I must ask Mother to keep the old girl sweet," Fiona added. "Roy adores her, and now that he's all she has got she won't want to let him go."

*　　　*　　　*

Roy Kingsland sighed that all was not as he had dreamed it would be with him. Here he was at home in spring with the lake cool at his door and the Easter lilies golden in the sun, Fiona expected at any moment and not a nerve in his body tingling in anticipation.

What was rotten in the state of Denmark? he wondered.

Fiona was still very lovely, but she reminded him of the snow queen in the old fairy-tale whose beauty masked a heart of ice. Fiona's gaze upon his at their surprise meeting last evening had been one of cool appraisal; judgment, almost. Her final capitulation offering him a little of her free time today savored of largesse spilled over from her bounty. He fancied she was "sparing him a penny", and God knew it was riches he had dreamed of back in El Belada whenever he dreamed of Fiona. He had once seen her laughing up at Adrian, at their engagement party, a glass in her hand and twin stars in her eyes, and that was the way he wanted Fiona to look at him, not speculatively as though he was a proposition she was vaguely considering. Perhaps people did change and one grew up from the heady kind of loving sooner or later.

"But heaven forbid!" he decided, pouring himself a drink.

It was at that moment the sound of a rending crash came from the front of the house. Roy rushed out in time to see a small red coupé disentangle itself from a portion of low garden wall, which now lay flat among the budding tulips.

"What the. . . !"

"So sorry!" called the driver of the car nervously. "I was reversing, and. . . !"

"So I see," Roy Kingsland observed dryly, and suddenly recognized under all the confusion an acquaintance of yesterday. "Miss Hayes, what are you. . . ?"

"Just a moment while I get clear!" Mac called, and swung about. Somehow she felt an utter idiot under Kingsland's eye and put the car into reverse again quite by accident. Roy felt himself pinned against his own gatepost agonisingly, and let out a yell. When he was silent and the small car had eased away he crumpled up and sank to the ground.

"Oh, Doctor Kingsland! What have I done?" Mac demanded, cradling the dark head on her lap. "What were you doing behind me? Oh, dear!"

Mrs. Kingsland and Fiona approached together.

"I'm a nurse," Fiona announced curtly. "Did you run over him?"

"Oh, no," Mac said miserably. "I *did* knock down a bit of your wall, and somehow he got behind me when I wasn't looking."

"I don't think you can have been looking anywhere," Fiona snapped. "It's people like you get women drivers a bad name."

"I'm a very good driver as a rule," Mac was stung to retort. "That's the first wall I have ever bumped in all my life!"

"Which can't be a very long time all told," Mrs. Kingsland observed kindly, and was intrigued to see her son open his eyes and then very quickly close them again. "Are you living, dear?" she asked, poking him with the stick she used to help her to walk.

A groan left the sufferer's lips and the head rolled a little in Mac's lap.

"I'm a nurse," Fiona reiterated firmly, "and we had better get help to take poor Roy inside. Can you phone Doctor Wilstrop, Mrs. Kingsland?"

"I—I'm a doctor," Mac said quickly. "I'll examine him if it's all right with you."

"It isn't thank you," Fiona snapped.

"But why not?" argued Roy's mother. "If this young lady's a doctor she's bound to be more up-to-date than old Wilstrop. He's as deaf as a post and will never know what we're talking about anyway. I'll just get Doogan to come and help move Roy inside. Will you want him undressed, Doctor?" she asked Mac, deliberately avoiding Fiona's fuming disapproval. "Oh, he seems to be better! He's getting up himself!"

Mac put her arms round the man's middle and helped to heave.

"How are you, Doctor Kingsland?" she asked in troubled tones. "Does anything hurt?"

"I thought you were going to examine me, Doctor Hayes?" he said coldly.

"Well, yes"—Mac flushed up to her ears—"I will if you like."

There was a faint smile in the brown eyes as Roy dusted himself down.

"I think there's been enough fooling around," Fiona said sharply. "You're obviously no worse, Roy. As you seem to know our visitor, wouldn't it be best if you introduced us?"

"Certainly. Mother, Fiona, this is Doctor Immacula Hayes, whose examination honors already put me to shame." He contrived a small wink in Mac's direction to put her at her ease. "This is my mother, and this is Sister Fiona Bardale, a neighbor of ours."

Over how-do-y'do's Fiona decided she wasn't enjoying herself one bit. Who was this "Doctor" Hayes with the color high in her cheeks and the freckles sprinkled on her nose? Why hadn't she been heard of at Coningwater before this? Was there any possibility that Roy had ceased to adore her, Fiona, exclusively? Roy's next words reassured her somewhat on this point.

"Now that you have literally dropped in, Doctor Hayes, won't you stay to tea, at least?"

"I suppose that would give us a chance to assess damages," Mac smiled, still a little shakily. "I'll pay for your wall, of course."

"And if I have punctured my spleen?" Roy Kingsland asked, feeling himself for tender spots. "What then?"

"I'll recommend a very good surgeon," Mac promised, and they turned laughingly towards the house together.

CHAPTER FIVE

MRS. KINGSLAND smiled wickedly as she settled herself in her wing-chair before the fire and opened the latest novel she was reading. Tea had gone off splendidly, and the house had once again rung with laughter, thanks to that Hayes girl. Fiona hadn't laughed much, and after Mrs. Kingsland had insisted that Mac should stay to dinner she had remembered an appointment she had overlooked and asked to be excused, taking Roy off with her on to the terrace, where she had kept him for a quarter of an hour while his second cup of tea went cold. He had come back into the room looking somewhat thoughtful, but had quickly cheered up again, especially when Miss Hayes challenged him on some medical observation he had idly made and actually argued with him bluntly and passionately, while he countered with confidence and finesse. It was good to see them treating one another as equals, not playing heavily on sex as man and woman but as doctor and doctor, and liking one another in a comradely way.

Now they were both off walking round the lake together, and Mrs. Kingsland wouldn't be surprised if Fiona wasn't watching them from behind her curtains, biting her knuckles and fuming, and wondering—as she herself was doing—where Immacula Hayes would finally fit into the picture?

*   *   *

"You must miss all this dreadfully when you're in the Sudan," Mac decided, indicating the pastoral spread of water and the purpling hills beyond. "I only have to work in a city for a while to become very nostalgic about home. But . . ."

"Yes?" prompted Roy Kingsland, thinking he would have liked a sister just like this girl.

"I was going to say—but it seems disloyal somehow—that I soon get tired of home nowadays. When I used to come home from school for the holidays it was absolute heaven. I want it to be the same now, but it isn't." She shrugged.

"I know just what you mean," he confided, "and I get it too. I travel joyfully, but arriving is always an anticlimax. It isn't that we're disloyal or love our people any the less, it's that home isn't our whole world any more. We have become independent of it. Really it's far better that way. Once one becomes adjusted to the change home takes its place as a welcome oasis in one's journeyings. If one is afraid to leave home, to suffer the initial wrench, one's horizons are bound to be narrowed considerably."

He thought briefly and frowningly of Fiona, who had always clung to her equally possessive mother, and who had rather shocked him by an outburst of childish petulance less than an hour ago. In that display he had recognized her mental immaturity, though previously she had sometimes challenged his, not always kindly.

"Roy is such a child!" she had complained when they had been seventeen together, and he had wanted to go and see a school cricket match in opposition to her wish to

31

swim in the lake, where the older brother, Adrian, might admire her developing figure in its new bathing-suit.

"Don't look at me like a bull-calf, Roy!" she had said in front of everyone at her engagement celebration. "You'll grow out of it in time!"

He came back with a jerk to the present, seeing Mac's speed-well-blue eyes on her own far horizons.

"I might even go to China," she decided suddenly. "I think I would be lost with all my special knowledge cooped up in Britain. Why, I should be looking out hopefully on the docks for ships flying the yellow jack just for my benefit! That would be a nice state of affairs, wouldn't it?"

Roy Kingsland laughed with her and gave her his hand to negotiate some stepping-stones across a narrow reach of water.

"Will your young man allow you to escape to China?" he asked.

"My young——!" Mac put a brogued foot squarely into the water in her surprise. "What young man?"

"Surely at our first fateful meeting—and fateful meetings we seem to have, you and I—you were being warmly embraced by a very resolute-looking character in Donegal tweeds?"

"Oh, Barney!" Mac flushed and twinkled. "He *isn't* my young man," she said archly.

"Oh? Appearances were deceptive then. Or do you allow your escorts equal liberty?" His dark eyes held a laughing challenge, but Mac's heart was in the process of turning quite over.

"I was telling him not to do it," she said in a breathless little voice. "In fact I made a vow never to be casually kissed again."

"A pity," he decided, with laughing regret. "You must be Mother Nature's most kissable creation."

"I am also a woman," Mac reminded him sharply, "and my appearance happens to be attached to a heart."

He stopped and looked at her in surprise.

"I'm sorry," he said at last. "I didn't mean to offend you. I'm truly sorry, Miss Hayes."

"You were calling me Mac a moment ago," she reminded him, trying to recapture the lightness in her tone. "Please don't go all stiff on me again. I am rather touchy about some things."

"Your privilege," he granted, as they rounded a floral bank and came once more within sight of Kingsmount,

32

"but I have never before met a woman who minded being complimented upon her obvious attractions."

"I don't normally," Mac told him. "In fact I think I only object to them coming from you."

"Indeed!" he sounded stung. "Perhaps you imagined I was flirting with you! I assure you nothing was further from my thoughts and I was merely trying to be nice to an unexpected guest. If you have inferred . . ."

"Please don't go on," Mac said in an unhappy little voice. "You have been very charming to me considering that I was so rude to you on our first meeting and knocked your wall down as well as nearly killing you on our next. I have expressed myself very badly and certainly didn't intend to rebuff you. You haven't been at all offensive to me in any way. What I meant to say was—well—I would rather *you* admired me for my work. Coming from you a compliment in that direction would really mean something."

They walked a little way in silence.

"Your coming here wasn't accidental then, Miss Hayes?"

We're being formal again, Mac thought wryly.

"No, it wasn't, Doctor Kingsland," she told him frankly. "Doctor Wynford phoned me last evening expecting I might soon be working with you at El Belada. This was news to me, and I felt rather foolish as you will understand. I'm afraid you hurt my professional pride. I came here simply to ask you—why? All my life I have looked like a doll in a box. When I was seven—with ringlets—they crowned me Queen of the May and danced round me: when I was nine it was a crown of roses, and I had two pages kissing my hand and seven little rosebuds holding my train. I got away to school then and they made me do my hair in pigtails. Still the other girls voted me 'Sportsqueen' one year, and I grew positively sick of acting Titania in school plays. Now I'm a doctor and I've earned all my laurels the hard way. No examiner passed me on account of my big blue eyes. Even my own father regards me as a bit of a freak. But nobody would raise an eyebrow if I was a sallow little brown mouse, would they?"

"Perhaps not," said Roy Kingsland, surprised by her sudden vehemence. He had paused to light his pipe and now puffed fragrantly. "But as a sallow little brown mouse you wouldn't be Immacula, and you wouldn't have all these wonderful coronation memories, would you? Womanly beauty will never be anything but an asset, Mac, and those who have worked with you must surely have feasted their tired old eyes on you many times in a day. Don't tell me you wish you were plain, now?"

"Well . . ." Mac hesitated. "No. Not exactly."

"In fact you like to take those glasses off occasionally and reassure yourself that those big blue eyes are really there."

Mac frowned, then her lips trembled into a mischievous smile and she removed the horn-rims, putting them into her pocket.

"That's better!" Roy Kingsland approved, and again held out his hand. "I have an idea we're holding up dinner, but I think you want satisfaction from me. Correct?"

"Correct," Mac agreed.

"Well, in the first place, I had this notion that you were engaged, and fiancés are not partial to their loved ones serving in the tropics: secondly I realized you had an ageing parent, a charming gentleman, who I thought didn't look too well. . . ."

"Daddy's all right, I think," Mac said, a little startled. "What seemed to be wrong with him?"

"Oh—I suppose he has his own doctor to tell him that. I would advise him to retire from active practice if he were my father. I don't want to alarm you, Mac. Please don't look so worried. It's just that I don't think he should have been worrying about a confinement with a young partner about the place."

"That's Barney," Mac said, somewhat relieved. "He's very willing, but Daddy will be difficult to retire, I'm afraid."

"I was merely trying to explain why I didn't introduce a certain topic to you yesterday, Mac. I thought I would be wasting my time. I need a pathologist badly at El Belada, and forgive me if I say you would brighten the place up considerably. Besides, you would be company for Fiona."

"Fiona?"

"The lady you just met. She might have appeared a bit standoffish with you, but she is really a very charming person, and she, too, might decide to give El Belada a trial. In all fairness I must say it's damned hot, but you get used to it in time and the heat is dry. It's fairly healthy for whites—of course we get our doses of malaria, but they come as a matter of course. We have improved native health in the area fifty per cent within a few years, and I hope to make it eighty-five in my lifetime. It's interesting work and in your line. As to staff, there's me; Red Bel-

34

linger, who's an American, and a bit of a reprobate; he had been drifting round the world doctoring on tramp ships until I discovered him in Massawa and abducted him to El Belada. He's our physician and anaesthetist. Then there's Zarek, our surgeon. He had an English mother and Sudani father. He's fabulously wealthy and very entertaining. Our radiographer is from the Belgian Congo, and our nursing staff are Sudani girls in the main. We get along pretty well together. I recently lost my pathologist, a graduate from Khartoum University. The educated Sudani doesn't want to bury himself in a scrub hospital: he wants city lights and amenities. Our pathologist went up to Cairo. So there it is!" Roy Kingsland shrugged. "I could certainly do with you out there, Mac, if you would care to consider it. Think of all the snags, because you won't be overpaid." He smiled ruefully.

"Would you mind if I asked you a very personal question, Roy?"

"Not at all. Fire away!"

"Are you and Fiona—er——?"

He didn't help her out but smiled encouragingly.

"I mean—you might think me impertinent, but if you are sweethearts it might account for her attitude earlier. I did rather burst in on you and she found me almost weeping over your 'dead' body. She might have misunderstood—concluded anything. If so I would like her to be enlightened. She might like me better."

"Fiona doesn't have to be enlightened yet," he reassured her. "She was once engaged to my brother who was killed in the air. I am at present, as you are, one hundred per cent engrossed in my work, though I have been looking forward to seeing Fiona immensely. Hallo! What's Mother waving her stick about for? She's telling us to hurry. Dinner must be ruined or something."

Together they ran the last hundred yards to the house where Mrs. Kingsland still stood gesticulating with some urgency.

"It's the telephone for Doctor Hayes," she called clearly. "I offered to take a message but the caller preferred it to be personal. The phone's in the hall, dear."

Without a care in the world Mac picked up the receiver. Doubtless it was Daddy inquiring why she wasn't home to dinner as promised.

"Hallo!" she called into the mouthpiece. "This is Mac. Oh! it's you, Barney!"

Then her voice died away as did the color in her cheeks. Passing through the hall Roy Kingsland hesitated and regarded her. He saw her mouth working but no sound coming out. With two strides he was at her side and holding her firmly as she would have fallen.

"What is it, Mac?" he asked, replacing the receiver. "Is it bad news?"

She tried to tell him. He held her very tightly while she mastered the power of speech again out of the depths of shock and tragedy.

"It—it's Daddy," she finally stammered in a voice thin and weak like a child's. "Barney found him—found him dead in his chair an hour ago. He said he"—she swallowed and almost choked—"was smiling, just as though he had gone to sleep." Her eyes blinked once, twice, sought reassurance in his. "This *is* true, isn't it, Roy? I'm not having some horrible dream? I feel dream-like and kind of funny."

"I want you to have a very stiff whisky, Mac, and let me take you home. I'm afraid it must be true and I'm deeply sorry. I'll help you all I can, my dear, even to keeping an eye on your father's patients if I'm needed. Down the hatch, Mac, and keep your chin up. Remember your dad was smiling. He can't have known a thing about it."

He was glad when she commenced to weep, and crept into his arms to do it. Somehow she didn't seem so sister-like now, but he was glad to lend himself as a receptacle for her grief, and give her his handkerchief for a final blow.

"I'm all right now," she told him, and her chin was up, jutting. "I won't feel as bad again. He had a bad heart and you spotted it immediately. I'll always remember. Somehow it wasn't as bad a shock as it would have been if your words hadn't in a way prepared me. Let's go, now. I don't think I can drive."

"I'll take you home in my car. Yours will follow later. May I leave you a moment to give a few instructions?"

Mac nodded, and stood at the window looking out over the darkening waters of the lake. She fancied she saw her father's gentle, whimsical face mirrored in the water, and he was nodding his head and telling her everything was for the best. It was only imagination, she knew, but somehow she felt comforted and not quite alone in the world of her bereavement.

CHAPTER SIX

THE FOLLOWING three weeks passed for Mac with all the accompanying confusion of a bad dream. People who had been normal everyday acquaintances now behaved abnormally, shuffling their feet and averting their eyes whenever she was in their vicinity. She wished heartily that mothers wouldn't insist on hushing the children whenever in their play they strayed too near the house of mourning, thus making the innocents aware of something they were better to be ignorant about. Even Barney looked heavily uncomfortable and inclined to stand on one leg like a stork, rubbing the toe of the other shoe against his trousered calf. Mrs. Tunney sniffed wetly for three whole days, wondering why Mac showed no inclination to do the same.

"You cry, lovey," she once advised the daughter of the house. "Bottling it up inside isn't going to do you any good."

"Thanks, but I'm all right as I am," Mac returned a little crossly, "and while Doctor Kingsland is here couldn't we have a decent curry, Mrs. Tunney? The sort you used to make for Daddy sometimes." She became aware of the housekeeper gazing at her reproachfully.

"Very well, Miss Mac," the woman said with a pronounced sniff. "If you can think of food at such a time I'll make a curry for dinner this evening." She turned away muttering under her breath, "But how you can be so heartless I'll never . . ."

"Mrs. Tunney!" Mac recalled her sharply, and the blue eyes were angrily bright as the woman turned, somewhat on her dignity. "What I feel at the moment is my own private business. I will not parade my grief in public for you or anyone else. And certainly I can and will think of food at such a time with two healthy and hungry men in the house. As a doctor I can't stand by and watch you serving up soggy lettuce leaves and patent sorrow every meal-time. My father would want this house —all of us—to carry on normally. A doctor's house is one place you can't afford to wreathe in gloom. The sick people coming to the surgery feel bad enough as it is. We can't unload our misery on to them as well." Her voice caught a little in her throat, then she coughed and swallowed quickly.

"You cried for a week after your mother died," the housekeeper reminded her.

"I shan't cry for a week this time," Mac said quietly, "and when I do cry you shan't see me. Now do go and find a hankie, Tunney, dear, and try to be a—a help and comfort as you used to be."

The last desperate plea had its effect on the housekeeper. She suddenly remembered the little girl trying to control her trembling lips and failing, burying her face into a cushion and sobbing wildly. Now she realized the little girl had grown twelve years older and learnt that physical control she had once lacked. This was the only difference.

"Very well, Miss Mac," she said respectfully, "I'll stand by you and try to—to cheer up. It isn't as if we can bring the dear, good soul back again, is it?"

True to his word, Roy Kingsland had stood by in the emergency, acting as locum, for Barney had perforce taken it upon himself to make arrangements for the funeral, had sent telegrams off to relatives, notified Doctor Hayes' legal representatives and generally proved himself invaluable and a friend in need. Mac spent the days going through her father's papers and clothes, surprised and touched to find snapshots of herself tucked away into old diaries and envelopes, snapshots she had forgotten existed, all neatly dated and labelled in her father's fine copper-plate hand, so unusual in one of his calling.

"Mac—aged three," in a somewhat leggy bathing-suit. "Mac aged seven—Queen o' the May."

"I had a decided pout!" Mac exclaimed in wonder.

"Mac aged ten—off to boarding-school."

"Did they really make us wear those dreadful hats?" Mac shuddered, seeing her small wistful face looking out from under a great, black-beaver, brimmed monstrosity. "We must have looked like a lot of little mushrooms!"

At eight o'clock each evening the three doctors met for dinner, sometimes for the first time in the day. Though Doctor Kingsland was a comparative stranger to the house and district he had pestered no one for information. The practice books were fortunately neatly kept and up to date, patients' notes filed away in alphabetical order by the "treasure" who had been Doctor Hayes' secretary for more years than her carefully henna'd hair admitted to, and who had become even more rejuvenated by the advent of Roy Kingsland. He had a camp bed in the study which was adjacent to the surgery, and rarely intruded into the house proper once he had taken his bath, a cold one, Mac discovered with a shiver.

Relatives—mostly distant, for both Mac's parents had been only children—arrived for the funeral and departed, then came the ordeal of the will-reading. Barney was dumbstruck when told he had inherited the considerable private portion of the practice, provided he stayed in person to administer it, and a small sum of money which would enable him to take a lease on this very house which now became Mac's property provided she handed over the tenancy to Barney. There wasn't much doubt that Barney would "inherit" the National Health patients also. The "old doctor's" will was so full of provisos intended to perpetuate the practice that it was almost amusing. Mrs. Tunney's loyalty was suitably rewarded, but was to be immediately enhanced provided Doctor Combe had the further option of her services as housekeeper, and the bequest to Miss Briggs, the secretary, was similarly worded.

"I wouldn't leave Doctor unless he told me to," Mrs. Tunney declared to all present, "and it's not the extra money, neither. So long as Miss Mac's properly looked after. . . ."

Mac looked rather small and forlorn in a corner of the big drawing-room sofa, the neat black suit she wore emphasizing her pallor. She scarcely heard the lawyer's verbose statements, for she had suddenly realized with a sensation of shock that from this moment life must go on for her, and she would henceforward be quite alone. Even now she was a guest in this house, Barney's guest: not that he would ever remind her of it, he probably hadn't yet fully appreciated the situation, but as her father had cunningly contrived to tie Barney to the practice and Silverdell, so in one fell swoop had he freed her from it. She hadn't a single tie here now. Her assets were all monetary and sufficient. Her father had given her a bank balance and taken the roof from over her head. It was as though through all the legal jargon his kindly voice was challenging her: "Right-ho, Mac. This is what you wanted.

39

Now get out and work wherever you like. The world is yours." But even at twenty-four, when you are a thrice-diploma'd doctor, the world can look a little frightening in its immensity when you can't lay claim to even one small corner of it.

There was a tea-trolley in the study, and as she poured herself a cup of the steaming liquid Mac heard Barney's voice in the surgery.

"Very well, Kingsland, I'll see your fees are paid into your account."

Roy appeared smilingly in the doorway. For the first time Mac noticed he looked tired and strained.

"I'll pour you some tea," she said a little self-consciously, feeling somewhat annoyed with Barney. What Roy had done was an act of friendship, and of course he must have his fees, but there was more to it than that.

"Mrs. Tunney tells me you're leaving, Doctor Kingsland," she said as she passed him a cup of tea. "I can't begin to say how grateful I am to you. . . ."

"Then don't embarrass me by trying," he pleaded. "I'm glad I was on hand in your hour of need, but as I am flying back to El Belada next week I must get home to pack, etcetera."

Mac's eyes were wide.

"So soon?" she asked. "I thought one had fabulous leaves on overseas service."

"Not where I work," he said ruefully, "and I came recruiting, remember? I can't go back empty-handed, so I must spend a day or two really looking around seriously."

"But I"—Mac began, when Barney suddenly appeared, looking larger and more assured than he had ever done before. It had suddenly occurred to Barney that he wasn't a junior partner any longer but "the doctor" to twelve hundred souls in the valley. He was the captain of his soul earlier than he had had any right to anticipate, and while being humbly thankful he could not help enjoying the sensation as he interviewed Kingsland finally in *his* surgery, and now entered *his* study to take tea with the others out of *his* tea-pot. He must remember to tell Mac she could have anything she wanted of her father's after Kingsland had gone: he wanted to give her much more, if she would accept it.

Mac experienced a near panic as Roy Kingsland finally shook hands in good-bye.

"Doctor Kingsland——!" her eyes were pleading as he clasped her fingers tightly. Why *did* Barney have to be looking on?

"I'll see you out to your car," she finished lamely.

"I'll do that," Barney volunteered. "It's cool and you've been developing a cough lately, Mac."

There was a slight pause which seemed eternity to Mac.

"I'll just give the old dog a pat, if you'll excuse us, Combe," Roy Kingsland said, dumping his cases in the hall. "Take me to him, Mac, will you?"

"He'll be in Father's room, I expect," she said, deliberately not meeting his eyes as they climbed the stairs together. "He's been fretting, I'm afraid. Thank you for . . ." she didn't know what she had to thank him for, and stopped speaking with a flush as they reached the old doctor's bedroom.

"Rogue doesn't seem to be here," Kingsland observed, looking round the room. "Maybe he's in the kitchen."

"He's here all right," Mac said dully. "He's under the bed. He—he's dead."

"Oh—I *am* sorry!" Roy Kingsland told her. "You seem to be having a packet lately, Mac. What can I say?"

"I don't want sympathy, thank you," she told him rather curtly. "I want a job. I want that job at El Belada. I'm serious, Doctor Kingsland."

"Are you sure?" he asked her keenly. "Have you really thought about it or are you wanting to find distraction from—from all that's happened lately? Forgive me if I'm frank, Mac, but in El Belada we have no time for self-pity in ourselves or others. The problems of our world outside are minimized by the problems of running a hospital beset by all the difficulties in the book. You have no idea what it's like trying to cope with an outbreak of say—blackwater fever, with the drug transport held up at the coast awaiting clearance by the authorities who are held up somewhere else. I can't begin to explain to you how the 'other half' lacks the efficiency of your beautiful Hospital for Tropical Diseases. We are fighting all the time against one enemy or another. It affects us as people. I, personally, have an evil reputation as Superintendent of El Belada. You didn't find me very likeable at our first meeting, you would like me even less if you worked with me."

He shrugged.

"I don't think my liking you or not will influence my work," Mac said coldly. "I *must* get a job soon, so why not El Belada? Unless you just couldn't care less," she snapped, turning away abruptly. "I am not going to plead with you for a job," she added with a return of her old spirit, "so take me or leave me, damn you!"

41

"I'll take you," he smiled, and held out his hand to seal the bargain. "You may have cause to regret your decision, but *I* won't. I'll get everything out of you for El Belada that I can get, even to your blood if I need it."

"I'm classified as A," Mac said drily, and found she could laugh again.

After surgery Barney was suddenly in pursuit of her, beckoning furiously.

"Can you give me ten minutes in the study, Mac?" he asked. "I'm expecting Mrs. Whitehead's baby tonight."

"That takes me back," Mac sighed, and then nodded her head. "All right, Barney, I'm coming."

Barney was pacing the small, book-lined room, examining the pipes in the rack and generally fidgeting. He coughed as Mac joined him and looked very pink after his second shave that day. Barney was inclined to be hirsute.

"Mac!" her bones positively creaked as she was seized in a stifling embrace, as unexpected as it was overwhelming. "My darling girl, I *have* to speak. You are not alone in the world, my dear, you have *me*!" Barney suddenly realized he was enfolding eight stone of feminine charm, and the knowledge went a little to his head. He kissed, kissed again and again, making little tender mother-hen noises between whiles. "God! but you're lovely!" he declared in an ecstasy of torment. Mac's eyes were closed and the lover suddenly panicked. He stopped squeezing and Mac swayed away from him, gasping for breath.

"I—I—I——" Barney blundered with her to the divan and laid her upon it gently. "Oh, Mac, I didn't mean to be so rough. I wanted to ask you to marry me. It will put us both out of our misery, I feel sure."

Mac felt herself down and found that no ribs appeared to be broken.

"Oh, Barney!" she gasped at him. "Who taught you to make love, may I ask?"

"I only ever kissed one girl before, Mac, but not like that. You drive me mad!" he accused her. "Don't you see we've got to get married, and then things can carry on as before, only you'll be my wife and—and——" The implication of his words made him feel suddenly faint, and he turned to the decanter. "Mac, I wanted you desperately just then," he told her frankly. "I'm afraid I might—might——"

She smiled gently.

"Oh, no, you never would, Barney," she assured him. "I'm not afraid for myself with you even if Mrs. Tunney wasn't in the house. There's nothing to stop you taking a wife, now, only it isn't going to be me. Now don't look so glum! Just because I'm here you can't see anyone else, but I know a few girls who'll be popping in to see you once I'm gone. You're quite a catch, Barney, my lad. You're nice-looking, and oh, what virility!" Her laughing eyes warned him off as he looked like proving this latter statement once again. "I'm going to work. I've got a job."

"Where?" asked Barney.

"El Belada, or Hades," Mac went on serenely. "Something tells me I'm going to be a lot older and wiser before I see Silverdell again."

"I hope a lot happier, too, Mac," Barney said sincerely.

"Yes," she sighed. "But Hades or Heaven, Barney, I've known I had to go from the beginning. Have you ever felt as sure of anything as that?"

Barney shifted his large feet, feeling out of his depth again.

"If you have to, you have to, Mac," he conceded. "I wanted to give you a home—your home—oh, I put things so badly!"

"But I understand," Mac said gently, "and thank you, Barney, dear. I would like to kiss you for it if you promise not to attack me again."

Barney held out his lips invitingly, and for the first time experienced the butterfly softness of a woman's willingly given tribute, which was so strangely exciting. But like a butterfly it was gone all too quickly, and so was Mac, leaving him large and lonely behind her in the old doctor's favorite chair.

CHAPTER SEVEN

IMMACULA HAYES did not see the arum lilies in the garden of Redcroft bloom that year, those same lilies which had so fascinated her father during his lifetime. He had been gazing at them on the day Mac was born, after ten years of what he had concluded was to be a childless marriage.

43

His hands had been trembling as he caressed the wax-like trumpets, and then a young nurse had come running to him across the lawn, her face bright with relief and happiness.

"It's all over, Doctor," she had told him, "and you have a beautiful little wax-doll of a baby girl, sir. I never saw such a darling. You can't call *her* John, now can you? Oh, and Mrs. Hayes is quite well, sir. You can see her—them—now."

His concern had been all for his wife producing a first baby in her middle-thirties, but women—he had discovered —are the most resilient of creatures and able to withstand a great deal more physical buffeting than their spouses. Helen had been radiant in the midst of her natural exhaustion, and finally he had looked on the child, seeing in its tightly screwed face an unopened lily bud.

"We'll call her Immacula—she came with the lilies," he told his wife on a note of inspiration.

So Mac got her name, a name she had always loathed and which was a never-ending embarrassment to her. A name like Immacula needed living up to, and she fancied she ought to have been tall, smooth-haired and stately to match it rather like one of those incredible ladies out of *Vogue*. But instead she was somewhat short of inches, slim and childlike, and though she had long ago dispensed with her curls and brushed her hair severely and with faithful regularity, it still perversely turned up round her nape and quickly became silken floss when the wind played with it.

Since she had been staying with Fiona Bardale these last weeks before they both were due to sail out to take up their new appointments in the Sudan, she had grown to envy Fiona her obvious physical assets. Fiona was all she had ever wanted to be, regally tall, dark and stately, a model figure on which all clothes looked rather special and elegant. Fiona looked like someone who had strayed out of Swan Lake, with that same quality of cool remoteness one associates with a *prima ballerina*. Mac, who had initially doubted the other's sincerity in proffering the hand of friendship, was now prepared to think she had been mistaken in Fiona on that first, fateful meeting. They had since laughed together about it.

"I thought you had killed Roy," Fiona flashed with a smile of reminiscence. "I was prepared to kill *you* if you had."

"You were once engaged to his brother, I believe?" Mac asked.

Fiona's quality of remoteness had suddenly descended; her face became mask-like.

"Yes. But one cannot remain attached to the dead. It doesn't do, does it?"

Fiona did not talk much about herself, but gently drew all her guest's past history out of her, romantic and otherwise. She was all sympathy when she heard about the affair with Gareth, which Mac had discussed with no third party before, apart from that merest reference in her father's somewhat embarrassed ear.

"Love is damnable!" Fiona said with alien passion. "It drives us into incredible situations at times!"

"You, too?" Mac asked sympathetically.

"No! No!" Fiona sighed hard. "If anything—but *any-thing*—came between me and the man I loved, I should die!"

"Then you are in love?" persisted Mac.

Fiona blinked her eyes and turned away with that innate elegance the other so envied in her. "Here we are talking of romance like two schoolgirls," she half apologized, "and I promised to take you out on the lake. Come on!"

Mrs. Bardale did not prove so reticent on the subject of her daughter's romances as Fiona, however. One day she had Mac summoned to her bedroom, where she had decided to stay for the day.

"One of my stupid migraines, dear," she explained, as the girl wondered whether to go back for her stethoscope. "I don't require your professional services. My own doctor has had me try absolutely everything for them, but bed and a darkened room afford me the only relief I can expect. I wanted to talk to you while Fiona is out. I'm so worried about my daughter, Doctor Hayes."

"Why should you be, Mrs. Bardale?" Mac asked gently. "I'm sure she's all right."

"Yes, but it's this dreadful place she's going to, and all it involves. I—er—don't mean the work. Fiona is a very capable Nursing Sister."

"I'm sure of it," Mac agreed.

"I have tried to keep life beautiful for my daughter," the woman proceeded. "She has always known this home, lived in luxury and elegance. I even had a governess for her rather than let her come up against some of those little ruffians they allow in good schools nowadays." Mac swallowed, wondering if she had been one of the "little ruffians" to whom Mrs. Bardale referred. She had certainly been a happy little tomboy once she had found her

45

feet at St. Winifrid's. "I gave her a season in town, and after that I was unfortunate enough to lose my husband and so the purse-strings were inevitably tightened." As Mrs. Bardale paused, Mac looked round the room with its deep pile carpet and regency furniture, and out of the window at the rolling lawns cascading to the lake. Did the Bardales realize what a tightening of purse-strings really meant, she wondered?

"Of course, when it became obvious that Adrian Kingsland and Fiona were in love, it made me so happy!" sighed Mrs. Bardale, her migraine forgotten. "It meant little physical change in my daughter's mode of living, simply that she would become mistress of Kingsmount and always be near to me. Adrian was a dear; so charming and volatile. You'd have liked him. But it was all not to be. Adrian got himself killed. . . ."

Mac almost asked what all this had to do with her, but desisted.

"Now Roy isn't like Adrian," Mrs. Bardale volunteered somewhat vehemently, "and I sometimes fear for my darling."

"But why should you?" Mac asked. "Fiona is old enough to look after herself."

"Some people never are, Doctor Hayes," the mother said firmly. "My daughter is not nearly so worldly-wise as yourself. You have had experiences"—for a horrible moment Mac feared Fiona had "blabbed" to her mother the confidences she had so recently outpoured—"your work and—and so forth. Why, you told me yourself you haven't had a mother to turn to since you were twelve. A girl must miss her mother dreadfully, but she does learn to stand on her own feet. I realize, of course, I have made mistakes in Fiona's upbringing. I too should have made her independent of me."

"Then she's going to learn how to be rather later than usual, apparently," Mac said cheerfully. "When you're three thousand miles away she'll soon get life in true perspective. I shouldn't worry about Fiona one little bit, Mrs. Bardale. She seems very self-assured to me."

"You don't know the half of it," the other said darkly. "She's emotionally—er—naive, for instance. Since Adrian she hasn't really been in love. Men have fallen in love with her but left her quite unmoved. Now Roy . . ." she paused as though faint for an instant.

"You mean Roy and Fiona are . . . ?" Mac's eyes were very round.

"I fear so," Mrs. Bardale nodded her head wearily.

"Why—fear?" Mac queried.

"Because I think Fiona is in love at last," the woman said. "I saw them together that last evening before Roy left for El Belada, and something tremendous had obviously happened between them. Fiona is different, and she refuses to discuss Roy with anyone, but if she loves him, and if he is taking advantage of it to drag her out there to him . . ."

"Surely she doesn't *have* to go?" questioned Mac.

"A woman in love is impelled to do almost anything, surely?" Mrs. Bardale countered. "If you loved a man wouldn't you follow him—even to El Belada?"

"But I'm going to El Belada without loving anybody!" Mac defended her argument.

"Yes, you're going of your own free will, Doctor Hayes. Fiona is going to be with Roy."

"But don't you ever want her to be in love?" Mac asked incredulously.

"Of course I want her to love, and marry. You don't appear to have seen my point, Doctor Hayes. Roy Kingsland is not as gentle-natured as his brother. He will exact every ounce out of Fiona for his wretched hospital. In public he will make no sign that he cares a fig about her. Fiona will be up against ugliness and horror for the first time in her life, and should Roy Kingsland not demonstrate the tenderness towards her I myself witnessed, I fear she will wilt and die like a flower. We can't interfere at this stage, but oh, Doctor Hayes, you can relieve my mind by promising to be Fiona's friend out there!"

"Of course I'll be her friend," Mac vowed out of the generosity of her heart, "but what can I actually do?"

"See that Fiona spends plenty of time with Roy to help her face up to the ugly side of things. As the only other white woman in the hospital you will probably be asked to accompany Roy and Fiona on occasions when actually they would much rather—er—be . . ."

"You needn't go on," Mac stated. "I have no desire to play gooseberry. I shall thrust the lovebirds together as much as possible."

"But don't make it too obvious," Mrs. Bardale said quickly. "Roy mustn't suspect—Fiona mustn't. They don't know we—er—know, Doctor Hayes. If I hadn't seen what I saw, and known my own daughter . . . !" And with a conspiratorial smirk Mrs. Bardale settled down to enjoy her day in bed.

"I wonder what the great love scene was like?" Mac asked herself as she went downstairs again. "I'm surprised Doctor Kingsland didn't guard against peepers. After all he should know all the hidey-holes round here. He has lived in these parts most of his life!"

She was surprised to find she felt a little disgruntled about the whole business. All day she imagined Fiona locked desperately in an embrace with Roy Kingsland, framed against the incredible beauty of the lake, and didn't enjoy the picture she mentally drew one little bit.

Fiona would have been amused if she could have heard her mother adressing their guest on her behalf. That she was emotionally fragile would even have struck her as a great joke. The invitation for Mac to stay with them at Water's Head was not motivated purely by kindness and sympathy for the girl in her bereavement. The Bardales had not liked the way Roy had dashed off to help in the Hayes' affairs and stayed away so long, leaving only a few scrappy days of his leave for friends of much longer standing. They had concluded Mac must be at the bottom of his interest. Purity of motive had so long ceased to be a Bardale trait that mother and daughter could hardly believe it present in anyone else. Mac had been invited to Waters' Head to be warned off the Kingsland grass, but it had to be manœuvred so that it was done most delicately, of course, and in the way least likely to alienate her from them. Mrs. Bardale took credit for having achieved her purpose admirably. If Roy Kingsland's eye roved in her direction at El Kadugli, it now behoved Mac, in sworn friendship's name, to rebuff him sharply, and if Mrs. Bardale knew anything about Roy, he wouldn't be in a hurry to invite such a rebuff again. Without competition it was up to Fiona to work hard and manipulate an engagement, at least. She was rather clever at fixing things. Playing on her vaunted innocence, she had often placed herself in a compromising situation with a member of the opposite sex. Roy was not one to compromise a woman and do nothing about it. He was already partially compromised in their eyes by the scene upon which Mrs. Bardale had dwelt so lovingly. Roy had been invited over to dinner on his last evening by an almost tearful Fiona, who had accused him of not "liking" her any more. "If only for old time's sake, Roy——!" she had pleaded with limpid eyes.

"Of course I'll come, Fiona," Roy had assured her. "I don't need to prove I 'like' you, either. I always have done that."

After dinner there had been music. Fiona played the piano rather well, and her shoulders were creamy in the flattery of the restrained lighting. She was in white and, he realized that the passing years had made her—if possible more beautiful. After the music Mrs. Bardale had waved them playfully out into the garden, and Roy had enjoyed the sensation of having Fiona on his arm as they stepped out through the french windows and took the path down to the lake where an old stone seat was set under the drooping fronds of a willow tree.

"Tell me about El Belada," Fiona had asked intensely, and to her mortification he had done so, at great length. Finally, feeling chilled, they walked back towards the house. Fiona now felt the sands of time were fast running out for her.

"Oh, Roy," she had appealed, seizing his lapels, "don't you want to kiss me even once before you go? I thought I meant something to you!"

The magic of the moment caught on. He was suddenly desperately aware of her beauty and her perfume, and the shoulders bared when her stole had slipped to the ground. He savoured and he sipped, pleasurably awaiting the awakening of the madness of his senses. But nothing happened at all. He left her and stood back, wondering why such feminine charm should leave him so cold. Still in an inquiring frame of mind, he tried again, pressing his lips hard against hers and even kissing her bared shoulders. In the middle of this—for want of a better word—effort, a discreet cough interrupted and Mrs. Bardale spoke out of the darkness.

"So sorry, dears, I didn't realize . . ."

At the time Roy had been glad of the interruption, for he was feeling rather a fool. Then Fiona spoke.

"It's rather unfortunate mother saw us."

"Why?" Roy inquired. "We're old friends, aren't we?"

"That was hardly an 'old friendly' exhibition, was it?" Fiona asked, to his surprise. "She will conclude we are—are——"

Roy had actually laughed.

"It will do you good to get away from here, Fi," he told her. "Your mother surely doesn't think you're engaged to every man who has kissed you? And don't tell me thousands haven't!" he changed his tone to a teasing challenge, and with that she had had to be content—for the present.

CHAPTER EIGHT

"IT CAN'T be true," Mac pondered some weeks later, standing at the rail of the *Indian Maid* as she slid imperceptibly through the oily waters of the Suez Canal; "this all just can't be true!"

Aboard the pilot ship a dusky-skinned individual roared Arabic imprecations up at a ginger-headed seaman who had just emptied a bucket of bilge accidentally on to the pilot's deck. "Ginger" was on a tanker which was hove-to while the *Indian Maid* crept past: Mac had always nursed an idea that the Suez Canal was about a mile wide, but now knew that it barely outstretched the Grand Union in parts, these being the dirtiest and smelliest parts, of course. It was the smells Mac was remarking on, her reactions to this adventure being all professional up to now. She wondered how any of God's creatures could possibly exist where the very air one breathed was a continuous stink, yet at Port Said the docks had swarmed with husky-looking individuals who did the work of cranes with muscular arms and shoulders, and the children— who must surely have been drawn together by some magical pied-piper of Islam (otherwise there couldn't have been so many children present at one time)—were cheerful and laughing as they pleaded for piastres, standing on their tarbushed or woolly heads for minutes at a time, pushing one another into the water, treating the honking horns of dockside traffic with a profound disdain and generally intent, apparently, on leading very short lives and superbly merry ones.

Fiona had spent most of her time shuddering since they had left the clean but hot little island of Pantelleria in the middle of the Mediterranean Sea: she had been in turn sea-sick, injection-sick and smell-sick. The canal was the end, she decided, and spent her time in the fan-cooled

50

lounges or state-rooms where air-purifier was sprayed, ice-cold, at regular intervals.

Mac, however, was keen to miss nothing. How could one learn how the other half lived if one stayed below all day avoiding the very air these people breathed as though one was a superior being from another planet? Mac was little bits of missionary, sociologist and doctor rolled up into one: she burned with a fierce resentment when she thought of the fellahin children diving for refuse from ship's bilges, while British children were compelled by law to receive adequate education and at least one square meal per day, at the State's expense, if necessary. No one seemed to be caring about the little fellahin. When one horrified passenger had demanded, "Where *are* their mothers?" a much-travelled gentleman had replied, "We have left maternal responsibilities far behind, Madam. Here—and henceforth—Allah will protect the faithful! And if he fails to do so all accidents are shrugged off as Fate!"

"Ginger" on the tanker suddenly tired of the Egyptian's querulousness, and called in a rich Glasgow accent, "Och! shut yer big mouth! Didna a say a was sorry efter a'? Get on an' shift this big bloomin' thing so we can get hame afore Hogmanay!"

The pilot's mate felt somewhat appeased by having drawn words, if not blood, from the Scotsman, and began to take an interest in their progress once more. The *Indian Maid* slid past the tanker without mishap, and on the road alongside the canal a camel caravan materialized, added to the general smelliness, and passed on towards Port Said.

"Hashish for the parson, hemp for the clerk!" misquoted a voice in Mac's ear, and looking round with a smile she welcomed Colin Ormby to her side. Colin was in Customs and Excise, bound for a new appointment in Aden, so he might well know what he was talking about.

"Does much dope smuggling go on?" Mac asked innocently.

"What?" the young man asked derisively, pausing to light his pipe. "I'll bet those camels are lousy with the stuff. I once shot a beast on the Jordan frontier which had a festering, fly-ridden sore on the flank. Tucked *into* the sore I found a wad of hemp."

"Dreadful!" Mac decided. "You mustn't tell that story to Fiona, Colin."

"Why?" He had flushed very slightly as though to

51

acknowledge that at the start of the voyage he had been more than a little interested in Miss Fiona Bardale.

"Well, I'm a doctor and can stand a lot more than she can. She doesn't like—ugliness."

"Do any of us?" he mocked. "Is that any reason for ignoring its existence? You'll be telling me next you enjoy the idea of the shrieks of an agonized dumb beast which had to be shot to quieten it."

Mac was silent.

Somewhat apologetically Colin Ormby spoke again.

"Excuse my asking this, Mac, but are you a very old friend of Fiona's?"

"No. I only met her a month or two ago. We are going to work together at El Belada Hospital in the Kordofan Province of the Sudan. That is the real limit of our association. Why?"

"Nothing. Just see that you *do* work together, that's all."

"You're being very ambiguous," Mac said, rather shortly.

"Then I'll put it more plainly, even though it's none of my business. Don't run around after Fiona in El Belada as you have done on this trip."

"But I haven't!" Mac actually laughed and looked up at Colin, who wasn't so laughing. Could it be the fellow was suffering from sour grapes because an Oxford-educated Indian princeling had begun to monopolise Fiona? It wasn't as if she had done much running about after the other, as Colin had suggested: when Fiona was sick she had naturally asked Mac to sit with her, so that the younger girl hadn't gone to the dance the crew had put on for the passengers, an even which had, apparently, proved most enjoyable. Then when the September heat had begun to tell, Fiona had wanted Mac to sit and play cribbage with her in the lounge, instead of joining in those overheating deck-games. It was just that Fiona was rather a rare flower and inclined to wilt easily. Mac—of the kind heart—was only too ready to help shelter such a bloom if it was in her power to do so.

"How about letting me show you a bit of Suez when we dock?" Colin suggested. "I was once stationed in Suez before they kicked us out."

"I'd love . . ." Mac began, then paused. "I'll ask Fiona if she wants to come."

"She won't," Colin said flatly. "I want to take you along to shanty-town, which would upset Fiona. You are a person capable of seeing life in the raw without blinkers on. I never met a girl quite like you."

"I believe you're prepared to carry on with me where you left off with my friend, Colin," she said on a note of warning. "I don't respond lightly to compliments—you had better know."

"I shouldn't think you respond lightly to anything, young Mac," he told her, smiling seriously, "which is why you are indeed mistaken in my intentions. I would as soon think of flirting with you as going up in a balloon. You're the kind of girl a man wants to marry if he wants anything. I can't afford to indulge such hopes—I am already married."

"Then no wonder Fiona threw you over!" Mac decided, remembering catching the two in an embrace and fading away from the scene in natural embarrassment.

Colin Ormby began to laugh.

"You *must* be joking, Mac! An estranged wife didn't turn Fiona against me. Why, the Maharajah, at twenty-two, has three wives waiting for his return to Palandrahore. Don't tell me Fiona doesn't know about *them*!"

"But there's nothing between the Maharajah and Fiona!" she exclaimed defensively. "He has tea with her and buys her a drink occasionally. They walk round the deck together. I'm sure there's nothing wrong in that! He's probably telling her all about Palandrahore, *and* his wives."

Colin shrugged and said no more, and Mac did her best to forget their conversation. "He evil does who evil thinks"—true enough; but Indian princes and diamond and emerald bracelets somehow go together, and she couldn't help wondering, sometimes, just what Fiona was getting out of that friendship and how far it was compatible with her avowed devotion to Roy.

•

CHAPTER NINE

THE VOYAGE was now almost over for the two girls, and in the writing lounge of the *Indian Maid* Mac was trying to pen a letter to Barney, which could be posted when the

Post Office officials came aboard with the pilot off the Eritrean port of Massawa. Barney's air-mailed letter had caught up with her at Jidda on the Saudi Arabian coast, where the faithful had disembarked for the pilgrimage to Mecca. Mac was keeping her letter strictly in the nature of a travelogue, though Barney's had merely emphasized the fact that he still couldn't see "other girls," and missed her terribly. If she ever regretted her decision to work in El Belada, would she consider a partnership with him— even though strictly on a professional basis?

"The whole valley misses your father still, and I'm sure your presence among us would compensate so many who remember him with an affection I could never inspire in them," Barney had concluded.

Mac nibbled at her pen, re-reading the page she had completed.

"I'm answering the last part of your letter first, Barney, dear, to say I will never join you in general practice in the valley. My resolution is firmer than ever since I have started this thing. It has started for me, you know, even on the ship. Wherever we have called I have seen the most dreadful human flotsam imaginable; blind and maimed children, young men who have grown up without a sound, healthy bone in their bodies, who drag themselves literally under the ship begging for piastres—as though they should have to beg for anything! They even put on a macabre entertainment for the benefit of us who are privileged to be normal. It has all made me feel very small and inadequate, but at least I can help a few of these stricken millions with my special knowledge, and this I intend to do. I think I can see what drives Doctor Schweitzer, bless him! and Roy Kingsland and all the others in this type of service. It isn't so much what they do, as the impossibility of going back to a way of life which doesn't allow me to do anything at all. I have collected the most horrifying statistics from various sources, but I don't want to shock you. Sufficient to say that an average, uneducated slum-type woman in these areas produces ten children and raises two who are more or less normal in every way. One or two will be still-born (because the mother was practically starving during pregnancy), three will be crippled by rickets, two will suffer from tuberculosis and one will be either blinded (by trichiasis) or mentally deficient. I don't expect Massawa to be as bad. I believe the Italians did a lot of good there. However, we'll see!"

Mac heard excitement growing out on the deck, and hurriedly scribbled:

"More next time from El Belada. I hear Massawa's just coming into view and I'm very keen to get ashore for good. One is so limited on a ship."

She signed herself as "Yours ever" and hurriedly rammed the letter in an envelope preparatory to purchasing the required stamp from the authorities.

She went out on to the promenade deck: the starboard side was deserted. As she passed the small reading lounge she caught sight of two people intimately conversing in a corner, and gave a sharp rap on the port-hole frame.

"Massawa, Fiona," she called.

Inside the lounge Prince Khalid Krishna of Palandra-hore leaned earnestly forward.

"Your answer, please, Fiona!" he pleaded. "There is much to do if you go on with me. The ship only stays here one hour. I must arrange your further passage, send telegrams and cables. Still you don't answer!"

He bent suddenly to kiss her white palm with an intimacy only Mac—and probably Colin Ormby—suspected.

"First you promise"—he accused her—"then you waver and perhaps change your mind. Are you not convinced that I love you, Fiona?"

She pouted.

"You have three wives already, Khalid, of your own kind. What future is there for me, a Christian, with you? Am I to be nursemaid to your children, perhaps?"

"Fiona, you break my heart!" the prince accused her. "These marriages were arranged in my childhood. Two of these 'wives' I do not even know. Maybe they are pretty"—he shrugged—"maybe not. You, Fiona, are real to me and very beautiful."

She struggled free of an embrace with him, saying virtuously, "Someone may come in. We must continue to be discreet, Khalid, and—and practical. Now, as I see it, I have very little proof that my future will be assured with you. Your ministers may well hate me, and make life impossible for us. . . ."

Mac sailed into the lounge like a breeze.

"Fiona, we're almost there," she warned. "Have you collected your bits and pieces?" She looked very coldly at Prince Khalid, who was feeling miserable enough already. "Good-bye, your Highness," she said from the doorway, "I do hope you find your family well?"

Fiona smiled as they went along the deck together. On the whole she had been rather glad of Mac's interruption. The Khalid episode was tied up rather neatly and she had some valuable presents to show for it. There might even be further gifts before he realized she had no intention of going to Palandrahore as a—as a—what would she be exactly? Fiona was far too refined even to think of the word which would describe her position in a thrice-wedded Eastern potentate's household!

Massawa looked clean, white and sparkling from the ship, but Mac realized that the same deadly evil of tropical disease might well have taken its toll in the areas behind the white façade.

"I wonder if Doctor Bellinger is down there?" she asked, looking down at the milling mob on the quayside. "I understood he would come aboard and claim us, but it doesn't look as though he's going to. Shall we go down and at least get our things through the Customs?"

"As you wish," Fiona agreed, aware of Prince Khalid's sombre glances from the lounge windows. As Mac turned away she blew him a butterfly kiss and made her escape in the other's wake.

Mac was a little worried as they allowed themselves to be shepherded into the Customs shed. The port authorities had brought the mail on board and there had been a letter for each new recruit from Roy Kingsland in El Belada. Mac imagined from Fiona's secretive smiles that hers was a love-letter, but the young doctor's was purely professional.

"I am sending our Doctor Bellinger to escort you for the rest of the journey. The name 'Red' aptly describes him. He is violently red-haired and boasts a nasal American drawl. He likes informality, so call him 'Red' from the start. I have given him the strictest information regarding you both, and sincerely trust there will be no hitch. If, however (and this is for your ear only), Red Bellinger does not contact you upon disembarkation, take a taxi to the Hotel Imperial, leave Fiona happily engaged and (without telling her) ask the manager—in my name—to lend Leonardo to you for an hour.

Leonardo will convey you to Mario's, where you will doubtless find Red and give him any treatment he requires. Red has a recurring physical complaint, which I won't go into now as it may not be necessary. I would have preferred Zarek to have escorted you, but again thought of Fiona, who will doubtless be slow to realize that she is a 'foreigner' now and therefore his guest.

"I place my complete trust in you, Doctor Immacula, to get yourselves and Red safely delivered to El Belada."

It was what Roy Kingsland hadn't said which worried Mac not a little; especially when it began to look as though Doctor Bellinger's weakness had apparently over-taken him. What kind of weakness could it be? Was he an epileptic, and subject to fits? Did he suffer from attacks of amnesia or blackouts?

"We're to take a taxi to the Hotel Imperial," Mac said as casually as she could when it became obvious that no escort was looking for them on the almost deserted dock side. "Doctor Kingsland warned me Bellinger might be delayed, but you are not to worry."

"I won't," Fiona smiled. "I was told on the ship that the Imperial is the Claridges of Eritrea. I don't particularly want to rush off to that dry-as-dust hospital. A few days here will be splendid. Did you see those magnificent beaches near the residential area? The Imperial has its own for bathing."

"Then you bathe," Mac advised, "while I attend to something."

They were rushed at more than fifty miles an hour through the broad streets of the city until they once more came within sight of the sea, this time incredibly green and sparkling, with little fronds of foam curling on the shimmering, silver sand. The Imperial was all that Fiona had boasted of it, with the addition of a fountain-cooled courtyard where vines bearing ripe apricots and grapes grew up the flower-starred walls. There was indeed a private beach where many guests of all nationalities, but chiefly Italian, were sprawling under striped umbrellas, somnolent in the afternoon heat. The newcomers were to discover that the Imperial boasted a roof-garden with a swimming-pool, which made it a favorite of the monied classes who could afford to pay for such amenities.

Mac was as impressed as Fiona with the establishment, but for a different reason. She realized the longer they were held up in Massawa the greater the cost to El Belada's pocket, or was it Roy Kingsland's own? So after a quick freshening up she sought out the manager, a Sardinian, who immediately assured her Leonardo was hers for the asking. Leonardo was somewhat of a surprise. He was a huge Ethiopian in scarlet satin trousers, who looked as though he was hired by a film unit to bang a gong and bring on the dancing girls at a given signal. His voice was an incredible *basso-profondo*, booming from a chest as deep as a barrel, and his geniality was boundless. The name Kingsland had the effect of an "open sesame"

57

to his ear. He seemed to know exactly what was expected of him and what to expect, which was more than Mac did.

"Doctor Bellinger him be Mario's," he told her, before she could explain the position. "Always he go Mario's. I take missie get him."

"Leonardo was once Doctor Bellinger's personal servant," the hotel manager explained. "As he has a wife and eleven children he prefers a more settled existence, however. He is, nevertheless, devoted to his former master."

Mac almost pinched herself when she was sitting in one of the hotel's station wagons beside the magnificent pantomime character of the dusky Leonardo, who must have been all of six foot seven in his thong-toed sandals, and as wide as a door to match. He drove the vehicle with an airy disregard for anything which happened to get in the way of it: dogs yelped, pedestrians shrieked and leapt aside, yelling imprecations in clouds of dust: as the streets became meaner they also became more congested, and Mac's heart was continuously in her mouth. Once she ventured, "Excuse me, Leonardo, but must we go so fast?"

"Fast, missie?" he asked with a great grin. "You want we go fast? Me Stirling Moss!" And down went his foot on the accelerator, which did her palpitation no good at all.

So this was it, she decided, as eventually they arrived in the meanest of mean streets once more in the vicinity of the docks. Here was no white façade to hide the evil. She had learned by now the very smell of vice: the more heavily curtained the doorway, the more fetid the air inside. People who didn't care for purity in the air they breathed had ceased to care for other good things as essential to health of mind and body. There was forgetfulness behind those curtained doorways; the forgetfulness of the opium pipe and the doped cigarette. Pain lost its meaning in the limbo of the drugged mind, and responsibility quickly became a thing of the past, to be shrugged off and left to others.

Mac was beginning to fear the worst when Leonardo cheerfully exclaimed, "Ah, Mario's!" outside the only establishment on the narrow street which boasted a striped awning. There was nothing to say what business the redoubtable Mario might be engaged in, but at least he had gone to the expense of putting his name up above the awning in strip lighting, which reassured Mac not a little. Surely no dope-den would advertise itself so obviously?

Mario was asleep in his doorway, under a large panama hat. Leonardo slapped him awake, and the two indulged

in a cheerful exchange in Italian, with a few hugs and
kisses on the cheek thrown in. Finally Mac caught the
name "Bellinger" and Mario laughed and cocked a thumb
over his shoulder while chattering on and on with shoulders, hands and mouth going fifty to the dozen.

"He is inside, missie. Come!" Leonardo invited when
the long harangue was over. "Mario say very sick," and
he shook his great head sadly.

"He sounded very happy about it," Mac decided,
frowning back at Mario, who was already in the act of
continuing his interrupted siesta. She followed the Ethiopian up a flight of dark but clean stairs, along a narrow
passage and—without ceremony—into a bedroom at the
end. There were groans coming from the bed, and Leonardo
leaned over it and crooned, "The head is sick bad, master?"

Mac dumped her bag on the chair and approached the
invalid. On the bedside table were ranged an assortment
of bottles and glasses: each bottle bore the same familiar
legend, Scotch Whisky. There were empties on the floor
and the room stank of alcohol. A carroty head on the
pillow rolled painfully from side to side in rhythm to a
deep husky nutmeg-grater voice declaring, "I'm dying,
Leonardo! Dying!"

With one almighty sweep Mac cleared the table of its
impedimenta and looked down, her lip curling.

"So this is it!" she declared. "This is what Fiona must
not be allowed to see! Doctor Bellinger in his cups.
Physical weakness my foot! Why didn't somebody tell
me he would be just plain drunk?"

CHAPTER TEN

NEVER, Mario's garrulous and plentiful wife declared, had
she been hustled from her hammock in the small yard at
the back of the premises and spoken to so before. In siesta
time, too. It wasn't decent. Coffee, the English doctor-
missie demanded; plenty, plenty coffee, hot and strong, as
though any self-respecting Italian wife didn't know how
coffee should be served. Francesca made the coffee nevertheless, grumbling in an undertone. The arrogant English.

Whose fault if Doctor Bellinger liked to drink whisky once in a while? Was it a crime to do what one wanted? Had Mario forced the whisky on him and tied him to the bed? If all Englishwomen were like this one, no wonder the British had such an Empire! There had to be somewhere for the men to run off to!

There was something about Mac, with a gleam in her eye, which persuaded even the most slothful of characters to come to life and serve her. As Francesca had been gently but firmly hauled into her kitchen and asked to provide coffee, so had Mario been jolted into action and told to remove all signs of liquor from Doctor Bellinger's bedroom and produce more at his peril. Mac had already learned that Mario's was the Eritrean equivalent of a fried-fish shop: Francesca cooked the fish her husband caught, in oil and soya butter; and sold the fish pieces cold, wrapped in palm leaves, in the evenings, when most people enjoyed their main meal. Mac had also realized, however, that with the fish there was a demand for the whisky with which Red Bellinger had been so well provided. Mario was, in fact, a smuggler, and it was this gainful occupation which had provided the striped awning and strip lighting, not the fried-fish pieces piled up in neat, green wrappings in the dark, airless kitchen opening on to the equally dark and airless yard.

Acting under instructions Leonardo had hauled Bellinger upright, the latter protesting mightily that he was dying and wanted to be allowed to die in peace.

"Use the bowl," Mac said curtly, when she realized he was about to vomit again. "When he has finished, Leonardo, bring him into the bathroom. I'll be waiting."

She had discovered, to her relief, that Mario boasted a bathroom with a shower cubicle, for Red Bellinger was by no means the only gentleman to occasionally   take the escapist route via the whisky bottle. Gentlemen liked to bath, however, and Mario was always ready to oblige when it paid him to do so.

Mac was waiting, the shower curtain wrapped round her middle apron-wise, when Leonardo dragged their moaning victim into view.

"Put his head under," Mac instructed.

Whoosh! streamed the cool jet over the sufferer. He became rigid with shock, gasped and spluttered.

"This is murder!" he declared.

Whoosh! Mac let him have more and more of it, then wrapped the dripping red head in a towel and told Leonardo to seat Doctor Bellinger on the cork stool. For the first time his eyes saw her, though he winced with the pain still cleaving his skull almost in half.

"Who is this virago?" he asked Leonardo sulkily.

"You'll find that out soon enough," Mac told him. "Meanwhile—coffee!"

Francesca had lumbered up the stairs, still grumbling. After dumping the tray she lumbered down again, and Red Bellinger suddenly decided, "I wanna drink."

"You'll get no drink"—Mac's blue eye was a dart of heat—"until you're decently dressed and attending to your proper business at the Imperial. I may let you have one small whisky after dinner."

"*You* may . . . ?" Red Bellinger had sobered up considerably in the past few minutes, but he was suddenly lost for words. "Who—who the heck *are* you?" he asked aggressively.

"My name is Immacula Hayes and I seem to be in charge of a party travelling to El Belada. I didn't intend to be in charge, but"—she indicated him with some contempt—"I don't appear to have much choice, do I?"

Red Bellinger gulped the hot, bitter coffee and blinked his eyes several times in disbelief.

"You mean the *Indian Maid* docked already?"

"Twenty-four hours late," Mac nodded pleasantly. "It was hardly reassuring not to be met."

"But I—how did you——?"

"Doctor Kingsland told me what to do in case you were—er—ill."

"I—I promised him I wouldn't do it." Red Bellinger rose to his feet a little unsteadily. "I was at the dock on time," he insisted, "then they told me she was overdue. If only you'd been on time this wouldn't have happened."

"I'm sorry," Mac said.

"It's not your fault, so quit apologisin'," the American went on gruffly. "I suppose I ought to thank you . . ."

"Don't trouble. I'm putting it down to experience. You are my first—er—inebriate, Doctor Bellinger. It seems cold water and coffee can work wonders."

"But what do you give a guy for his conscience?" Red asked miserably. "Roy will . . . Where's the lily?" he demanded, suddenly in a panic. "There *were* two of you?"

"The lily being Sister Bardale, she is probably swimming over at the hotel," Mac said somewhat bitterly, surveying her own afternoon's activities. "Will you bath and dress now, Doctor Bellinger? We're keeping Leonardo from his work."

61

"You"—Red halted her in the bathroom doorway, looking like a grotesque baby with red curls sticking to his brow under the striped towel—"needn't worry about me now, Doctor Hayes. As soon as I remembered Roy waitin' back at the hospital I was cold sober, and that's the way I'll stay. Do you want the privilege of telling the boss of this?"

"Of course not," Mac almost snapped. "As far as I'm concerned it's over and done with. You were delayed for an hour or two—that's all. Sister Bardale doesn't know."

"Oh, then, you mean I——?"

"I mean I leave all that to you, Doctor Bellinger, to tell or not to tell. It's how you feel about it yourself. Do hurry!"

"You know darned well I'll tell, if you know Roy," he shrugged. "There's one guy you can't kid for long. I admit I was playing with the idea of you and me keeping a secret, but . . ."

Mac went downstairs to wait, liking Red Bellinger better for the difficult decision he had made.

*   *   *

Fiona, in yellow chiffon, came across the dining-room to meet Mac, a cocktail in her hand.

"Where *have* you been?" she demanded, and without waiting for an answer, "It's absolutely wonderful here. I couldn't tear myself away from the swimming-bath and I actually feel wonderfully cool for the first time since we entered the Med. You look awful, darling. So hot." Mac almost bridled, but controlled herself with an effort. "I met a charming American who has been teaching me the crawl, and one can actually get tea here. I had some while the girl was setting my hair. Do you think we can stay here for a few days? I hope that wretched Bellinger never materializes."

"Ahem!" came from behind her.

"Doctor Bellinger—Fiona Bardale!" Mac introduced the two briefly. Fiona was almost childishly upset by the encounter and failed to offer her hand.

"I didn't mean you to overhear," she said defensively.

"So who's worrying?" Red asked with a laugh. "I'm always dropping bricks and things. It's understandable to prefer the Hotel Imperial to El Belada Hospital if you're looking for a social kind of existence. You look like a typical social exister, Sister."

"What do you mean by that?" Fiona demanded.

"Quit raising your hackles," Red pleaded tiredly. "I had a heavy day. Don't give me female tantrums on the top of it. Will you take a chair—Fiona?" He tried her name out on his tongue experimentally, wondering if he would be repulsed or not.

Mac was the observer throughout dinner. Fiona didn't appear to like Red Bellinger at all, and this being so she made no effort to be pleasant or enter into conversation with him. Once or twice when he turned away she studied him darkly, veiling her thoughts. He—on the other hand—was quite gay and apparently carefree: his recovery surprised Mac not a little. Fiona's American came to claim her for after-dinner coffee in the roof-garden.

"If she can be spared?" he smilingly questioned the others.

"Certainly." Red had risen and smiled at Fiona encouragingly. "Do make the most of it for the little time we have left to us. Tomorrow we go on into the interior, to the toil and sweat, the flies, the stinging sand, the miseries to which we few faithful have devoted our lives."

"Shall we go?" Fiona asked her escort, as though eager to escape present company.

"I think you and Fiona should at least try to hit it off if we're all to work together," Mac pointed out as the waiter brought their coffee to the table.

"But we have hit it off," Red smiled. "That's the trouble. Sister Bardale and I love each other."

Mac actually laughed.

"Scoff if you must," Red invited. "I tell you, Mac, that girl and I crashed head on. *She* doesn't like it, because lovin' means givin', an' she's no giver; and I don't like it because it would mean an end to my excursions to Mario's forever, and at least I know the hell I get into with Mario's hooch. I know myself, and Fiona knows herself, and doesn't it take the devil to recognize his own?"

"I refuse to listen to rubbish," Mac said shortly. "You were talking more sense with alcohol coming out of your ears. Forget Fiona: she's Doctor Kingsland's department."

"I owe Roy a great deal," Red said thoughtfully, "and this could be one way of paying some of it back. Anyhow, we'll see."

The next morning Mac was the first to plunge into the swimming-pool, determined to enjoy a brief hour of sheer physical delight before resigning herself to the fact that such amenities as cool, tiled pools would lie behind from now on. She went into breakfast shaking her short, damp hair like a puppy, only to be met with an almost tangible depression emanating from a silent Fiona and a perversely cheerful Red, his defection forgotten in the puckish promise of today's mischief.

Shortly after ten they were speeding along in the train, looking out at terraced vineyards and elegant white villas. Occasionally they ran into and through an all-native village with straw and mud huts built in a circle round a larger central house, where one presumed the social life of the village went on.

Fiona cheered up when she discovered Red Bellinger had not forced himself upon them. They had their own private compartment. Iced drinks were brought at intervals, and once a man came to repair a blind they were having difficulty with. Asmara, Keren, Agordat—places Mac remembered vaguely from the war reports her father had collected and kept—took on reality as they were overtaken by the iron monster and left behind. It was now cold, mountainous country, and Red appeared briefly to dump rugs and blankets with them and inquire if there was more they required. Lunch was served between Bishia and Barenta, and then followed a somewhat tiresome hold-up while they waited in a siding for the express travelling to the coast to pass them.

It was evening when they finally chuffed into Kassala and changed into one of the magnificent Sudan State Railway trains. This was surprisingly modern with a fine diesel oil-burning engine at the motive end. Mac, who had imagined that all human comforts lay behind, was pleasantly overwhelmed by the sudden spotlessness of seat covers and a wholesome smell of pine disinfectant in the washrooms. The Sudani attendants were also obviously encouraged to take a pride in their appearance, and red tarbush and cummerbund stood out sharply in contrast to the snow-white, loose, ankle-length shirts they wore. Of course, Mac realized with a smile, the British had only recently moved out, but their excellent example was whole-heartedly adopted and possibly improved on. The Sudan was determined that travellers should see the hand of progress now that she was managing her own affairs.

"But we gave them a good shove off," Mac decided, as she climbed into the sleeping bunk above Fiona and settled down for the long night's run to Khartoum.

Sightseeing was necessarily brief when they arrived in the fine modern city on the banks of the Blue Nile. Fiona pleaded to be allowed to stay a few days in a hotel, saying she was unwell.

"Send Roy for me when you two arrive," she suggested.

Red smilingly tossed a coin, asking Mac to call.

"One of us examines her and finds the trouble," he said. "Much cheaper to treat her ourselves than put the boss to the expense of coming here for her."

Mac looked questioningly at Fiona.

"Are you really seedy?" she asked.

"Of course. I don't tell lies. But I'm not bothering either of you with my health. I suppose I'll have to go on."

It was not so fine a train out of Khartoum and bound for the last outpost of the railways, Jebelein. Red said they had better keep together in case of armed bandits, delighted to observe Fiona's immediate agitation.

"You can lean on me any time, honey," Red told her, ignoring her patent shudder. "You know, Fiona, I just can't see you at El Belada. I can't seem to see you at all. Why?"

"Why—what?" Fiona almost snapped.

"Just why crucify yourself like this?"

Fiona looked forlornly at Mac.

"I even have to remind myself," she said, quickly lowering her eyes.

"We'll all be happier to arrive, I think," Mac opined. "It's living in suitcases I find so wearing. Trying to keep up feminine appearances without a portable iron is my number one grouse."

"You always look as fresh and sweet as a daisy, Mac," from Red.

"Well, thank you, sir!" Mac contrived a curtsey.

"Oh, we'll get on one another's nerves if there's much more of this," Fiona said with a cold fury, and stalked away down the corridor, apparently preferring the possibility of a bandit attack.

"You see"—Red told Mac, with a smile—"she loves me! She can't bear me to pay a compliment to another woman."

"You are a fool, Red!" Mac laughed uninhibitedly. "If Fiona is an example of a woman in love, no wonder a rolling-pin is such a necessity in the wife's kitchen!"

"You'll see!" Red warned, amused by her mirth and liking and respecting her far more than he would ever like and respect Fiona Bardale, though he wouldn't have told her so for the world.

Part of that day and all night they spent on a chugging steamer battering its way up the Nile. There was no privacy and no peace on board. The mosquitoes bit one incessantly. Mac was relieved to disembark and leave the green belt of the river to its pests. Fiona looked almost stunned, and for the first time in her life reflected her age, with the skin below eyes and mouth positively sagging.

The heat during the day was burningly intense, and Mac watched Fiona visibly wilting as they climbed into a small, converted ambulance for the last lap of the long journey by desert road.

"El Belada next stop," Red told them. "I'll sit up with the driver and leave you girls to divest yourselves of anything divestable. Loosen your stays, Fiona, or whatever is making you look green!"

"I don't wear stays, you disgusting creature!" Fiona lashed at him. "Oh, Mac, what am I to do if I can't stick it?" she asked when Red had left them.

"Go back home, of course," Mac said, surprised by the question. "It's not going to alter Roy's feelings for you because you tried and—and failed."

"Roy's feelings?" Fiona asked, and the other suddenly realized her blunder.

"I mean he won't think any the less of your friendship. That's an established thing between your families, isn't it?"

"You didn't mean that at all, Mac," Fiona said, her dark eyes glowing. "You know about Roy and me. Mother suspected and told you, perhaps?"

Mac shrugged ruefully.

"I promised not to blab," she said, "and I forgot."

"It doesn't matter," Fiona sighed. "I rather like you knowing, Mac, though Roy wants us to keep it secret for the time being. Never let him know you—suspect. He's very good at hiding his feelings."

Roy certainly hid any feelings of an intimate nature when he met the party as it drove into the hospital compound. Mac tried not to think she was as glad as she was to see him again, out of loyalty to Fiona. He greeted both girls with equal enthusiasm, and dismissed them to a white bungalow which had been specially built for them. Mac was so weary she remembered very little about their arrival, but she did remember going to sleep to the tune of someone strumming a guitar under her window, and that Roy Kingsland—after interviewing his second-in-command in private about the journey—said three words to her which made her very happy indeed. They were "Well done, Mac!"

CHAPTER ELEVEN

THERE HADN'T been much discussion about anything on that first evening. Fiona's behavior precluded even the normality of an introduction to the hospital proper, which Mac had been eager to investigate even before they partook of very necessary refreshment. The new sister had collapsed into wild hysterical weeping, as though the sight of Roy and the knowledge that she had reached the end of an ordeal was too much for her. Mac was beginning to feel slightly impatient with Fiona: she had shown little sign of delicacy on occasions which had proved purely pleasurable, and Mac knew only too well what a nurse's training involved. The weak just couldn't survive it. That Fiona had not only survived in her profession but prospered in it was obvious, and this allergy to El Belada had started as a seed in her mind when they were still three thousand miles distant. A place that is undesirable is not necessarily unendurable, Mac argued: Fiona was making heavy going of a task to which she was not yet committed. Mac's slim shoulders had practically carried her to El Belada: from that elevated position she was now content to fall as though exhausted into Roy Kingsland's arms and let him assume the burden. She seemed to have no intention of standing on her own feet if she could help it.

Fiona had gone to bed with a sedative and was still asleep when Mac opened her eyes with that sense of anticipatory joy one often experiences in childhood, but all too rarely in adult life.

"Here I am!" Mac told herself, and looked round her room with interest. A couple of lizards scuttled up the wall as she stirred, regarding her with beady frog-eyes and darting out their long tongues at the flies which somehow by-passed the netting over the windows. The bed was comfortable—Mac wondered if all the staff at El Belada slept on interior springs—there was a dainty cedar-wood suite of modern design with an ample wardrobe and a white Abyssinian sheepskin rug on the red cement floor. Mac was also glad to see a small bureau-bookcase where she could write up her notes or read in the relaxed atmosphere of her own quarters. Upon further investigation she discovered the bathroom. There was a fine, deep bath already filled and waiting, and she had no hesitation in sinking into the cool refreshing water and washing away the last vestiges of the dust of travel from her hair, fingernails, everywhere. Last night Roy Kingsland had been emphatic that they both get into bed and find relaxation in sleep.

"Now I'm ready for anything!" Mac decided, throwing her wrap loosely about her and going back into the bedroom.

"Oh!" she cried out involuntarily, and clutched her wrap over her chest. "Who—who are you?" she demanded.

The fly-screens had been thrown back from the windows, and leaning confidently forward into the room was a very handsome young man. Mac had an immediate impression of startlingly white teeth in a gash of a grin, a fair, sunburnt skin, sun-bleached fair hair and a pair of eyes sombre and deep like sepia velvet.

"I am Mustafa Mohammed Zarek, at your service," he introduced himself. "Last night when I was free of the hospital I played you some music. Did you like it?"

"It was very nice of you, Mr. Zarek," Mac ventured, proffering a tentative hand. "I—I'm hardly dressed for entertaining, I'm afraid. If you'll wait until I'm dressed?"

Zarek smiled engagingly.

"I hoped to find you not dressed, Miss Mac, if you will excuse the liberty . . . ?" Mac's eyes were watchful, but she fortunately waited for him to continue speaking. He somehow didn't look like a roué. "I have horses waiting and I wish to take you for a ride. We have breakfast in one hour. Can you dress suitably, now?"

"I have shorts," Mac said, and Zarek promptly salaamed and backed away from the window, closing the screens after him.

Mac thought as she dressed, "I'll go with him this once, but I must tell him I'm here to work and like to make my own plans."

But the handsome Zarek was so utterly charming that Mac hadn't the heart to repulse him this early in their acquaintance. He had a boy standing holding two magnificent Arab stallions, one a grey and the other a strawberry roan. It was surprisingly pleasant so early in the morning to ride out of the white-walled compound and gallop across the desert while the air was still cool from the night. Mac was not very comfortable in her shorts, and she hadn't realized that riding might be part of the hospital's routine. She really knew very little about El Belada, and—thanks to having Fiona for a travelling companion—had been inclined to fear the worst. But this was better than anything she had expected, she decided, as she laughed at Zarek's quips and the quaint English in which he expressed himself.

"The Superintendent says I drive him crazy. I do not get my sexes right no matter how I try. I say 'I do' when I should say 'I did.' Little things like that, you know?"

"You mean tenses, not sexes, Mr. Zarek," laughed Mac. "Don't worry; I get them wrong too, quite often."

"You are more and more a girl after my own heart, Miss Mac," he told her, his eyes openly admiring her. Mac pressed her knees and felt the sudden surge of power in the beast beneath her. "When Roy told us you were coming I was very happy. Now I know why."

"You mustn't say such things to me," Mac warned him. "I have an idea Doctor Kingsland wouldn't like it. I'm here as a member of the staff, and you must think of me as you think of—well—Red, shall we say?"

"Impossible!" Zarek said incredulously. "Red is not so pretty as you are!"

"Hadn't we better be getting back?" Mac asked.

"If you like. I will see much of you in future, so will be content to let you go this once. Perhaps we do this every day?"

"No, not every day. In fact not again until I get some jodhpurs." She eased her chafed thighs cautiously, glad to see the hospital come into view. The sun was beginning to stab like a burning spear, and a shady hat was another essential to outdoor occupation.

Breakfast was served on the wide veranda adjoining Roy Kingsland's bungalow. A steward, immaculate in the usual loose white shirt of the district, waited until the medical staff were all seated, then served ice-cold rice with stewed apricots.

"I observe there is no need for introductions between you two," Roy Kingsland said quietly, as Zarek admired Mac's forget-me-not sprigged dress with his voice and the whiteness of her throat with his eyes.

"An introduction would be somewhat pointless, seeing

that we have been together since the crack of dawn," Mac smiled. "I am saddle-sore, thanks to Mr. Zarek."

"Mac is all that you have told me, Roy," declared the young surgeon, "and much more."

"Oh, and what did you tell him, Doctor Kingsland?" Mac inquired innocently.

"That you are a clever pathologist, of course," the Superintendent smiled. "The 'much more' he appears to have discovered for himself."

"Last evening I sing Mac to sleep," Zarek persisted. "Then I did not know her. Tonight my song will be——"

"Non-existent, for all our sakes," Roy said equably. "Mac is well able to sleep without your efforts, my boy. You mustn't take any notice of this fellow's compliments," he told Mac, "they roll off his tongue far too glibly."

"I have discovered that and I won't," Mac said blithely. "How are you today, Doctor Bellinger? You're very quiet."

"Ahem!" coughed the American, and turned with a wry smile to Roy Kingsland. "Permission to speak to the lady, sir? She has addressed a remark in the direction of the dog-house."

The Superintendent flushed for a moment as though in anger, then he swallowed and turned to the other.

"Since you wish to make the matter public, Red, we had better tell Doctor Hayes that you and I had a few words last night."

"He means we had a flaming row," Red nodded in Mac's direction.

"I thought we had said everything necessary on that occasion," Roy went on. "Do you want to open it up again?"

"I'm a slow healer," Red said grudgingly, then shrugged his shoulders. "Oh, shucks! Sorry, Mac! I guess I hate myself today."

"If it's about that business in Massawa," Mac said, "I wish everybody would forget it. It's over and done with, surely?"

"And thanks to you the party caught the one and only weekly train out of Khartoum," Roy told her, "so no real harm has been done. Rajab?" he called, clapping his hands, and the steward appeared with rolls, a tin of butter and marmalade, while a small boy whisked away the used dishes.

"We eat very lightly to work on," Roy Kingsland went on pleasantly, for Mac's benefit. "Eight o'clock dinner is served in my house, but liquid tea or coffee you may have

70

any time for the asking. Is there anything you want to know while we're all here?"

"No, only to ask where the lab is. I'm dying to get started."

There was a momentary flash of appreciation from the Superintendent's dark eyes.

"Straining at the leash already, Mac?" he asked, in a voice more like the Roy who had stepped in so readily to help after her father's death. "My dear girl, you can't rush into your job like that! I insist upon three days' absolute relaxation for you. I have to give you a couple of injections, also, which might bowl you over a little."

Mac grimaced.

"I am operating this morning," Zarek said quickly, "but later I will take you to see my estate if you will like. That is good relaxation for you. I——"

"Mac will stay here today," Kingsland said rather ominously, daring his young surgeon to say more. "I thought I made it clear that I wish to give the necessary injections to both ladies?"

"I am sorry," Zarek apologized pleasantly. "It is that I am so happy to see a pretty girl here in our midst like this. She goes to my head."

"Mac's got enough feet on the ground for both of you," Red Bellinger said ambiguously, and while the Sudani was considering this a woman's scream rent the air.

"Fiona! What . . . ?" Roy Kingsland jumped to his feet.

"Get away!" Fiona could be heard shrilling. "Get out! Go!"

A magnificent, coal-black specimen of manhood came tearing across the compound, raising the white, sandy dust in a cloud about him.

"Tia Kafi!" Roy exploded. "Has a snake got into Sister's room? I told you to guard her with your life!"

The man was too excited to reply in English, but Mac had already discovered that the Superintendent was an excellent Arabic speaker. He listened to the man's explanation patiently, then patted his shoulder kindly.

"You stay here and I'll explain to Sister."

The servant folded his hands into his sleeves and then regarded Mac for the first time with round-eyed, uninhibited interest.

"Good morning!" Mac greeted him.

*   *   *

Roy Kingsland strode grim-browed across the compound, wanting to hurl a stone somewhere hard, but resisting the impulse. He counted to ten before entering the women's bungalow, then marched into Fiona's bedroom without more ado. She was in a pale, gauzy wrap, her long hair hanging down almost to her waist: her cheeks were like alabaster and her eyes questioned his appearance, then took him for granted.

"Darling! I wondered when you were coming to say good morning. But I'm hardly dressed. . . ."

"You'll do for what I have to say, Fiona. I won't keep you long. You have upset Tia Kafi, who is our best and most faithful servant. Of course he's black. He's a Nuba. But the Nubas are very fine tribesmen from the Lower Sudan, and proud. He tells me you hurled the tea he brought you at him and that you told him to get out. Fiona"—he swallowed hard—"you assured me you knew what you were doing when you took this step. I would have thought you'd have read up the Sudan—all about it—its peoples and so forth. But apparently you haven't troubled even to find out that the Sudan is peopled by Sudanis."

"Darling"—Fiona's eyes were even more round now—"are you ever so slightly scolding me for something?"

"I'm telling you to watch your step. You are the stranger here, not Tia Kafi. His experience of Europeans is limited. You have hardly enhanced us in his eyes."

"Am I to worry my head about this servant?" Fiona demanded aghast.

"He is a good man, a Nuba," Roy patiently explained, "and he is more purely bred than you or I can claim to be. His skin is provided by nature to withstand the rigors of the climate, and he is an excellent steward. Now I must go."

"Just a minute, Roy"—Fiona's voice was almost menacing, but she managed a smile as he turned to regard her—"aren't you forgetting something?"

"I don't think so. I didn't bring anything with me. You interrupted our breakfast."

To his horror he watched her eyes fill with tears and heard her voice plaintively whisper, "I—I thought you might at least have kissed me, Roy. You're different here."

"I don't think I am, Fiona," he said more kindly. "I don't mean to be."

"Yes you are," she still accused, "but don't expect me to change. I shall always be the Fiona you used to know and—and like!" With which her tears spilled over. When he reached out clumsily she thrust him away and was furious when—repulsed—he went away into the sunlight without another word.

CHAPTER TWELVE

MAC WAS shocked to realize she had been at El Belada for three whole weeks. It didn't seem possible somehow. Where did time disappear to in these latitudes? It wasn't as if she had idled away the hours: she was now an accepted member of the staff and the routine of the hospital was proceeding almost too smoothly to be true. On duty she didn't even notice the heat, though the big thermometer on the veranda was monotonously registering a daily maximum of a hundred and ten degrees, but she was finding it increasingly difficult to take any interest in off-duty activities. Between the hours of one and three p.m., when the medical staff left the hospital to its very necessary siesta, barring emergencies, she was succumbing to that rather wonderful complaint, tropical hypnosis, the symptoms of which were lying full length on one's bed and allowing the mind to become a complete blank. Her books were still in her trunk and she hadn't written a single letter home, but it seemed in this wonderful state of sublimation that there was no hurry for anything; let them all wait. In good time she would get round to these things, but for the moment the only pursuit was a physical and mental dismembering which could only take place in a climate so torrid it seemed forcibly to demand inanimation in one.

Promptly at five to three Tia Kafi would appear with the inevitable tea-tray, and Mac plucked her mind out of the atmosphere and became mobilized once more. After the first cup of tea she told herself she ought to be ashamed that Barney was—quite naturally—wondering how she was getting on, and that she could have attended to all her outstanding mail during the free period. After two cups she was glaring round the room, annoyed by the empty bookshelves with which the Superintendent had so thoughtfully provided her, and determining to do something about everything on the morrow. Usually at this moment Fiona dropped in to complain about something, and Mac was glad to finish her third cup and get back to work. Fiona hadn't started work yet. She had—true to expectations—taken to her bed for a week following the preventive injections the Superintendent had considered necessary for the newcomers' health, but Mac had disdained to lie up for more than twenty-four hours, though she had a very sore arm from one injection and was internally upset by the other. Fiona became interestingly slender because she refused food for a while. It took a lot of the Superintendent's time to talk her back on to a reasonable diet once more. Roy was noticeably gentle with her, and always attended her himself, even though staff health was really Red Bellinger's concern.

"Does anybody know when our Sister-in-Charge is gonna take charge of anybody but Roy?" Red asked one day when Mac and Zarek joined him for mid-morning coffee in the staff-room of the hospital. "She's surely gotta take the blinkers off soon and realize there's a hospital going on here!"

"Do not criticize the fair Fiona," Zarek said in his pedantic English. "She looks not of this world. Not like my beautiful Mac, who, like the English rose she resembles, blooms as well here as there. What matter if Fiona works or not, so long as she keeps Roy happy, eh?"

"I never knew him take so much saccharin before," Red mused. "He's gonna sicken soon."

"Doctor Bellinger," Mac said firmly, recognizing in the American a puckish desire to make mischief, "I think you are being rather offensive about Fiona. I believe you are partial towards her yourself, and that all these acid comments you make are just sour grapes on your part."

"My dear Doctor Hayes," Red's sarcasm was riven wide open now under this verbal assault, "it seems you are laboring under a slight misapprehension. If I wanted the said fair lady, I have but to whisper a few sweet somethings into her ear and you would notice an immediate change in our relationship. You see, I have something even our dashing Super hasn't got, and you can bet your sweet life it's what she wants more than anything. But I don't intend to tell her what is is unless"—he shrugged— "I decide to want her. It's up to me for the state of my health that I never do." He strode off sulkily and Zarek shrugged.

"No one understands Red," he told Mac. "No one tries any more. How can one understand a man who speaks of wanting a woman as one speaks of wanting an orange? He does not speak of love. . . ." Here the surgeon looked up at his companion from under heavily lidded eyes. "When will you come to see my house and stables, Mac?"

"Soon," she promised. "Is it a big house?"

"Pretty big," he smiled, "and cool. My father made much water to play. You call . . . ?"

"Fountains?" Mac supplied.

"Yes. Fountains. My mother was English, you know."

"I suspected you didn't get that blond hair from a packet of dye, Zarek."

"You joke. My mother was a British officer's daughter, and my father a junior officer in the regiment. A subaltern he is called. They fell in love and wished to marry, but British parents very angry with my father. There is much unhappiness and soon that girl is to be sent back to England in disgrace for loving my father."

"Shame!" said Mac, but realized at the same time the age-old problem which would always arise, when love recognized only the beloved and not the color of his skin. "What happened then?"

"My father breeds the fastest horses in the world. Stella, my dear mother, tells him, 'Come for me when darkness falls and take me on your white stallion to your house. They will let us marry then.' My father asks, 'How is this so?' but surely enough, when it is discovered my mother has been all night in that house the parent says they will be married and be damned to them! You know the British?" Mac smiled. "It was all too easy, I think?"

Mac said naught.

"They are very happy together," Zarek went on, "and I am born, my father's son with my mother's face, but of course my mother is prettier. A pity I only know her for five years. She died when my sister is born. Not enough doctors in Sudan at that time."

"And your father?" Mac inquired.

"I would say he died with her. It is that he does not try to live after her death, there is no interest in anything, not even his horses."

"Children surely come before horses?" Mac asked indignantly.

"You do not know my father," Zarek smiled. "Children are just—children. Anyone can have children. But only

75

my father in all Sudan has such horses." He laughed at her wide-eyed expression which begged him to assure her he was only joking. "Shall I love you like that, Mac?" he asked casually.

"So that you can neglect my children?" she demanded. "I should think not. I'm going back to work, Mr. Zarek!"

"*Ma'essalaameh!*" he bowed mockingly after her. "You do not leave me so forever, dear Mac!"

* * *

Roy Kingsland appeared looking boyishly gay, heeling the mesh-screen of the path. lab. into place behind him.

"What do you mean by it, Doctor Hayes, on your day off, too? I insist you take your free time for your health's sake!"

He didn't look too forbidding, however, and Mac smiled as she took her eye away from the microscope on the slab in front of her.

"I didn't intend staying long. I was interested to see how this culture was coming along, and relieved to find it's still neutral."

"You have taken such a load off me since you came, my girl, even I can claim some free time today. Do you know I haven't had a real chat with you since you arrived, Mac?"

The girl felt like saying this was through no fault of hers, as Fiona was invariably edging her off the Superintendent in innumerable ways, but she let it slide.

"Get your bonnet on and we'll run up to Dilling," he went on. "You can enjoy some military pageantry, see somebody else sweat for a change, and we'll have lunch with the C.O. Ten minutes from now?"

"Thank you, sir," Mac said gladly, putting the culture away in its sterile container and preceding him out of the laboratory. "It all sounds delightful."

"Informality off duty," he reminded her, "or are we not on Christian name terms any more?"

She looked at him suddenly, met the dark eyes and flushed, for which she hated herself. Why did his glance have to be so warm upon her when Fiona was always hinting an engagement was only a matter of time?

"It has been nothing but work for both of us up to now," he went on, as though the moment had to be overcome for him also. "I have almost forgotten that delightful creature who chased me up to Coningwater and tried to run me down against my own gate-post."

76

"I have almost forgotten that girl myself," Mac said quietly. "I'll get my 'bonnet,' as you call it—Roy."

"Yes, do. I'm taking an open tourer. I don't run to the luxury of an insulated saloon like Zarek. But then, Zarek owns a quarter of the Sudan, even this land we're built on."

"But he works hard," Mac mused. "I wonder why?"

"For the best of reasons, my girl. He happens to like it. Also he can keep an eye on his plantations and other sources of revenue from here. I'll see you in seven minutes from now."

Mac ran almost light-heartedly across the compound, breaking into song as she reached the shade of the bungalow and entered her bedroom by the veranda windows. She was pulling on her lightest, coolest white dress when Fiona suddenly appeared.

"Where are you going?" she asked sulkily.

"It's my day off and I'm going up to Dilling or some-where. Why?"

"Oh!" Fiona almost stamped her foot. "Has he asked you, too?"

"If you mean Doctor Kingsland," Mac said, her heart suddenly sinking, "yes, he has. Are you well enough to go, Fiona?"

"Perhaps you hoped I wasn't," the other snapped.

Mac controlled her exasperation.

"Now look here, Fiona, you know that isn't true. I merely looked upon this trip as a refreshing change. I've worked hard for a month. . . . "

"And I haven't done any work at all, eh? Well, you know how ill I've been. I've felt half dead most of the time."

"I have been sorry for you, Fiona," Mac went on gently, "but lately I've been thinking it would be better for you to make a bit of an effort. I'm sure you wouldn't feel so bad if you could only see some of the patients we've got in just now, especially the kiddies. We have two with sleeping sickness, and I've been making tests on one for smallpox, but thank goodness the first test has proved negative! When little scraps of humanity are so poorly it gives you no time to think of yourself, if you see what I mean? Roy will be tooting any minute. You had better get your hat."

"I'm not going," Fiona sulked. "Three's a crowd. I should feel even more depressed to hear you two discussing some disgusting tropical disease half the time. You carry on and enjoy yourselves."

Mac suddenly remembered the conversation she had had with Mrs. Bardale. "See that Fiona spends plenty of time with Roy, won't you? There may be occasions when— because you are the only other white woman at the hospital —Roy may ask you to accompany them out of politeness." Perhaps this was one such occasion when she was merely being asked "out of politeness," though Roy Kingsland needn't have appeared so gallant while he was doing it, thus completely disarming her.

"You get your hat, Fiona," she said suddenly. "I'll stay."

"Really, Mac?" Fiona had suddenly come to life again. "Sure you don't mind?"

The younger girl deliberately avoided the extravagance of an embrace.

"Of course not," she said. "I'll get my books sorted out, and this afternoon I'll play badminton with Zarek. I'm getting quite good at it. You enjoy your trip."

"Thank you darling. I'm sure Roy will be relieved by your decision, and I'll make your excuses. Leave it to me."

Leave it to Fiona, Mac did, and as the car went away without Roy Kingsland appearing in person to demand an explanation, she presumed he was, as the other had said, relieved at not having her along with them after all.

The day suddenly stretched in an endless vista, and though she refused to admit her disappointment, there was no activity she could think of which seemed as attractive as the "real chat" Roy Kingsland had promised her once they were both away from the hospital scene. Had he really wanted to find the girl she had once appeared to him again, or was this part of his patter? Mac wished she didn't mind so much the fact that he was spending the day alone with Fiona. What was it to her, anyway? She had come to El Belada to work, not to fall in love with the Superintendent. He wanted her purely in a professional capacity, and had once told her so.

CHAPTER THIRTEEN

ON THE DAY that Fiona started work Red observed to the others that *madonna* had consented to walk the wards.

"Sister Haifah scrubbed the patients specially," he went on relentlessly. "I nearly expected the black ones to be blancoed."

Zarek laughed.

"Red always jokes," he told Mac. "I find Sister Bardale charming. She looks so cool—like water."

"She acts pretty cool, too," Red nodded; "or hadn't you noticed it particularly, Bud?"

"Please don't!" Mac pleaded. Somehow she couldn't bear the idea of Fiona's snubbing Zarek, of all people. He was so proud of his mixed parentage, the father who had given him his fiery blood and the power he now wielded, the gentler mother who had graced him with her fair skin and hair and certain tendencies towards romance and sentimentality. Zarek was ingenuous, popular with everyone: the prejudice against the mixing of racial blood inherent in people like Fiona he just wouldn't understand. Was he not the product of such a union? Was he not Zarek, with hands as skilful as any and a brain to direct them? When the surgeon had first been introduced, Fiona had acknowledged him with an inclination of her head, ignoring the brown outstretched hand, and since she had joined them for meals she pointedly kept her distance nor ever addressed him willingly. All these occasions Roy Kingsland had so far smoothed over: Zarek was still blissfully unaware that he was not as other men in Sister Bardale's sight. Mac remembered that Fiona's color prejudice hadn't operated where Prince Khalid was concerned, and couldn't check the thought that perhaps no one had told Fiona that Zarek was even richer. Mac was more chummy towards him whenever Fiona was present, and realized this might have been a mistake when the young man waited patiently until her off-day coincided with his and then suggested she spend the day at his house as his guest.

"I—er—have letters . . ." she said lamely, but the sepia eyes burned deeply into hers.

"Why do you always make excuses, Mac, when I ask you to come with me? Are you afraid of Zarek, that he will eat you?"

"No—that wasn't my fear exactly," Mac smiled. "Maybe the letters could wait if you think the Superintendent won't mind?"

"But why should he mind what you and I do?" the surgeon asked.

Mac couldn't answer that, but she was still convinced that Roy Kingsland minded this particular excursion in that he had on several occasions gently but firmly vetoed the idea without giving offence to anyone.

"We'll take Mac to see your humble abode at a more convenient time for all of us," he had said on the last occasion, and the surgeon was so delighted by that "humble abode" he hadn't gone on to argue the matter. Mac felt it scarcely behoved her to go and ask permission to go off with Zarek: she was, after all, of an age when one is considered capable of taking care of one-self, and she was also a thrice-diploma'd doctor who had already seen much of the seamy side of life. The worst that could happen would be that Zarek would make love to her, a situation which would have to be handled tactfully so that it would not endanger the existing friendship. Mac thought she could deal with her colleague should the need arise, and didn't have to ask Roy Kingsland how to do it.

It was therefore quite blithely she stepped into the insulated, mechanical wonder that was Zarek's limousine, which a chauffeur had brought to the hospital in the early morning and had since fussed over like a midwife with a baby. She looked back as they swung out of the compound and beheld the Superintendent looking after them from the top of the veranda steps, his brow puckered into a frown. Since the Dilling episode he had been somewhat withdrawn from her, not unfriendly, but coolly professional in all their conversation. Once he asked if she was often beset by incapacitating headaches at short notice, and she had flushed and said, "No, sir. Why?" He hadn't replied, and she had suddenly realized Fiona must have used this ridiculous lie as her excuse for not going on the trip.

"I could have done better myself!" Mac decided contemptuously. "I never had an incapacitating headache in my life. And anyway, wasn't I doing him a favor by dropping out? He had his precious all to himself all day."

The car sped along at almost eighty miles an hour, Zarek at the wheel, raising a wake of white, sandy dust which remained suspended in the hot, still air. At one point Zarek slowed down and pulled in to the side of the road as a white cloud approached from the direction in which they were travelling. Mac saw a green pennant emerge from the dust topped by the arrogant, coffee-colored countenance of the standard-bearer of a detachment of the Sudan Defence Force, mounted on camels.

"Is it true that those animals can go for days without water?" asked the girl as the cavalcade passed and the car slid forwards again.

"They can, as you can if you have to, dear Mac. But it is a fallacy to suppose they enjoy it. A camel is as greedy for his water ration as any other beast. His hump is the rainy day he saves for—yes?"

There were now some signs of cultivation, whole areas were neatly enclosed within needle-sharp thorn hedges. Mac remarked that the thorns were as big as darning needles and she wouldn't like to run into them in the night.

"Neither, I hope, will the nomad tribes who steal from me," Zarek said promptly. "This land is being prepared for cotton growing. I have tried wiring the area, but wire can be put to so many domestic uses by thieves. They can pen their chickens and their animals at my expense So now my workers have planted the thorn which is indigenous to the district and serves well. There, now you see cotton under crop." He hooted the car's horn, and immediately several half-naked figures appeared from nowhere and started to work furiously at nothing in particular. "Just to let them know the master is here," Zarek said blithely and with a certain arrogance. "After all, I pay them."

There were a few thousand acres monotonous with cotton, then scattered junipers appeared at the sides of the road, casting pools of inky-black shadow. These were soon joined by sweet palms and wild bananas, then the air became fragrant with orange blossom, and the car slowed down in the shade of an enchanting grove so that the visitor could enjoy the scent, which was positively breath-taking.

"Oh, Zarek!" Mac exclaimed.

"You like?" he was delighted by her reaction. "I introduce the orange from Palestine. You are sorry now you make so many excuses not to come?"

"Maybe to make up for it I won't want to go back," Mac smiled, and the other's eyes became swiftly expressive with unspoken words. Only the presence of the chauffeur in the back, heavy-liddedly enjoying the role of passenger, prevented an impulsive declaration on Zarek's part, but he became very quiet and Mac felt as though a wall had risen between them. She was glad of the chauffeur's presence at this moment, but knew her host had only to speak to dismiss any servant peremptorily from his presence once they were in his house if—for any reason— he wished to be alone with her. This was a land of master and vassal still, and Zarek had early learned all the arts of lord and mastership.

She was somewhat reassured, however, when her companion appeared his own cheerful and friendly self as he introduced her proudly to his domain. The house was designed in the Moorish style with a central dome and small canopied windows *ad infinitum*: the façade blazed white in the sun, but thereafter sank into the welcome shade of olives and cypresses: the drive curved round between tough bahama-grass lawns, but the very sight of green grass was welcome after the glaringly white sandy plain reaching to the hospital's very door. The façade was actually merely a wall enclosing an inner courtyard where the vaunted waters played coolly day-long, and pink lilies lay flat-cupped among their plate-like leaves, providing cover from which multi-colored fish darted when the water in the pools was disturbed. Here were cool, moss-damp walls, and growing in profusion bougainvillea, hibiscus and apricots, some in blossom and some bearing tiny, forming green fruits.

"This is a real oasis in the desert, Zarek," Mac said, keeping her voice deliberately impersonal.

"You think so? Come. . . ."

She followed him through a floral archway and saw in the distance a long, deep stretch of natural water, rimmed by palms and looking like a picture postcard with its depths of reseda and aquamarine.

"How right you were!" he told her ringingly, laughing at her astonishment. "Or did you know?" he teased. "We will swim."

Mac explained she hadn't a costume, but Zarek waved that one airily aside, and as she was gathering her courage to tell him she absolutely refused to swim in the nude, a woman-servant appeared, shyly beckoning, and took her off into a dim, cool room where she helped her to disrobe. After this the woman produced a length of shimmering

82

silk which she wound expertly round Mac's fair young body, making a creditable one-piece bathing-costume out of it. Mac had seen coutouriers who did wonders out of a length of material and a few pins, but she hadn't even a pin about her: nevertheless she felt quite secure and the thought of a swim was delightful.

If she had imagined they would be swimming in the lake she was mistaken, for this was sacred to animals and to travellers who needed drinking water. Zarek had provided himself with a swimming-pool, blue tiles and all. For a wonderful hour Mac swam and splashed to her heart's content, admiring Zarek's bronzed, strong young body performing feats beyond her prowess from the diving-board. The woman-servant appeared to take her off in a bath-robe and dress her again. Mac was beginning to realize that this was one of those households where some people worked and the more privileged didn't have to raise a finger for themselves unless they were so inclined. The woman finally brushed her hair and pla'ed in it with her fingers, half expecting a rebuke, for she jumped visibly when Mac addressed her.

"Do you speak English?"

"Oh, yes, miss. Zarek effendi makes us all to speak the English."

"Well, my hair is very nicely done, and thank you. What happens now?"

"I will take you to my master."

Is this it? Mac wondered, unconsciously tensing herself as she rejoined her host in the courtyard of the fountains. Under a striped awning a servant had set the inevitable coffee and a dish of sugary dates. Zarek had changed his role: he was now the Sudanese, wearing a loose white robe and a turbaned headdress.

"For lunch we have cheese omelette," he told her triumphantly. "I hear you say one day you like this, and I wish to please you, dear Mac."

"Well, thank you very much," the girl smiled.

"Zarek always tries to please," he told her. "When Roy comes here we have goulash, and he makes it himself. My servants think he is mad, but then—one more mad Englishman is not noticed, you think? Red does not think so much of food as——"

Mac quite understood and Zarek did not enlarge upon his statement.

After coffee they went to see the horses. There were five magnificent stud stallions and a dozen or more brood mares, some with their current foal gangling alongside them: then there were the geldings which were sold as riding horses, all magnificently groomed, sleek and shining. In the veterinary stall were two sick beasts, one obviously in great pain. Zarek raved for a while at the attendant groom and then dismissed the fellow on some errand.

"Will you help me operate, Mac?" he asked urgently.

"You mean"—Mac pointed—"on a horse?"

"Why not? Am I to let Ibrahim die for want of surgery?"

"I'm not objecting, Zarek, I meant I haven't done any veterinary work before."

"It is all the same in Sudan," he said airily. "This poor fellow has swallowed his bit. Not very digestible, eh?"

The next two hours passed fantastically for Mac. She found herself clad in a shroud-like garment engaged in anaesthetising the stallion, Ibrahim, who rolled his eyes pathetically at her when a boy sat on his head to quieten him. The boy, too, was dizzy with the anaesthetic by the time Ibrahim was unconscious, and Zarek immediately made an immense outer incision in the broad belly, groped for the stomach and then made a smaller incision from which he quickly withdrew the offending bit, already rusting from the effects of natural acid, and a length of chewed leather harness. All the while he upbraided his staff in Arabic, telling them exactly what he thought of them. Then he joined arteries, removed clips and swabs and began stitching, leaving at the finish a long tidy weal in the leathery skin of the belly which he put under adhesive plaster. He was still jabbering, his brow like thunder, as he shot a large dose of penicillin into the broad rump and went over to a trough to wash his hands.

Mac thought she must have dreamed such an afternoon's work, but saw that it was indeed true when—after their belated lunch—they went back to see the patient and found him already back on his feet, looking a trifle unsteady and sorry for himself but minus an outsize belly-ache.

"Now I will take you back to El Belada and you shall tell Roy effendi how good I am to you."

It was an order rather than a question, and Mac smiled.

"I certainly will if he asks," she said blithely.

"But he will," the young man told her. "However, I have not eaten you, eh, Mac?"

This time the question was there in his dark eyes, but it was not the one framed by his lips.

"You haven't eaten me, Zarek," she told him, "and— and thank you for it. This has been absolutely delightful."

84

"Even including Ibrahim?"

"Even that," Mac laughed joyously. "If there's a new admission waiting for you at the hospital, don't forget he isn't a horse, will you?" again she laughed, and this time Zarek studied her appreciatively.

"I think you have very pretty teeth, Mac," he decided.

CHAPTER FOURTEEN

"THIS TIME Hafiz will drive and I will hold your hand, Mac," the surgeon suggested as they climbed once more into the limousine. "It is permitted that I hold your hand?" he asked.

"I think a surgeon should keep his hands cool," she said quickly. "Don't you?"

"You do not like me," he said a little sadly.

"Of course I like you," she told him. "I like you enormously. But I don't have to hold your hand to prove that, Zarek. I am more puzzled about you than ever today."

"Yes?" he asked eagerly. "Tell me!"

"I don't understand why you, who are all this"—she waved her hand at the estate flashing past—"should be working in a small, poorly staffed hospital on the edge of the desert. It seems to me you could command a position in Khartoum—at the university, maybe—being what you are. Not that I wish to deprive Roy of your services," she added hastily, "he has few enough of us as it is."

"And so you are puzzled, eh, Mac? I am happy you think occasionally about Zarek, if only of these things. I am all you say, I have excellent degree: not only Khartoum but London would open her arms to me. But I also have a heart"—he tapped his chest—"and my heart serves that man Kingsland. As long as he needs the services of Mustafa Mohammed Zarek, I will be honored to serve him. It was that man who gave me back my sister from the living dead."

"Your sister?" Mac inquired. "Was she ill, then?"

"My sister Fadia is five years younger than myself, but she does not have my mother's looks. Fadia is, nevertheless, a beautiful girl." He sighed as though with painful remembrance.

"What happened?" Mac asked tensely. "I don't want to pry," she hastened to add, "don't talk about it if you'd rather not."

Zarek shrugged. "Not to talk is sometimes a bad thing," he mused. "I will tell you, Mac, because you are my friend. To Sister Bardale I could never tell such a thing. You understand?"

Spontaneously Mac reached out and there was the forbidden holding of hands after all.

"My sister, like all educated women, newly emancipated, wishes to spread her wings and fly a little. Because her brother is studying medicine she will be a nurse, and because I can see her often this is very good. We are both happy. Then one day I see she is"—he held his free hand up to his cheek—"not so pretty, perhaps. Her mouth is sore, her nose swollen. She says it is nothing, but I take her to see my teacher who—to my horror—tells me that Fadia has contracted leprosy." He began to shudder, and Mac put an arm round his shoulders and tried to comfort him.

"I understand how you must have felt," she said softly. "But that's not the end of the story, is it?"

"No, thanks be to God! I take her to one supposed specialist after another, but all the time she gets worse. She doesn't say much, she jokes and once again wears a veil, but all the time her heart is breaking, and one day she tries to kill herself." Mac didn't speak, she merely squeezed the hand she held very tightly. ". . . On that day," Zarek went on, "I heard of a man named Kingsland who was recruiting young housemen for a hospital he ran at El Belada. They told me to steer clear of this man as he consorted with lepers. I met Roy Kingsland, I took him to see Fadia, and he gave her hope for the first time in many months. It might well take three years to effect a cure, he said, but there was work for my sister at the colony, if she cared to help, and the time would soon pass. He said it was best I did not see her in that time. I went newly inspired back to my studies, and strangely ashamed. I am to be a doctor, my friends are doctors, and all of us turning a blind eye to the curse hanging over our very heads. Leprosy is a curse of this continent, but who studies its beginnings and works to find a cure? The English, Irish, Americans and French . . . we nationals behave as

86

though it wasn't there! We turn our backs on the enemy whose strike is the most deadly of all. But I digress. I get up on my soapbox, you say?" Mac smiled. "Fadia is happy to go with Doctor Kingsland and for three years I do not see her. I take my degree, I practise surgery and go to London for my diploma. Then I am called to El Belada to see little Fadia. That is indeed a day! Not only is she cured but beautiful again! I hardly believe this thing. I look for scars but I do not find any. Fadia laughs at me and we give thanks to God together. We also thank Roy Kingsland. But words . . ."

"I know," Mac told him. "they seem poor things at such a time. Where is Fadia now?"

Zarek shrugged. "Still nursing the lepers. I—her brother—cannot drag her away, and now she is married to the doctor whom Roy has trained to run the colony, so she does not consult me what to do any more. Neither do I forget a man who has made such life and love possible for my sister. I offer to work for him. Does this now unpuzzle you, dear Mac?"

"Yes," slowly she pulled her hand clear. "I didn't realize Roy Kingsland had such a personal hold over your affections. He seems to hold Red in much the same way. I sometimes feel I hardly know him myself."

"Then much is missing in your life," the other said quaintly. "Get to know him, Mac, I beg of you. You will not only be a better doctor for it, but a happier woman. I promise you."

Mac thought wryly, "I might, if only one could get near him for Fiona!"

* * *

One o'clock in the afternoon was the hour the patients took their naps after being washed, injected and generally subjected to the treatment handed out by Sister Haifeh and her staff. It was also the time the medical staff went off duty for two glorious hours of relaxation. Of course this was not always possible, for being an official free time it allowed for one to catch up on innumerable jobs not included in the routine. Abdel ibn Rahman's blood transfusion, for instance, not being a number one priority emergency, had to be fitted into an odd moment, and this was as good a time as any to transfuse him. Abdel was a professional hunter who worked in the forests bordering the banks of the Nile in the Lower Sudan, but his blood's lack of red corpuscles was not due to any battle with an enemy's tooth and claw, but to an inherent physical deficiency which—as he explained it—took away his strength and left him to die. Abdel, however, had awakened one day to find himself in this place where people were encouraged, sometimes unwillingly, to take hold of living again. This would be his fifth and final transfusion, and there was already talk of his being discharged as fit in the near future. Abdel was worrying a little about the cost of all this treatment. As Sister Haifeh strapped his arm to its rest and the saline was exchanged for the rich, red blood in the upended vacolitre, he thought it best to inform her that he was a very poor man who came of a very poor family, that he had a wife and seven children who must by now be starving: how could such a family pay money for doctors and beds with sheets upon them? and anyway, he hadn't asked to come! Sister Haifeh called down shame upon his head. If he didn't want to pay the doctor effendi nobody would trouble him. He was free to go when he was discharged. God knew how much he could afford to pay, and if he wished to live at peace with God it would be as well to make the effort.

"*Salaam aleykum!*" Abdel responded devoutly.

Sister Haifeh had her own methods of dealing with her countryfolk: knowing the native mind, torn eternally between God and Mammon, she subtly played one against the other, and was personally responsible for much of the hospital's revenue. She knew by a man's dress, his speech, what his status was, and mentally docketed him as being worth this or that in terms of cash or goods. She had long ago discovered that it was not always the poorest who shirked payment: a man who has little is often quite content to go with less. There was the case of old Amin ibn Hassan, known in the Arabic fashion as the son of his father long past middle age because his wife had borne him no child. Amin was poor, a farmer who scratched a meagre livelihood from the sandy soil as his father had done before him. Because his wife scratched willingly alongside him through the years Amin remained faithful to her, and only after her death did he take another and younger wife with but one idea in view, that to become a father and be known as Abu Amin for the rest of his days. Surely enough the couple were soon blest with a son, and now there was someone to scratch for: life had a purpose, a meaning, a joy about it. The child was named Hassan after his grandfather, and Amin ibn Hassan became Abu Hassan Amin in his sixtieth year, and was well content with his lot. Alas! the child was stricken by sickness before it was two years old, and when Roy Kingsland saw the mite, its beseeching-eyed parents who had brought it to him, one of whom looked old enough to be its grandfather, his heart sickened. He knew there was very little he could do. He allowed the parents to sit by the cot in the isolation ward, hold the child's hand and smooth its brow, and though this went on for nearly a week there was only one possible end to the business. The child died peacefully—Roy Kingsland at least saw to that—and while the stricken parents sat silent and submissive in the compound he embalmed the tiny body and bound it so that it could be taken on the long journey to the home village for burial without becoming offensive to anyone. The old man and his wife went off carrying their burden on a litter between them, and that appeared to be the end of that.

No so, however. After several months old Amin re-appeared in the hospital compound driving a sleek, well-fed she-goat in small payment for all the doctor effendi's kindness to the small Hassan: Amin regretted the delay in making payment, but the effendi would realize it took some little time to get the goat in such condition as this.

Roy Kingsland duly admired the goat and formally accepted it so as not to offend the old man: he had his steward make coffee and they drank the ceremonial three cups together, during which time the superintendent decided that such a handsome she-goat should have a mate and be used as nature intended her: unfortunately there was no he-goat at the hospital. Would Amin therefore return to his village with the goat and keep it for the effendi until such time as he could claim it?

"I will always know I have a goat at your house," Roy Kingsland concluded, "and that I will not have to worry about it, you being so obviously a man who can look after goats if this is a specimen."

Thus the incident passed with the greatest amicability all round, and when Amin was blest with a daughter and then twin sons, he sent a messenger with the glad news to the doctor effendi, and at the same time told him his goat herd now numbered twenty-and-two.

Sister Haifeh was thinking about Amin as she watched the blood dripping slowly into Abdel's vein. They weren't all like this man, thank God, out for all they could get and making a great show of empty purses while they were getting it.

The Superintendent materialized beside her.

"How's it going, Sister?"

"All right, sir. You should be off duty by now."

"Yes, I know. Where would Sister Bardale be?"

"The Sister-in-Charge will be in the office I expect, sir. She usually is." Sister Haifeh was smiling a little as she spoke, and Roy asked: "Are you finding Sister a help?"

"Oh—she does the reports which is certainly a help, sir," the other said generously. "I hate writing, and anyway I never find time."

"Good." He went off down the ward wondering how he could suggest to Fiona that she should do a little more than write reports on patients she hardly ever saw. All day he had wanted to speak with Fiona, but he had learned never to rush at anything. It would keep. He felt out of humor ever since he had seen his surgeon disappearing with the new pathologist. He knew where they had gone and he didn't like the idea at all. Mac was of more than average intelligence and he thought she must have understood his efforts to hedge Zarek off. She didn't know what she was biting off and might well finish up by having to chew it. He would tell her a few of the facts of life when she returned, and if she didn't like it, well—she could jolly well lump it! Also the morning had brought the weekly mail, and he hadn't enjoyed his letters from home one little bit. His mother had written:

"Darling,
"What indiscretion have you committed with Fiona that I don't know about? Her mother was over here yesterday hinting that you were as good as engaged to her ewe-lamb (or is Fiona a sheep by this time?) or ought to be by now. . . ."

There had also been a letter for him from Mrs. Bardale herself.

"Roy,
"(You dear old busy bee, you!) I have my friends dithering on the brink of an announcement and still no definite news of you two naughty things! You haven't quarrelled, have you? Let me know in good time about the wedding (I've whispered a hint to the vicar, hoping you won't mind) and you are sure to come home for it, aren't you?"

Yes, Roy wanted to see Fiona very badly indeed after that lot. Now he tapped on the office door and entered. Fiona was sitting doing her nails: she looked very lovely in her plain white tailored uniform dress and army-nurse's type of cap. Her dark hair peeped at intervals, her grey eyes looked cool, like rain pools.

"What a lovely surprise, Roy!" she greeted him.

"I'm afraid it's not so lovely, and would you please remember to call me 'sir' when on duty?"

She looked a little less certain of herself.

"I didn't think it mattered between old friends like you and me. . . ."

"It matters in the hospital—on duty," he told her firmly. "Within these walls I am the Superintendent Medical Officer and you are my Sister-in-Charge. I don't want you to have any illusions about your status, either. You are appointed as Sister-in-Charge of this hospital, and the hospital is your concern, not merely the office. The nurse in the women's ward is struggling to change a heavy patient who is incontinent. I don't think anyone else can be spared at the moment. When you have given the girl a hand will you come over to my house, please?"

Fiona fumed as she watched him go out into the white-hot glare of the compound. How dared he speak to her like that, as though she was a mere probationer! And to ask her to give a hand changing an incontinent patient, of all things! She hadn't done that sort of thing for years, and wasn't going to start now for him or anyone. Always well versed in by-passing all forms of unpleasantness, Fiona took over from the staff-nurse who was taking temps, and sent her along to help where help was most needed.

Fifteen minutes later Fiona joined Roy Kingsland on the veranda of his house, accepted an iced drink from the steward and observed, "I'm here, sir, if you want to bully me again."

Roy smiled.

"I don't, Fiona. I hope I never bully you. It's just that with two of us off duty together there's so much to do and I get rather short-tempered, I suppose. You'll have to forgive me."

She eased herself into the long chair and put her feet up.

"Are we on Christian-name terms again, then?"

"Of course. We're not on duty. We can be ourselves now, which is what exactly, Fiona?"

"Whatever do you mean?" she demanded.

"I mean am I your sweetheart, or just a friend of long standing, my girl? That's what I mean!"

CHAPTER FIFTEEN

FIONA SIPPED slowly through her straw, collecting her scattered wits. As her companion didn't speak again and was obviously waiting for an answer to his question, she decided to play along with him.

"Are you giving me a choice?" she asked coyly.

Roy insisted, "What are we, Fiona? You tell me because you know perfectly well."

"Then why ask me to confirm it?" she snapped. "I don't understand what this is all about. Why the third-degree?"

"Because of this. . . ." He handed over Mrs. Bardale's letter and watched her read it, her brow furrowed.

"How stupid of Mother!" she exclaimed, and for the first time he felt sorry for her. "How impossibly stupid!"

"I thought you'd agree with me on that," Roy said. "You must write your mother and tell her to stop weaving romance around us, Fiona. Tell her in no uncertain terms."

"But how can I ever face them back at Coningwater? The vicar thinks . . ." She lowered her eyes, then raised them slowly to meet his. "Naturally he'll think Mother had some reason for hinting."

"What possible reason?" Roy almost exploded. "Anyone would think you and I had—had"—he almost choked —"and you know perfectly well there has been nothing at all between us. I admit I grew up loving and idealizing you, Fiona, as any young man has one perfect image in his mind, but you—naturally enough—had no eyes for me. There were always too many other attractive chaps around, even after Adrian. We can't have your mother arranging our lives for us because she is so damned posses-sive that she wants you within hail all her days. She wants you as mistress of Kingsmount, not particularly as my wife: it wouldn't matter if we never saw one another as long as she could continue to run your life as she has been doing. Show some spirit, Fiona. Tell your mother you'll arrange your own marriage as and when you decide on a partner of your own choosing!"

"It all sounds very simple," Fiona said sharply.

"Didn't you come out to El Belada to break away from"—he tapped the letter—"this sort of thing? I thought you did. It seemed to me you were stifled. Crying out for help, as it were. I fancied if you were prepared to take on El Belada you must be pretty desperate about something."

"I must have been," Fiona agreed.

"Well then"—he shrugged—"if you've made this gesture for freedom I'll be glad to help you achieve it. Start by telling your mother to undo all this mischief and to stop causing you embarrassment. I'm not a nineteen-year-old boy any more and I have no intention of rusticating at Kingsmount. I shall live—and most probably die—right here in El Belada. If you tell your mamma that she will immediately rush to the vicarage and break our mythical engagement without loss of face to anyone."

Fiona was painfully swallowing the bitter pill of knowledge that Roy Kingsland was nursing no secret tender feelings towards her: the grain of comfort in all this was that he appeared to consider that this state of affairs was mutual. If she threw herself on his neck now, declared herself, and he still put her from him, even this shred left of her pride would be gone. She must at least cling to what was left, become aloof from him and hope to awaken his interest and desire by the age-old act of withdrawal. Anything but reveal to him her true reasons for coming out to join him in the wilderness, that she had not been escaping from her over-possessive parent at all, but blindly following out that same mother's unmistakable instructions to do something about Roy Kingsland as an assurance against the future, even at the dreadful expense of laboring in El Belada for a while.

"All for nothing!" she fumed, and was suddenly conscious of Roy's eyes upon her. Swiftly masking her true feelings she observed somewhat wistfully, "We both seem to have decided on a single state, don't we?"

"Oh, I don't know. . . ." he mused. "I am rather like Mr. Micawber in a romantic way, always hopeful of something turning up one day. I wouldn't like to renounce all thoughts of marriage, though of course the field of possibility is considerably narrowed by the work I do here. Not many white females come my way, and I don't suppose I'm particularly attractive to women: I'm by no means a polished or experienced lover."

"Would you care for a little practice while we're both otherwise disengaged?" Fiona asked slyly.

He did not take this seriously, however, believing that no nice girl could be serious about such a thing.

"Your mother might well have a spy even here," he smiled. "Maybe Red is her spy," he teased, seeing the physician eyeing them morosely from his own veranda about twenty yards distant.

"What is the matter with him?" Fiona demanded peevishly. "He always makes me feel uncomfortable."

"You mean to say you don't know?" Roy was still smiling as he patiently lit a pipe and puffed away. "I thought any woman knew when a fellow was in love with her."

"You're mad!" Fiona snapped. "Doctor Bellinger isn't in love with me. He gets too much enjoyment out of annoying me."

Roy merely raised his brows and sucked at his pipe.

"That could be a symptom with Red," he finally decided. "I may be wrong, of course, but since you came on the scene Red hates my guts. He's sitting there hating me now because he thinks what your mother wants everyone to think—that we're more than 'old friends.' It's up to you to enlighten him if you're interested. If not I don't mind being the buffer between you and letting him hate me to a reasonable extent."

"He's nothing but a tramp doctor," Fiona declared, intrigued nevertheless by the idea of a secret burning devotion towards her in anyone. "He never seems to be properly dressed, and red hair—ugh!"

"Red is just—Red," Roy said flatly, "and he's no tramp. In fact he's like you in some respects: he ran away from an over-possessive father who was insisting on pushing his square-pegged son into the round hole of the family enterprise. Red rebelled. He wanted to be a doctor, but his father wouldn't spend a penny towards gratifying his ambitions, so Red left home and worked at just about everything—in the American way—and paid his own way through medical school. I admire him immensely."

"But why is he here?" Fiona demanded.

"And why shouldn't he be here, young lady? El Belada isn't the bottom of everything for all of us, you know!" Roy was smiling again.

"You know what I mean. Why should an American be

here in the Sudan if he isn't still running away from something?"

"I'm afraid I can't answer that. I only know he appears to prefer this continent to the one where his family's name is now a household word."

"I suppose his father has now disowned him?"

"No, indeed. 'Pop' Bellinger is very proud of the fact that his son made the grade without his help. He once came to Massawa in a fabulous yacht to tell him so. He also tried to 'square the deal' and give him a lot of money. I know he didn't succeed. Red is very proud."

"It seems silly to refuse money, though," Fiona said in a musing voice, looking across at the long, loose-limbed recumbent figure on the other veranda.

"Some people can't handle more than they can hold," Roy decided. "Red is one of those. He is a case that a good, understanding woman could work wonders on. She could persuade him back into the bosom of his family without anybody being conscious of having climbed down, and she could act as liaison between the almighty dollar of industry and Red's pride and skill in a notoriously underpaid profession."

"I didn't realize Doctor Bellinger had such an interesting background," said Fiona, thinking of the ocean-going yacht and all that must go with it.

"Even at El Belada we have our story-book characters," Roy went on. "Take Zarek...."

Fiona shuddered. "My mother would have a heart attack if she knew I was mixing with such people."

"You haven't done much mixing yet," Roy said dryly. "The day you were asked to take theatre with him you trumped up a paltry and obvious excuse. I won't have you playing God here, Fiona, so let's settle this thing once and for all. Zarek is a Sudani by birth and an Englishman by inclination, and he's the very best of both worlds, take it from me. You won't meet a finer gentleman anywhere on earth. Forget these mean little prejudices of yours and join in, for goodness' sake!"

Fiona had risen offendedly.

"If you think you can bawl at me whenever you like you're mistaken, Roy. I think it is you who are playing God. You would rather be thought somebody in this forgotten place than a nobody in England." Her eyes flashed with temper and the Superintendent rose also.

"Are we letting our hair down, Fiona?"

She turned her back and felt his hands strong and persuasive on her shoulders. Though she would dearly have loved to fling him off she studied the effect of the scene on Red's scowling countenance. It was as though he couldn't tear his eyes away from them, and he was not to know this was a quarrel.

"You are being horrid to me," Fiona whispered. "It was a mistake for me to come here. I'll never 'join in' as you call it with the natives. They scare me. Zarek scares me."

"You should share the confidence of your house-mate," the Superintendent said more acidly than even he realized. "He doesn't appear to be such an ogre to her. She has gone off with him alone to the Zarek private residence."

"You sound as though you mind," Fiona accused him.

"Of course I don't mind my staff being friends, but I don't think young Mac understands Zarek as I do. He has always idealized the union between his parents. He is—unconsciously—prepared to fall in love with any girl in his mother's image, and Mac just about fills the bill in this respect for him. She may find, in making gestures of close friendship, that she has a situation on her hands. I don't think our little pathologist has had much time in her short life for *affaires de cœur* and may not be awake to emotional danger."

"Ha! ha! our little pathologist has had more experience than you think," Fiona jeered. "You are out of character as her guardian angel, so don't worry about those two being together any more, unless you're worrying for Zarek. Mac told me herself about an affair she once had with a married man: he was a doctor, too, and because of the damage a scandal might have done their respective careers they called the whole thing off. Your pathologist isn't quite the little innocent you presumed, eh?"

Roy had turned and was staring at her as though uncomprehending.

"It's quite true, I assure you," Fiona declared, not liking the expression in the dark eyes.

"Should you have told me?" he asked in a voice he scarcely recognized as his own. "Surely such items are classed as highly confidential?"

"Well—I didn't say I wouldn't tell . . ." Fiona blustered. "Anyhow, you have been talking about everyone yourself this afternoon."

"I have repeated nothing of an intimate nature," Roy insisted. "I feel shocked by this thing you have told me. I'm sure Mac didn't mean me to know of it."

"Are you sure you're not just shocked?" Fiona's voice held a jarring note for Roy Kingsland now. "Maybe you were nursing a secret fancy for Mac yourself, and feel badly about someone having got in ahead of you."

"I think you had better go back to the wards," Roy said coldly. "It's past two o'clock and the work must be mounting up. I'll be along shortly."

With a toss of the head Fiona turned and walked down the steps and across the compound. Her steps were slower as she passed Red Bellinger, as though she was very deep in thought.

"Sister"—she started at his voice—"would you have a cure for a blinder on you?"

Fiona went up to him, her brain working furiously but none of it obvious in her serene countenance. She laid cool fingers on his brow and a thrill of his masculinity passed into her being like a current of electricity.

"You must have a bad head, Doctor Bellinger," she said sympathetically. "I'll send one of the nurses over with some codeine. Try to sleep for half an hour."

"After you have just pepped up my circulation, honey? You must be joking!"

"I'm going back to work, Doctor Bellinger," she said almost sadly. "I've wasted enough time already. Keep quiet with that headache, now."

He found the grey eyes in their fringe of dark lashes strangely hypnotic and lay back dutifully on the long chair while she gently pulled a cushion into place under his head.

"There, now! Is there anything else before I go?"

"No, honey. Nothin' else, I guess. If this is a dream just let me keep on dreamin', fer Pete's sake! I'd better put this down before I forget. 'Dear Diary, today the fair Fiona looked at me for the first time as though I wasn't something the cat had thrown up. I am well content with my lot!' "

CHAPTER SIXTEEN

ROY KINGSLAND'S brow was dark with unpleasant thoughts for the rest of the day. Fiona couldn't have made that up about Mac's affair with a married man, could she? She had seemed so viciously sure of herself, as though—having become aware of a deterioration in their relationship—she seized upon someone to drag down with her in his estimation, another's defection being some justification for her own to her way of thinking. Women—he supposed—did discuss their love affairs with one another, even down to intimate details: they had to indulge in romance, which was as necessary to their well-being as food, apparently. Maybe he would never really understand the opposite sex, and had better stop trying for his own peace of mind. He hesitated to admit that his pathologist's past amours were any real concern of his: he prided himself upon being broad-minded in general, but had been surprised to find that his reactions had been narrow-minded in the extreme in this particular. Fiona had somewhat wildly suggested he perhaps nursed a secret regard for Mac, which he pooh-poohed immediately as ridiculous, but upon investigation of his feelings he realized that the cloud which had fallen across his day would not have assumed such proportions if he had been entirely impersonal on the subject. In fact he found himself actually brooding over Mac's romantic past, wondering how far this affair with the married doctor had gone? Had they been "lovers" in the accepted sense, meeting in hotels at weekends and skilfully employing all the subterfuges necessary to keep their private joy in one another from the all too damning glare of the public eye? Roy tried to wriggle away from these thoughts, but they beset him like demons. He had held Mac to be a shining, pristine creature who had found her professional skill at the expense of her heart's yearnings. He thought of her as untried emotionally, someone who must be protected from love's onslaught, who must be encouraged by a lover to approach and offer her first shy kiss, rather than be subjected to passion's ravaging demands. He hadn't exactly pictured himself as this lover, but it was this shadowy figure, courteous and gentle, for whom he was prepared to guard her from Zarek, until—knowing better the surgeon's intentions towards her—he could tell his colleague to wait patiently for Mac's own indication as to which way her heart was inclining. Now he could have kicked himself for being such an old woman. Protect this girl from a healthy, warm-blooded young man whose loving would at least be honest? She who was prepared to rob an innocent woman of her rightful place in a man's heart and had desisted only in time to guard her professional neck? She both had her cake and had eaten a goodly slice too, and he would not concern himself in the future with any misguided effort to protect one whose emotional experience was so obviously greater than his own.

Mac was all but a scarlet woman in the Superintendent's sight by the time the big car slid sleekly to a standstill in the compound and she was handed out, still laughing at some joke or other, by the gallant and still garrulous Zarek.

"We do this again sometime, eh, Mac?" he demanded as he watched the car reverse and slip away once more in a cloud of dust.

"Certainly. But now I'm going to change for dinner. Thank you for a lovely day, Zarek, dear!"

Roy heard this and a sneer marred his handsome countenance.

"Do it all the time," he muttered. "Hand yourself around like a plate of cakes, my girl, and see if I care!"

Only Mac and Zarek appeared lighthearted over dinner. They made merry exchanges until it became obvious that the other three were more silent than usual. Red was trying to digest this new Fiona along with his food, this goddess who had actually tolerated him on several occasions since he had returned to his duties this day, had smiled coolly at his somewhat malicious asides, and who had once addressed him as "Red" before quickly apologizing and substituting his full title with an embarrassed lowering of eyelashes.

"You can call me Jeff, honey, if it'd make you feel more cosy," Red had suggested, still watchful for the "catch" he felt must be present to account for this *volte-face* by the new Sister. "That being short for Jefferson, my real name."

Fiona had smiled again, the rather sad smile of the unearthly creature who has just been introduced to earthly whimsies for the first time.

"On duty I must remember to call you 'Doctor,' and how is your head now?"

Yes, indeed, Red had plenty to occupy his thoughts during the meal. He usually spent his time doing battle for what he wanted, making mischief for amusement's sake and generally surveying life from the viewpoint of an overgrown pixie: now he was under the spell of a mysterious enchantment: a woman's grey eyes and cool fingers had bewitched him temporarily. But Red had no illusions that Fiona was in love with him. The bewitchment he suffered was that effected by a snake about to strike, and Red was interested in his reactions to the situation and strangely unafraid. When the beautiful cobra decided to make her strike he would seize her if it so pleased him, and they would devour one another in an ecstasy of self-destruction.

Fiona, too, was thoughtful, though she did not indulge in mental metaphors. Debit and credit to her account she could reason out in words of one syllable. She had already reasoned that Roy Kingsland entertained no latent feelings of a warmer regard for her than those of a friend of the family, nor was he likely to develop these now. They had spent much time together during these past weeks, especially before she had started working, and he had displayed a natural concern over her health. Not once had he hinted a desire to step into the role of lover, though she had done everything to encourage him bar making the most obvious of advances. No—he must be written off as a total loss, and this meant the loss of an insurance policy against the rigors of the future. Mrs. Bardale had been left adequately provided for, but her extravagance was always above her means, with the result that she had sacrificed many of her securities to provide for herself those comforts from which she refused to be separated: these included a full staff of servants, the holding of large dinner-parties at over-frequent intervals and unnecessary excursions for weeks at a time to places renowned for the medicinal properties of their natural elements. What Fiona was to exist on after her mother's demise was a mystery. Occasionally Mrs. Bardale allowed herself to dwell on the problem, but it invariably brought on one of her migraines and laid her low for a while, so she didn't allow herself to get really worked up about it. Of course Fiona was sure to marry one day, and that would be that. There was always Roy Kingsland in the very last extremity.

Fiona had thought much along the same lines, and she had also accepted Roy as her final bastion of defence against a lonely and poverty-stricken old age. Now there was not even Roy, and she had known moments of actual panic since the somewhat heated exchanges of the afternoon. The idea of having to work all her life in order to even exist was humiliating to her and could not be seriously considered. She even thought of young Khalid—from whom she had heard that very day and who had promised her all manner of luxuries. But even Khalid wanted value of his money—he wanted her. If she went to Khalid it was as good as a step over a precipice, and meant she would be barred forever from the genteel drawing-rooms of Coningwater.

Looking up from her plate where she had been merely picking at her food, Fiona met Red Bellinger's questioning green and amber-flecked eyes. Red had only entered her thoughts as a remote possibility against greater disaster a few hours ago: she didn't really want to have to consider him at all. Red would not purchase a woman's beauty, as Khalid was prepared to do, neither would he accede with gallantry and dignity to her whims and fancies as perhaps Roy—as a husband—might do. Red would see to it that whatever she got out of a union with him—ocean-going yacht and all—she would put her full share in, by jiminy! Fiona sometimes felt as though she had known Red all her life: he was Nemesis who had always been on the tail of her own shadow. This she had recognized even in Massawa when they had first met. It didn't seem much use, looking into those challenging, malicious eyes, to run away any longer. Fiona felt suddenly tired of the effort to sidetrack fate. She looked back at Red, and her eyes were large and strangely soft in capitulation.

*   *   *

"The atmosphere was as thick as butter during dinner," Mac observed, selecting and putting the record of Grieg's Elegiac Prelude on the turntable of the old-fashioned portable gramophone. "Has somebody had a row while I was out with Zarek?"

Fiona became immediately alert—defensive, almost. This was a heaven-sent opportunity to straighten herself out with her housemate.

"Roy and I did have a small difference of opinion about something. Mac—my feelings are changing towards him. What shall I do?"

"If you're sure, tell him, of course," the younger girl said in some surprise.

"I did try to," Fiona said in a pained voice. "That's the trouble. He can't believe it. I don't want him to be hurt so that El Belada would suffer."

"I can't see him allowing that to happen," Mac argued. "He wouldn't be satisfied with your tolerance of him. People who love want love in return, not pity. You must tell him frankly, Fiona."

"Give me time and I will," the other agreed. "I adore that part in the music, don't you? It's sort of lost and lonely like a breaking heart."

Mac glanced obliquely at her companion,

"If you hadn't just told me you were falling out of love I would have presumed the worst after a remark like that, Fiona. I've never known you to wax poetical before."

"Maybe you're right," Sister Bardale mused, looking at herself in the mirror. "Maybe you're right in your presumption. I could be falling in love, I suppose."

Mac decided not to press the matter further.

"I thought perhaps Zarek and I had offended in going off as we did."

"Silly girl! Your day off is your own concern. Did Zarek make love to you?"

Mac merely stared her surprise.

"Well, he was obviously only awaiting an opportunity to get you by yourself," Fiona smilingly justified her question. "He absolutely adores you. You can surely tell me all about it?"

"But there's nothing of that sort to tell," Mac said simply. "It is possible to go out with a man and enjoy other pursuits than love-making, you know. Zarek has a marvellous swimming-pool and there's a real oasis, too. Oh, and we saw a patrol of the Defence Force!"

"Lovely!" Fiona decided without interest. "If you'll excuse me now, dear, I promised to go and have a cigarette with . . ."

The name was lost in her perfumed exit, and Mac shrugged and settled down to re-read the day's mail. She was especially interested in a letter from Gareth: the sight of his handwriting had the power to stir her still, but once she began reading it had been all right. Gareth wrote in terms of gratitude and friendship, and she was relieved to find she could read of his activities dispassionately.

"I have just become a father [he wrote] *and now that we have a son things are just about as well with us as they can be. I'll never forget that dreadful time when Claire left me and I groped around blindly in the dark, Mac, until I found you. It may have been wrong not to tell you about Claire from the first, but you were such a comfort to me, such a welcome little port in the heart's storm. I shall always be glad it was you, and that you persuaded me to make a fight for happiness with my wife. Any other woman might have led me right away in the opposite direction. But what did you get out of it all, my dear? I fear nothing but pain and disillusionment. . . ."*

Mac stopped reading and pondered. There was no pain left now, but at the time of Gareth's confession that he was a married man with a wife he had tried in vain to hate, the pain had seemed more than a heart could bear. It was difficult to be strong at such a time, to put away selfish happiness and pursue the only right course. But Mac had never given in to weakness, her character was built around an inward light which would never allow her to compromise with the illicit or the sly. She and Fiona Bardale were the female counterparts of chalk and cheese.

Gareth went on to say that he had secured an appointment in Kenya, and that when he had had time to prepare a suitable house for them, Claire and the boy would be flying out to join him.

"*I am taking the long, slow route myself* [he told her]. *I shall disembark at Port Sudan and motor the rest of the way in my veteran jag. I shall plan my route to take in El Belada and look you up.*"

So they were to meet again. It was a good thing no one at the hospital knew the story. . . . Mac's brow furrowed as she thought of Fiona and that foolish exchange of confidences in the early days of their acquaintance. Fortunately Fiona was primarily concerned with her own affairs and might well have forgotten about Gareth. Mac hoped so. Such a confidence could be a double-edged weapon in the hands of a confidante who was not a friend.

CHAPTER SEVENTEEN

MAC GENTLY drew down the edge of a snowy sheet, gazed into a pair of liquid brown eyes and said softly, so as not to awaken the other sleeping women in the ward, "I want a sample of your blood, Fatima binte Abdullah."

The Moslem name fell easily now from her lips, and she prided herself upon knowing the names of every patient in the ward who had been there for more than a day. Fatima, she knew, meant the faithful one; binte Abdullah, that she was the daughter of Abdullah, whosoever that lord and master of a household might be.

"It is very good, Doctor Immacula," the girl whispered back. "You want my arm or my ear?"

"Your ear will do this time. I won't take much."

Mac quickly and efficiently got on with her job and noticed a new face in the next bed. "Who's that?" she inquired, not yet able to read the Arabic script on the head-plate.

"That is Jamila binte Ibrahim, Doctor Immacula." Fatima smiled, anticipating the doctor's next question. "Jamila means the beautiful. You should be known as Jamila binte Immacula, if I may so."

Mac flushed and dimpled in genuine pleasure.

"Well, thank you, Fatima! How nice that you should think so!"

She took her innocent delight out of the ward with her along with her equipment. It was too involved a business to go into an explanation that Immacula was her christened name only. From the very beginning she had been known as Doctor Immacula: it was Roy Kingsland who had introduced her to the hospital thus, and the patients addressed her so without question.

Her rubber-soled shoes made no sound on the red cement of the corridor: as she passed the partly open door of the linen-room she saw two figures therein standing—in her opinion—far too close together for comfort in this heat. The tall, somewhat gangling figure of Doctor Bellinger almost blotted out the white-capped, snowy-clad figure of a woman. Mac hadn't to guess twice to know who that would be, though she immediately looked ahead and commenced whistling like a blackbird, a thing she hadn't done since her schooldays, but there seemed so much of intrigue in the air lately one didn't know what one might come upon next, so it was as well to advertise one's presence continually.

Those two were obviously carrying on an affair, Mac pondered darkly, and the Superintendent was so black-browed and snappy, it appeared as though he half suspected what was going on and didn't like it one bit.

"He does rather take it out on me, though," Mac thought ruefully. "I haven't had a friendly word out of him for ages."

She backed herself into the laboratory, guarding her trays, and observed, "Here comes Jamila binte Immacula according to young Fatima. What do you think about it, Ahmed?"

She expected her young assistant to laugh shrilly: he was always amused by her Arabic learnings. But there was no response and Mac concluded Ahmed must be taking the blood-sample she required from Abu Khadra in the men's ward. She set down her trays and turned to the powerful microscope, only to start abruptly as strong arms seized her from behind and wheeled her around. She gazed questioningly into the almost black eyes of Zarek, which looked at this moment wholly Arab, burning and sombre. She didn't quite understand the situation or the friendly, light-hearted young man who had suddenly changed into a physically dominant stranger; but no one could mistake that crooned, "Mac, *Jamila, el binte hiya ya habibti.*"

In any language that tone implied a declaration of love.

"Zarek, let me go instantly!" she demanded.

The surgeon's reply was to crush her lips impatiently against his own. The more desperately she struggled the more tightly he held her, alternately laughing and kissing with an almost savage delight in the fury he had aroused in her. Weary and almost weeping, she at last grew limp in his arms, and again Zarek's voice took on that velvet tone.

"*Ya habibti*—my love."

She closed her eyes as the sensuous lips again descended: they flashed open wide, however, as a new voice demanded, "Am I in the right place? This is the path. lab., I presume?"

It was the Superintendent.

Zarek released Mac as though she were a hot brick and she floundered against the table, finding her legs weak and her head light. There was a brief, sharp command from the staff senior and Zarek—with a rueful shrug of broad shoulders—left the laboratory. Mac tried to collect her scattered wits and awaited the onslaught which never came.

"Did you get those samples I asked for?" Kingsland asked coolly.

"Yes, but I—I haven't classified them yet, sir. I'm sorry. I'll do them right away."

Mac hated her voice for trembling so, fearing that the Superintendent might conclude she was suffering the after-effects of stirred emotion instead of impotence and rage. Why didn't he make a reference to the scene he had just witnessed instead of pacing about silently like a tiger in a cage? He had probably seen the couple in the linen-room on his way here, and what he must be thinking. . . !

Forthright Mac could stand it no longer.

"I'm sorry for what just happened, sir," she said with some difficulty, not knowing how to put it into words. "I'll see it doesn't happen again."

"Oh, my dear Miss Hayes, don't deny yourself life's simple joys on my account! I merely ask that they are not indulged here in the hospital while you are supposedly on duty. It is somewhat embarrassing to be about one's legitimate business and suddenly come upon such a scene. After all, you see enough of Mr. Zarek out of duty time, you ride together and you have even gone along with him to his house. I would have thought sufficient opportunities are afforded you for demonstrations of an intimate nature without trespassing on the hospital's time."

Well . . . ! Mac had asked for it and she had certainly got it. She felt her strength returning fivefold, the strength of honest to goodness anger. She stared at Roy Kingsland, hardly believing her ears.

"Now look here, sir," she said, breathing hard, "I don't quite understand what this is all about. I didn't go to Mr. Zarek's house to—to . . ." she floundered for words.

"Well, I would much rather you did it at his house than here," the senior told her, preparing to leave the laboratory. "If I may have those blood groupings as soon as possible, please?"

Ahmed entered at that moment and stood uncertainly looking from one to the other of them, sensing the stormy atmosphere.

"Sir"—Mac said desperately—"I've got to see you in private. May I have five minutes of your time after dinner tonight?"

"If you wish, Doctor Hayes," Roy Kingsland's smile was like ice on the blaze of a volcano. "At eight-forty-five sharp I shall be in my office."

In his office! Mac sought for control as she turned back to the table. He was on his high horse indeed when he granted interviews in his office. There was to be no cosy chat in his bungalow over a cup of coffee for her, it appeared.

For the rest of the day Mac worked furiously yet with little satisfaction. She was consumed by a burning wrath against mankind in general: even Ahmed did not escape the lash of her tongue on occasions, being the most available target, but he remained blithely unruffled by it all. Red Bellinger, coming into the lab. and wanting a job hustled through, got short shrift also.

"I'm fully occupied, as you can see, Doctor Bellinger. It'll have to wait."

"But it can't wait, young Mac. If you can't give it number one priority, shift along and I'll do it myself."

"You'll do no such thing!" Mac flared. "Why the sudden haste? I didn't see you exactly hustling half an hour ago!"

Red looked as though something had hit him between the eyes. He was very self-conscious upon the subject of himself and the Sister-in-Charge, and—like an ostrich hiding its head in the sand—was inclined to hope no one had noticed anything. Now he colored up to match his name, apologized for the interruption and left the laboratory without another word.

Mac tried to feel sorry and couldn't. Her day had been upset for her, an innocent victim of circumstance, and the guilty weren't going to push her around if she could help it.

Dinner was another rather dreadful experience. Only the Superintendent appeared much as usual, but he never allowed his feelings to show in public. Fiona looked as though she had been weeping; torn between her lovers, no doubt, Mac thought bitterly and impatiently. Fiona needed to grow up and realize one had to make a decision sometime about something and accept the consequences. Zarek was morose, and Mac had no doubt he was brooding more about Roy's disapproval than her lack of response to his advances. Red made ambiguous and sometimes cruel remarks during the courses, looking around as though sensing that for once everyone was in disfavor with everybody else. He felt maliciously intrigued by it all.

Mac was the most anxious to put her world back to rights, and as chairs were pushed back and there was the usual indecisive standing about, she approached the Sudani and confronted him squarely.

"Mr. Zarek. . . ."

"Yes, Doctor Hayes?" he copied her tone in some amusement.

"May I have a word with you, please?"

There was nothing furtive about this conversation: all could hear if they so wished.

"You want we should go to my house?" Zarek was all for dashing off there and then to the bungalow he shared with Red, but Mac was shaking her head.

"A walk round the compound will do. I have to see the Superintendent in five minutes."

"Very well, dear lady."

Zarek took Mac's arm and led her away into the half-light. Roy Kingsland coughed and, with a word of excuse, went across to the hospital. Fiona, unexpectedly alone with Red, stepped out on to the veranda and—sensing the physician close behind her—turned suddenly and surrendered herself to his arms.

"Fiona, honey," he said huskily from the fragrance of her throat where he was burrowing, "what madness has gotten into me? I just cain't understand myself lately. What are you doing to me?"

"Are you in love with me, Red, darling?"

"Nothin' so straightforward. I'm just insane about you, I guess. Have you told his nibs yet?"

"Er—no. Not yet."

Swiftly he put her from him.

"I could'a sworn he wasn't himself at dinner. Look, Fiona, I cain't hurt that guy of all people. I cain't steal from him. You gotta sort things out between you before I take over. It's gotta be off with the old love before it's on with the new. That man gave me back my self-respect, gave me a job when I was . . . well, never mind what I was. I won't do any sneakin' in by the back door with him. I'm beginning to hate myself for wanting you like this, Fiona, when by rights you're his."

"By what rights?" Fiona asked sulkily. "We're not engaged or anything."

"By the right of your given word, you told me," Red said sharply. "Fiona, if ever you gave your word to me and broke it, I'd break your pretty neck, so help me! You'll tell him tonight, do you hear?"

"But . . ." her eyes wavered.

"You'll tell him tonight, or I will."

"I—I'll tell him, Red." Fiona smiled to herself as he took her across the compound to her own quarters, holding her as though she was something precious and fragile which might disintegrate suddenly before his dazzled eyes.

*   *   *

"An absolute barbarian!" Mac exploded under the lone prickly pear which grew in the compound. "I was ne'er attacked like that before in all my life, Zarek, and it better hadn't happen again. I'm not in love with you. I'm prepared to be friends and that's my limit."

The surgeon was silent for a moment, then he replied ruefully: "I am sad you think so badly of me, dear Mac. I hoped you would like me a little. The moment arrives and I do not think, only that you are very sweet to my lips. What more can I say? That I am sorry, perhaps? But no—I could not be sorry for something as delightful as kissing you. Maybe you change towards me, eh?"

"Never, Zarek. I can't make myself love you."

"You have not known me very long," he insisted. "How can you be so sure of this? Maybe you love someone else?"

"No. I—no," she finished lamely.

"But a woman must love or she dries up like the pomegranate. There is an Arab saying, it goes, 'A woman must veil her face in order to hide the light of her love.' All women are beautified by love, Mac. You must not miss this very necessary thing so that you wither away. Zarek will wait and hope. We take the rides together and be friends until——"

"I can't go riding with you any more, Zarek."

"But yes," he insisted. "You cannot take all away from me together, your love and your friendship. I accept your friendship for time being," he said magnanimously.

Mac sighed, realizing the futility of explaining the impossibility of taking away something he had never possessed.

"I have to see the Superintendent now," she said, and marched grimly away in the direction of the hospital.

"She will come round," Zarek told the rising moon confidently. "Sister Bardale told me an Englishwoman, for all her apparent coldness, enjoys being swept off her feet. I will wait a little. Have the patience. Then I will sweep. . . !"

CHAPTER EIGHTEEN

WAITING OUTSIDE the glass-panelled door bearing the legend Senior Medical Registrar, in both English and Arabic script, Mac felt as nervous as she had done on long-past trips to the dentist during her schooldays. She knocked on the door and was bidden to enter. Roy Kingsland looked as though he had just hurriedly donned a pair of horn-rimmed spectacles. Mac hadn't seen him wearing glasses before, and was reminded of her own efforts to conceal the soft feminity of her looks behind severe horn-rims. Was this man also reduced at times to having to employ aids to add sternness to his countenance? Surely he wasn't as human as all that? Still he was obviously self-conscious about the glasses and fingered them as he spoke.

"I believe you wished to speak with me, Doctor Hayes?"

"Yes, sir. It's about this afternoon. We were rather cut off in the middle of a somewhat unsatisfactory conversation."

"Were we?" he smiled reminiscently. "Then you will have had time to get your feet on solid earth again, I should imagine."

"They were never airborne," Mac said sharply, determined not to be provoked. "What exactly did you mean to imply by your remarks about Mr. Zarek and myself? Are you suggesting that I make a habit of—of that sort of thing?"

Roy Kingsland took off his glasses, polished them on his handkerchief and set them down on the desk in front of him.

"Surely it's not my concern whom you choose to favor?" he ventured. "I am not here in the guise of either your Father Confessor or your guardian, and I do apologize most sincerely if you imagine it was your actions which came under criticism from me. These, I repeat, are not my business. Perhaps you do on occasion take me aback. When I first met you I was inclined to think of you as a somewhat precocious schoolgirl, but I have had to reassess you in the light of events. You have come half-way across the world more or less under your own steam and you are a fully active member of the staff here. I have no right to intrude into the pursuits of your spare time. I assure you it is not what occurs between yourself and Zarek which concerns me, merely where it occurs. It's hardly good for discipline to have the staff indulging romantic episodes within the hospital precincts. It might have been Ahmed who interrupted you."

"That I fully realize," Mac said, her voice trembling despite herself. "Sir—Doctor Kingsland"—it seemed a long time since they had been "Roy" and "Mac" together —"your magnanimity in this matter is just a trifle offensive to me. It doesn't appear to have occurred to you, even as a remote possibility, that I was being embraced against my will."

"And were you, Doctor Hayes?" His voice held a sudden challenge. "It seemed to me you were absolutely compliant when I saw you. If it had appeared otherwise I would have dealt most severely with Zarek, you can be sure!"

Mac swallowed. So this was an ultimatum. She either told the whole truth and "carpeted" the surgeon, or she stayed silent and allowed this cold-eyed stranger to think the worst of her.

"There seems to be nothing else to say," she decided, rising and smoothing herself down. "I can only repeat that I'm sorry, and . . ."

"Ah!" Zarek's blithe voice broke in on them from the doorway. "I catch you both together. That is good!"

"What is it?" Roy demanded a little impatiently.

"I think perhaps you are not understanding about this afternoon, my friend," Zarek pressed on. "Our little Mac is unhappy and you are angry with her, so I tell what happened. Speak up to shame the devil, I think you say? I am hiding behind the door when Mac comes into the laboratory, and—as always—she pleases my heart." He put a long, brown hand dramatically on his chest. "So I creep up behind to seize the little one and she is afraid and cries, 'No! no! Zarek!' and beats me with her fists. I think I have captured a bird and I will not let her go; I keep her so until she can beat me no more and then I am stirred to pity. This is when you come in, effendi, and tell me to be off, and I go." The surgeon shrugged and looked for approval in Mac's eyes.

"Well, thank you, Mr. Zarek," she said with a faint smile. "You couldn't have made the situation more clear. Not that I'm interested in trying any more," and she went towards the doorway.

"Just a moment, Doctor Hayes—Mac!" called Roy Kingsland. She heard him coming after her down the long corridor, but her heart felt like a flint and she didn't once turn her head. At the main door he caught up with her and said in a sincere and apologetic tone, "Mac, I'm sorry!"

"So you ought to be you—you prig!" she blazed, suddenly rounding on him. He was very tall, his brown eyes almost wistful in the restrained night-lighting of the hospital. Mac saw the shadowy, flitting figure in the background of the staff nurse who was in charge at night. With a swift, mischievous movement she reached up and drew his head down to her own, planting her lips upon his for an instant.

"There!" she said triumphantly. "Let's have the boot on the other foot for a change! Try explaining that away to Nurse Meryam!"

She didn't allow for Roy Kingsland, however.

"Then Nurse Meryam may as well have her money's worth," he said coolly, and holding her to him with one

111

firm arm he tilted her chin up with his free hand and proceeded leisurely to make a real job of the salutation.

* * *

The little procession wending its way into the compound did not strike Mac as being in any way peculiar. Patients did not roll up in expensively equipped ambulances here, they came as this one did, carried upon a litter by their relatives, or struggling along upon their own two feet only to collapse weakly once succor was in sight. Two men were bearing this litter, and two women, heavily veiled, walked behind carrying everything but the kitchen stove about their persons.

"Hakym! Hakym!" the man on the litter was groaning, rolling his head from side to side. "Hakym!" he suddenly shrieked, then more softly and desperately, "*Dawa, w'allahi!*"

Mac knew he was asking for a doctor, and, as though in sudden unbearable pain, for medicine, calling on God to witness and have pity on him.

"The poor laddie will get both now," Mac said compassionately to Ahmed, turning her eyes away from the window.

It seemed to be only a moment later that the Superintendent came rather desperately into the laboratory, his usually smooth dark hair almost standing on end.

"Isolation A," he said urgently; "take full precautions and secure a culture, query smallpox, will you? An almost certain smallpox," he added, and dashed out again.

"Oh, lord!" gasped Mac, and Ahmed swiftly invoked Allah in sympathy. "This looks like the real thing! I wondered when smallpox would turn up."

She donned a sterile gown, cap, mask and gloves, picked up her equipment and went along to the small ward known as Isolation A. The young man who had been on the litter was now between clean sheets on the long, high bed. His skin was a continuous mass of suppurating eruptions, evil-smelling.

"Hallo!" Mac smiled reassuringly as his eyes rolled fearfully in her direction. "Hakym," she pointed at herself and he relaxed once more, going back to dwell on his various physical miseries, his gaze turning inwards as she watched. She went back to the lab., having been divested of her outer clothing by the isolation nurse, and made two tests simultaneously. These took some time to complete.

112

It was midnight before she was able to send her report on her findings to the Superintendent, and by that time the patient was dead.

*   *   *

Three patients with smallpox in the hospital, more, in all probability, on the way. This was the situation facing the staff as a meeting was called for nine o'clock the following morning.

"All those affected come from the same village, fortunately," Roy Kingsland announced. "The village of Wadi Nahla, which refused vaccination when we were in that area eighteen months ago. You remember, Red?"

"Sure," said the physician grimly. "Now look what they got!"

"Exactly," nodded the Superintendent, "so somebody's got to go to Wadi Nahla to see to the sick who haven't come to hospital, and vaccinate the rest. The news must be spread by all means possible to coax others in for vaccination also. You will see to the propaganda side of things, Zarek?"

"I will so, Roy effendi. Do not trouble."

"You might also check the staff records. If anybody is getting remotely near to booster time, do 'em."

Again Zarek nodded.

"You, Red, take charge here, and may God help you! Mac and I are shoving off for Wadi Nahla, stat. Give us one orderly and one nurse. Tell them to get moving. Any questions?"

There were no questions. Everybody knew precisely what was required of them and that a situation had arisen which needed to be overcome by sheer will and effort. Only Fiona kept somewhat fearfully in the background, hoping for once not to be noticed. She had not seen—let alone nursed—a case of smallpox in her life, and didn't want to become involved now if she could help it.

Red somewhat worriedly helped his chief assemble all the Wadi Nahla party's needs for the hundred-mile journey and an indefinite stay in camp. He had much on his mind, and did not trust his newly acquired lady love further than he could spit. Fiona had now assured him that she had told Roy any intimate association between them was a thing of the past, but Roy had not appeared unduly subdued, neither did he behave like a man who has just been jilted. Red decided this was as good a time as any to tell his superior he had lost in the love stakes to

113

a natural-born heel, and ventured: "Roy, I sure appreciate the way you've taken it about Fiona and me."

Roy Kingsland was watching Tia Kafi loading the sterile containers of vaccine, and glanced at his colleague only half-attentively.

"What about you and Fiona?"

Red felt a consuming, murderous anger towards the Sister-in-Charge mounting behind his eyes.

"We—we're in love, sir."

How he wished to God it wasn't true!

"Congratulations!" Roy said mildly, then with more enthusiasm, "I hope you'll be very happy together."

Red couldn't believe his ears. The Superintendent wasn't as good an actor as all that. He just wasn't affected one way or the other by the Great News, and in order to find out why, Red might have to look foolish. To be Roy's fool, or Fiona's? Which was the most unpalatable?

"Do I understand you are giving us your blessing, sir? I thought I might'a been treading on your toes, maybe?"

"Not at all, old chap!" Roy actually patted him on the shoulder. "I believe it's symptomatic of love that a lover imagines fondly everybody else is in the running. I assure you the charming creature is all yours, and now I must go."

Red went back into the hospital, the mobile unit on its way, with one thought eating like a worm into his brain.

"She lied to me. She was never in the running with Roy. And if not—why not? What's wrong with Fiona? What am I letting myself in for?"

As Fiona slid out of the office to confront and wind her arms suggestively around him, she reeled suddenly against the wall, spurned and thrust aside. Her eyes were wide as the spare figure went on towards the isolation block without a backward glance.

CHAPTER NINETEEN

MAC RAN A hand through her damp hair and, taking the tin mug of tea from Tia Kafi's urging hand, sank down thankfully in the welcome shade of a wild fig-tree. Before her stretched the village of Wadi Nahla, which had been suddenly stricken with the evil scourge of smallpox. Mac felt she now knew Wadi Nahla as intimately as she knew Silverdell back home, but at home this sort of thing just couldn't happen. There might be the annual outbreak of measles and mumps, but the killers had been tackled and now were mostly under control by the mere job of a hypodermic needle available for the asking, and in most cases accepted as a routine protection for the young. Here, however, in the Southern Sudan the people mainly lived very close to nature: lack of education resulted in their attaching more importance to the past. They lived as their grandfathers and fathers had before them, bowing to old superstitions and nursing the old beliefs with a tenacity from which they refused to budge. The elders of the village welcomed the mobile unit gladly, for half the adult population was sick and there were fewer to do the work. The sooner Hakym effendi and Hakym binte cured the sick people, the better they would all like it, but be vaccinated when they were well? The effendi was joking, surely? Didn't the effendi know it was God who numbered the days of a man's life? It wasn't smallpox or the sleeping death—any of these things.

"Then if God numbers our days"—patiently argued Roy—"will vaccination change things one way or the other?"

The argument had gone on far into the night while Mac supervised the erection of the hospital encampment. There was a big, white hospital tent and a dozen camp-beds within it nearby, the bath-house for the patients was erected of the local mud-bricks, also a field-kitchen where Tia Kafi bossed two cooks who had come along with the party. At a safe distance were the staff tents and the canvas-rigged bath-tent they would share. All water must be drawn from the village well as the wadi—a river-bed—was dry at this season of the year. Mac saw to the boiling of many gallons of water which was then stored for drinking purposes: tanks holding water for washing were heavily chlorinated.

Nine beds were occupied almost immediately, in the hospital, and of the nine Mac found one patient, Karim ibn Basil, was not nearly as sick as the others. Upon examination she saw the minute scar upon his upper arm and said eagerly, "You have been vaccinated, Karim?"

"No, Hakym"—he hesitated, and decided to shame the devil—"if Hakym binte will not tell I will confess something."

"Confess away," Mac bade him eagerly.

"I was in army little time. I do not like so I come back to my wife. I desert. That is all."

"But that's wonderful, Karim, and just what we need to know. You're not going to die, the infection is very mild because of the vaccination the army made you have. Do you see what this means?"

Karim didn't particularly, but Mac positively raced away, plunged in and out of the chlorinated water, changed her clothes, and joined the meeting where Roy was bitterly arguing the virtues of vaccination. She told him what she had discovered and in less than an hour the battle was won.

"Quickly, before they change their minds!" Roy told her triumphantly, and children were awakened from their beds before they could realize what was happening and put back again sleepily protesting at the minor discomfort they had endured. All the fit adults were then done, except one who looked as though he might be incubating the disease. He was isolated and placed under observation.

"It has been a good night's work," Roy observed with satisfaction, and Mac—whose eyelids were drooping heavily —suddenly realized there was to be no sleep while the situation was so desperate.

"Here!" Roy said, observing her, "take one of these every four hours until I can let you off duty. They do help."

It was not the first time Mac had taken benzedrine, but it was the first time she had been reduced to taking it continuously because there simply wasn't anybody to fill her place while she slept. She and the Superintendent grew lean and haggard together as one death was followed by another in the encampment: the adult who was under observation became a positive case within twenty-four hours; two of the vaccinated succumbed to a mild form of the disease, but soon recovered, fortunately, and then the worst of the horror was over and the funeral pyre behind the grove of gafalfa-trees—from which frankincense is procured—actually burned down to grey ashes for lack of more victims to devour.

"How do you feel?" Roy Kingsland asked, joining his colleague in the black shade of the wild fig-tree, and accepting the mug of stewed tea from Tia Kafi's pink-palmed hands.

"Awful," Mac said miserably.

"How awful?" he asked in sudden concern. "You're not sickening for something, are you?"

"No," she said, impatiently waving away the hand that would have sought her brow for signs of fever. "I mean I feel awful about the way I look. My hair . . . see my hair . . . what's left of it!"

"It'll improve once you're back to decent water and shampoos," he told her. "Anyway, I thought you rather resented your comely appearance. You certainly warned me off the grass when I once tried to compliment you upon it."

"That's a long time ago," she insisted, "and you haven't attempted to offend me since."

He glanced at her obliquely and scalded his mouth with the burning tea.

"Damn that Nuba!" he choked. "He will insist on boiling the *shai*. Now, where were we? Oh, yes . . . do you mean to imply you've taken the sign off that particular patch of grass?"

Mac ran the sandy dust through her fingers, watching a column of ants busily involved in log-rolling with a discarded matchstick.

"You do like everything put into plain words, don't you?" she asked in some annoyance. "I merely want to know if I look as awful as I think I do?"

He looked hard and frankly at the heart-shaped face earnestly turned up to his. The skin was parched and dry from the effects of chlorine, the eyebrows and brittle hair were bleached almost white, the lips were drawn and the cheeks sunken with weariness: indomitably, the blue eyes looked forth, challenging him to give his verdict without sparing her feelings.

"You look as awful as you think you do," he said quietly, and her eyes promptly fell before his. "But"—he went on gently—"you will never look lovelier to me, Mac, old thing."

That "old thing" was completely sexless. She found she could look up again, questioning his words.

"I made the right choice when I brought you along," he told her, and offered her a fat American cigarette. "Just look what Red included in the stores; king size, too! I don't blame you for not smoking them. They're horrible for the first five hundred, then they rather grow on one. You're all right, Mac. You look like a doctor who's been busier than usual about her business, and that'll always be a sight for my sore eyes!"

Mac sighed sharply.

"I like a woman to look like a woman at the right times," he went on reflectively, "a suggestion of perfume, hair softly disordered against a bright cushion, a flowing négligé, perhaps!"

"Fiona, in fact," Mac said crisply.

"What?" he was startled, then a slow smile broke across his countenance. "It could be," he agreed, his head on one side, "but I was trying to picture you like that. There must be times when you're not a doctor, Mac. It would be nice knowing you then."

"I do have a day off occasionally," she said, her heart doing unaccountable tricks within her breast.

"Yes, I know. It's a pity there is such a demand for your company at these times, and a swimming-pool is such a pleasant inducement."

"I don't need any inducements to go anywhere with anyone," Mac said irritably. "You have been rather busy yourself."

"You think so?" he rolled over on to his side, his dark eyes challenging her. "I wonder if this somewhat intriguing exchange is the result of lack of competition in our respective orbits at the moment?"

"You must decide that for yourself," Mac said, and selected a cigarette after all. Hiding behind it and the puffs of smoke she blew somewhat inexpertly she managed to avoid his eyes and her racing heart calmed a little.

"I seem to remember I received an outraged slap on the one occasion my behavior fell short of the professional with you," he mused. "That was an entirely new experience for me."

"Me too," Mac said between puffs. "I never slapped anyone before."

"Then"—he observed mock-ruefully—"the 'keep-off-the-grass' sign is obviously meant for my eyes alone. *Touché*, Doctor Hayes, you have made your point. Never mind, you'll soon be back with your Zarek!"

"He is not 'my Zarek,' and I am not particularly fretting to get back to him or anyone. Maybe you are pining to rejoin Fiona—if she still wants you!"

There was a long silence, painful to Mac who feared she had gone too far with that angry gibe.

"I shouldn't imagine she does," Roy said at length slowly. "She has Red. He told me before I left that he wished to marry her. I gave them my blessing."

"Oh! I—I'm sorry!"

Mac burnt her fingers and threw her cigarette away into the dust.

"Why should you be sorry, Mac?"

"I thought you and she were . . . I understood . . . Oh, I don't know what I meant!"

"Yes, you do," he insisted, and rising drew her also to her feet. "Why does everyone assume that Fiona and I are anything more than friends? Red hinted as much. Zarek makes references coupling her name with mine. Good lord! Am I supposed to be jilted or something?"

He looked angry, breathing hard, his nostrils almost flaring in his lean, brown face.

"Did Fiona tell you we were engaged?" he demanded.

"No. Not exactly. Mrs. Bardale . . ."

"Mrs. Bardale! It's to be hoped Red marries Fiona before Mrs. Bardale has a chance to materialize in his life. I must say I'm hardly flattered," he went on meditatively, "to be thought of as scorned by a lady who prefers the attentions of my second-in-command. In fact my self-esteem has taken two dips in the past few minutes. Firstly I'm told I'm the only repulsive male in one lady's life, then——"

"I didn't say that!" Mac exclaimed, flushing hotly. "You do twist everything! I said it was the first time I had slapped a man who kissed me, and I slapped you because I was angry at the time and because I thought you should have been making a fight for Fiona if you cared about her. It wasn't as if the kiss was meant. It was merely retaliation."

"Theoretically it was supposed to be. In practice I rather enjoyed it. How about you?"

"I—I don't remember," Mac said, seeing *Danger* written on every leaf of the tree over their heads. "I think I'm wanted. Safa is expecting her baby any moment."

"I'll see you later then," Roy said pointedly, and strolled off in the direction of the hospital tent.

Mac allowed her body to relax and felt suddenly weak. It was as though she had just been emotionally involved with someone who had been slowly battering down her defences, allowing her to escape just in time. The point was, did she want to keep this particular assailant out? Roy Kingsland was difficult to assess. He was the non-pareil of Medical Superintendents, but how much of himself could such a paragon spare for love?

"I suppose it was all just idle conversation on his part," she shrugged, watching him earnestly discussing Abu Mohammed's convalescence with Nurse Uwongi, who came from Kenya and laughed her way through all her duties, onerous or not. "To take him seriously would be fatal for my own peace of mind. If he fancies a small flirtation to while away the time he'll find he's got the wrong girl."

But Mac knew in her heart that if Roy Kingsland made even the smallest advance towards her she was as good as lost. He had kept her quivering and palpitating like a caged bird this past half-hour, and sooner or later he would read in her eyes that she was his for the taking.

Mac acted midwife in those early evening hours, delivering a fine baby boy in a tent specially erected for maternity. Her head had begun to ache and she felt a little sick as she finally left Safa to think up a name for her new son. She had not eaten but decided she would be happier in bed. When she had taken a few steps, however, her legs began to feel like jelly and she stopped in her tracks as though dazed. She must have cried out, though she didn't consciously know this, and it was strong, gentle arms which picked her up bodily and carried her to her quarters.

"You brave little idiot, you!" a voice crooned into her ear. "I thought all day you were sickening for something. Been forgetting to take your paludrine, eh, and let malaria overtake you? Never mind, dear, I'll look after you. Don't worry, little Mac! Don't worry, my pet!"

CHAPTER TWENTY

RED BELLINGER noticed the pale shadow lurking on his veranda and deliberately looked away in the opposite direction. He was not surprised, and his thrill was conscious as fingers touched him lightly and a voice spoke.

"Red . . . what have I done? Why are you being horrid to me?"

"Horrid to you, Fiona? What makes you think that?" he smiled in the darkness.

"You have been cold and distant and made me do awful things in the hospital. Why can't Sister Haifeh take charge of Isolation? I have never done such duties in my life and it terrifies me. I'm afraid I'll catch something and die."

"Aren't you afraid somebody else will die if they take over?" he taunted.

"Well—I . . ." she tried again. "Red, don't you like me any more? Look! I—I put this dress on specially for you. I know you admire it."

He turned coolly and surveyed her. She wore an evening gown of pale yellow, strapless and moulded to the figure, hardly suitable for the limited social life of a hospital on the fringe of the desert, and much less so for this present occasion when everyone was worn out with fatigue and desirous only of being allowed to sleep the night through without fear of interruption.

"Going somewhere?" Red inquired.

"No. I . . ." Fiona realized the futility of banging her head against a brick wall and tried a fresh approach. She collapsed into tears. Weeping had never left anyone else unmoved in all her varied career, but Red proved to be the exception. He regarded her heaving shoulders dispassionately and then observed, "You need all that salt, Fiona, honey. Don't waste it in crying or you'll be sick tomorrow, and I sure can't spare you from Isolation at the moment."

Fiona quivered into silence, then she looked up with eyes full of venom.

"I hate you!" she almost spat. "I hate you and despise you, you oaf! I could——!"

He seized her white arm as it was raised to strike and twisted it a little, his mouth smiling round his cigarette. She writhed and squirmed in his grasp like a mad thing but could not escape: her tongue lashed him incessantly. It was as though the harridan—suppressed in her for so long—came up at long last for air and had its fling. The revealing dress tore during the struggle, her hair shook loose of its pins and tumbled down to her shoulders: she suddenly humanized before her tormenter and became more desirable to him in her primeval fury than with all her vaunted sophistication.

Zarek, coming across the compound in the direction of the bungalow after visiting a post-operative patient, paused irresolute as he witnessed his colleague apparently wrestling with a dishevelled Sister-in-Charge. Red was laughing fiendishly as he swept the slender figure suddenly up into his arms, kicking legs and all, and carried her inside the house to his quarters.

Zarek waited for a moment, whistling softly and kicking stones idly from his path. It was quiet now in the house, so the fighting was obviously over. With a broad-minded shrug of wide shoulders the surgeon—who just wanted to sleep—turned in the direction of the Superintendent's bungalow and smothered a yawn with his hand.

*   *   *

Fiona was moodily picking at her grapefruit when Zarek arrived at the breakfast table shining with *bonhomie*.

"Good morning, my dear Fiona! Did you sleep well?"

"Of course I slept well," she said sharply, her dark-shadowed eyes belying the statement. "Why shouldn't I?"

"No reason, my friend. I just make a routine inquiry. Ah, Red! You are late. Come, sit here!"

"Where did you get to last night?" asked the American, deliberating resisting an urge to meet Fiona's eyes.

"I slept here in Roy's bed. I slept very well."

"But why on earth . . . ? I thought something had happened to keep you at the hospital."

"Oh, no. It is that I just do not want to be"—he smilingly indicated Fiona—"a blackberry when you have such charming company with you."

Red smote his thigh and guffawed while Fiona colored up to her eyebrows with embarrassment.

"I don't know what you mean, Mr. Zarek," she said indignantly. "How dare you suggest . . . !"

"She means I put her out at midnight," Red smilingly explained. "I was tired. Another time you might not be so lucky, honey," he taunted her.

"I shall be glad when Roy is back," Fiona said chokingly.

"So shall we all, my sweet, then your interrupted engagement can continue for all our good."

"I like Roy to be engaged to Sister, also," Zarek said from his heart. "All this time he is with Mac, alone. . . ."

"If you want the girl why don't you take her?" Fiona asked savagely. "That seems to be the rule around here. Absolute savages——!" her voice trailed away and caught in a sudden sob. Red dismissed Zarek with an urgent kick on the ankle and the Sudani slid away to ponder on Sister Bardale's words.

"If you want the girl why don't you take her?" He imagined Mac behind him on a white stallion, the way his mother had once sat behind his father to gallop away into the night. Mac was not very heavy and Ibrahim, now almost recovered, was a notoriously powerful beast. He could make her happy, he was sure, if once he could break down the barriers of her reserve. It was no life for a woman

122

to be a doctor all her life, poking about in test tubes and preserving other people's appendages in alcohol. He would really be doing her a service in taking her away—by force if necessary—from these unfeminine occupations.

Red leant forward and said softly, "It's all right, Fiona. Don't cry, honey."

"I'm not c-crying."

"But you are, and I like you for it. You're not pretending nor nuthin'. But why, Fiona? I let you go like I told Zarek."

"I know. But I'm ashamed when I think of my m-mother."

"What about your mother? I didn't even know you'd got one."

"She—she's very strict about behavior, things like—like last night, for instance. I feel I've let her down in some way. You see I"—Fiona looked at him for the first time with her heart in her eyes—"didn't want to leave you. I didn't seem to care. . . ."

Red's hand reached out and sought hers, squeezing it in a savage ecstasy peculiar to the moment.

"I understand, honey. Listen! I've just been on the field-radio to Roy. Young Mac's down with malaria, but they're practically through with Wadi Nahla anyway, so in a day or two when she's fit to travel they're coming back. He told me the Anglican padre's coming our way today, if any of us God-forsaken creatures are interested. I suppose that sort of thing's important to you, Fiona?"

"I attended church at home, if that's what you mean."

"Yes, and these guys can marry a couple at a moment's notice. They carry licences—everything. How'd ya like to be Mrs. B. by tonight?"

Fiona knocked her coffee over: she stood up looking startled and suddenly afraid.

"You're mad, Red! We hardly know one another. My—my mother . . ."

He came inexorably towards her, holding her gaze almost hypnotically in his own.

"We're sure gonna know each other better next time, Fiona, and you know it. Your mother will be told in good time, same as my folks."

"It's sheer insanity, Red, what you're suggesting. I don't know what your parents will think, but my mother would never forgive me. She has always planned my wedding."

Red's mouth curled a little.

"That's why it never happened, I guess. Well, it's for you to say, Fiona: I'm not gonna force you into anything against your will. Take me or leave me. It'll be six months before the padre comes this way again—his is a mighty big parish—and just anything might happen in six months. I'm due for leave. I might go up to Massawa and not come back."

"You wouldn't do that, Red!"

"Oh, but I would. I'm a creature who acts upon impulses. This marriage is one of 'em. I'll probably regret it by tomorrow. In fact I'm beginning to regret it now . . ." he turned away to hide his amusement at the torment of doubt and chagrin in her face.

"Red, I—I'll do it!" she said desperately, seizing him by the arm and searching his countenance for approval. He looked merely bored, however.

"Right, we'll start our honeymoon with a trip to El Arak. . . ."

"The leper colony?" Fiona asked in a whisper. "Don't joke like that, Red, darling, please!"

"I'm not joking, honey," he told her. "El Arak's no joke to us here. I've gotta go see, and you—you wouldn't let your brand-new husband go alone, would you? Would you?" he challenged.

"No. No—of course not. I had better go and start work now, hadn't I, Red?"

"That's right, Fiona."

He watched her go across the compound and guessed at the conflict of emotions in her breast. He had now seen Fiona helpless, afraid and in love: it all gave him a wonderful feeling of power and well-being.

"Best to start off on the right foot," he mused. "She's gonna give and give till it hurts. When she stops jibbing I'll take time to show her what a nice guy I can be. Just so long as she plays four aces from the pack. . . ."

*   *   *

The Rev. John Chalmers Watkyn wriggled out from beneath his car and flagged down the approaching vehicle which was faintly visible in its cloud of dust.

"Hi, there!" he called desperately.

"Hallo!" It was an English voice, thank heaven. The padre's Arabic was suspect, being a weird and wonderful mixture of various dialects picked up phonetically during his travels. "Having trouble?" the newcomer asked.

124

"I think I've had it," the padre said ruefully. "My boy has gone ahead on foot, but I hardly expect to see him before nightfall, if then. In fact as I didn't pay him last month-end he might desert me. I've broken a fan-belt and my battery's flat. Do you think the rest is worth towing away?"

"Hardly." Gareth Hendon strolled round the wreck of the ancient Ford and observed, "I'm heading for El Belada. Is that any good to you?"

"Certainly. I was going there myself. The hospital houses a sprinkling of my scattered flock."

"Good. Have you salvaged all you need?"

"I think so. By the way, my name's Watkyn. You wouldn't be another Welshman, would you?"

"I am, though I was born and bred in Liverpool until I went to Edinburgh to study medicine. I'm a doctor."

"Oh, good! They'll be glad to see you at El Belada. There's been a bit of an emergency. Smallpox!"

"My God! Forgive me, padre. None of the staff affected, I hope?"

"Not so far as I know. The Superintendent went out and isolated the village where the outbreak began. He's a good chap, Kingsland."

"H'm. We'll push on then. As you say, an extra pair of hands might be welcome at such a time."

CHAPTER TWENTY-ONE

MAC SWAM up into consciousness, loth to leave the dream where she was cradled in two strong and protective arms. As she opened her eyes the feel of arms was still there, however, and she breathed a little sigh of thankfulness.

"Hallo, Mac!" Roy Kingsland's voice greeted her. "Do you know where you are?"

She nodded weakly. A tear spilled over on to her cheek which he wiped away gently with his handkerchief.

"Don't try to talk. You've had a malarial attack. I've been waiting and sitting with you all night expecting that temperature to break. Thank heaven it did before you boiled over! You had the padre worried when he called here yesterday. He nearly waited to see you off, but I assured him you could take it. You've neglected to take your paludrine, you rascal. I'll watch you in future."

She wriggled a little and looked fretful.

"Roy—" she gasped out.

"Don't try to talk, Mac. You're weak."

"Roy"—she insisted a little petulantly—"don't treat me like a child. Don't treat me like a child, do you hear? I'm not a child." Her eyes closed with the effort of speech.

He put his lips to her ear.

"I know you're not, Mac," he whispered. "I know darned well you're not." He touched his lips to her temple and she sighed again and slid into an exhausted sleep.

Roy Kingsland laid her back against the pillows, motioning Nurse Uwongi alongside.

"She's sweating freely now," he explained. "See that she doesn't get a chill. Call me if there's the slightest deterioration in her condition."

"I will, sir."

"And remind me to give you a rise in salary after this lot, Nurse. You deserve it."

The girl laughed delightedly and settled down beside the camp-bed where the patient lay. The fair, sun-bleached hair was damp with perspiration. Nurse Uwongi fingered it, wondering at its texture and softness, then felt her own black stubble, gave a philosophical shrug, reached into her pocket and drew out a paper-backed volume bearing the alluring title *That Tropical Night of Love.*

Forty-eight hours later Mac herself was able to laugh and thinking life couldn't be better. It didn't matter where one was, she had concluded, it was the company every time that mattered, and Roy Kingsland's was the only company she really cared for at the moment. Wadi Nahla had risen from its ashes like the phoenix: it had buried its dead and built new houses for the living, which was no great labor when one's materials for building were always at hand, the earth and reeds and water: moreover its inhabitants had virtuously submitted to vaccination, immunization and inoculations of various types and these had the psychological effect of making them feel like a super race, invulnerable to everything except the onset of old age. Even the pock-pitted countenances smiled again, glad at their deliverance from the horror which had struck so suddenly and ruthlessly. On the day Wadi Nahla was officially declared out of quarantine, Roy came up to Mac and offered her his arm.

"May I have the pleasure, Miss Hayes?"

He led her to a clearing where a table had been laid for two. Giggling women were still busily decorating the cloth with small clusters of golden acacia bobs and scarlet pyrethrums: they fled shrilling with laughter, and as Roy stood courteously behind Mac's chair while she sat down wonderingly, Tia Kafi appeared bearing a platter upon which lay a succulent-looking "habbash."

"Wild turkey," Roy explained, "a present from the village. They wish to honor us."

"It smells delicious!" Mac exclaimed, her appetite returning for the first time since her illness.

While Roy carved and served up the inevitable yam and French beans, Tia Kafi returned carrying a bottle of rich red wine and two medicine glasses.

"I save for this day," he said proudly. "For effendi, for Haykm binte. *Salaam aleykum!*" he bowed, grinned and disappeared.

"Well——!" Mac felt deeply touched without knowing why. "What is this day, Roy?" she asked.

He poured the wine before he replied, then held his glass up to her.

"Happy Christmas, Mac!" he wished. "You little thought you'd be spending Christmas like this with me, did you? I'm sorry I can't make snow for you."

Mac had an overpowering desire to weep suddenly and held on to her lower lip with her sharp teeth. When she was in control of her voice again, she too raised her glass and said sincerely, "It doesn't matter about snow, Roy. This will do very well, and"—she looked around her, at the wild fig and gafalfa-trees, the dried-up wadi and the new brick houses where the women crouched gossiping in their doorways nursing the inevitable small child and watching the antics of the toddlers—"I shall always remember it. But how did Christmas sneak up on us like that?"

"You must watch your calendar in future," Roy smiled, "it's all one has to go by out here. The leaves do not fall from the trees to warn us, the sun scorches every day. We usually celebrate Christmas with an epidemic of one sort or another, I've discovered, and there's another in June in the middle of the rains. How's it working out, Mac, this new job? Are you utterly fed up, or . . . ?"

She paused before she answered and his heart sank a little.

"To say I like it wouldn't quite be true," she pondered. "One can't like retrogression in anything. It's upsetting to start at the top and then find oneself at the absolute bottom, figuratively speaking. I suppose it's similar to choosing poverty after riches—quite the wrong way round. But I've worked more happily in El Belada than anywhere else and I can't think why that should be so."

"Zarek is in love with you," Roy said clearly. "I believe any woman is naturally stimulated by such knowledge."

"Can't we leave Zarek out of our Christmas celebrations at least?" Mac demanded. "Would you like me to marry him to get it off your mind?"

"I have his interests at heart, naturally. He hasn't had much experience with women and you—by the very nature of your profession—are a woman of the world."

"Hag-ridden in fact," Mac contributed nastily. "You needn't worry about your protégé, Doctor Kingsland. I can handle any man who doesn't interest me. My problem is . . ."

"Yes?" he prompted.

"Oh, forget it! The turkey is delicious," she said firmly.

"You were going to say"—Roy insisted—"that you are not so experienced in handling the men who do interest you."

"I was. Do you write under a pseudonym for some lonely hearts column or other?"

"No, I merely have a fellow feeling with you on this subject. I, too, am not so fortunate in pursuing a positive advance towards a lady who charms me."

"I'm glad to know such a creature exists," Mac said airily. "I thought when I was ill you were almost human on occasions, but you're back to normal at this moment with a vengeance."

"You, also, are displaying tooth and claw, my dear girl. Why? Why do we fight, Mac?"

"Naturally allergic, I suppose."

"Or naturally sympathetic. . . ."

"Are you in sympathy with me at this moment?"

"Extremely. I want to take you in my arms and kiss you."

Her gasp was too revealing as she rose from the table and walked away towards the acacia grove beyond the hospital quarters. She was conscious of him one pace behind her, his voice pleading.

"Mac, I'm sorry! I shouldn't have startled you like that. Please forgive me. Come back and eat."

"Eat?" she said tremulously. "After that?" So that he

would not misunderstand she groped blindly for his hand and under the golden-blossoming trees faced him.

"Do it, Roy," she invited. "Just do it, as you said."

"Oh, Mac! May I?" he felt the cool surrender of her lips turning his own into fire; her pliant young body gave itself into his arms and clung against him in a desperation of joy and revelation.

"Mac," he murmured as he sank his face into her hair, "I should never have believed anything against you. You're not capable of actions which are mean and furtive."

"I've told Zarek where he stands with me, Roy. You needn't have worried."

He didn't tell her he hadn't been thinking of Zarek at that moment. He was content to seek her lips again and treasure the moment for its own worth.

"Ought we to go back for our Christmas dinner?" Mac inquired dreamily, some time later.

"Only if you're hungry, dear. Our hosts will know what we're up to. This grove is for the lovers' meeting, and they all know how it affects the appetite."

"I said earlier that I would always remember this Christmas Day, Roy. I must have anticipated a little. Do you remember knocking poor old Rogue for six and then coming to see me?"

"I do. Five-foot-three of stiff-necked resentment. I caught a chill from you that day."

"And yet . . . it was odd . . . I told Barney in a round-about way that a man had affected me strangely. I said I ought to kick him but would much rather be kissing him. Poor old Barney thought I was referring to him and asked me to kick so that we could get on with the other thing." Mac smiled reminiscently.

"I thought at one time you were never going to stop kicking," Roy said ruefully. "Don't tell me you actually liked me a little all the time?"

"I was always too conscious of you to feel dispassionate. You were the barometer of my emotions. I had a dreadful time with you."

"Dear little Mac! I do love you and yet I can't really believe it has happened. Will it all still be real when we go back to El Belada tomorrow?"

"If it's real now, Roy, it'll be real anywhere."

"Other people can affect one, though; it's other people who have kept us apart so long. Fiona and Zarek both contributed."

"You're to promise you won't be jealous of Zarek ever again," Mac said gently.

"I'm beginning to resent that young man," Roy declared. "How dare he be in love with my girl!" The realization of the implication in his words revealed to him the further need for assurance in the feverish seeking of her lips. Trembling and shyly acquiescent, she pleaded, "Don't rush me so, Roy, darling. I won't suddenly disappear, you know. I want to enjoy all this slowly, from the chrysalis stage onwards. I feel utterly content for it to have happened at last."

"And I won't be content until you're mine, dearest Immacula. You will have to be patient with me. I want to get married now—this Christmas Day—but unless you agree to a ceremony involving only a common consent I will have to be patient. Maybe weddings are contagious. I was so wrapped up in my—our—affairs I forgot to tell you that Red and Fiona were married three days ago when the padre visited the hospital. Red told me over the field-radio this morning."

"I hope they'll be very happy," Mac said sincerely.

"That will depend . . ." Roy said non-committally, then, with sudden eagerness, "we'll get up to Khartoum together somehow, Mac, and I'll buy you a ring. It seems rather silly now, but I always liked looking in the jewellers' and picking a ring for my imaginary girl whenever I went on leave."

"Was she anything like me?" Mac smiled.

"No. She was tall—brunette——"

"Fiona-ish?" Mac teased.

"Fiona was all I had to go on. I never knew any other woman. I little thought I would finish up with a snub little wax doll like you!"

He caught her to him as she frowned her indignation.

"——and a pathologist!" he teased her. "Oh, my darling, I could be profound at this moment: I could ask what is happiness such as this? It's tangible because I can feel you in my arms, but it's somehow ephemeral too, a wisp of straw that could blow away in the wind."

"It mustn't blow away, Roy. Don't let it."

He looked down at her with a new glorious awareness of responsibility: her future was in his hands. If it pleased God so was her happiness. They might even be blessed with a child or two in time. . . . This latter thought captivated him and he squeezed her shoulders as they turned to walk from the acacia grove together. This slightly built, lovely little fairy a mother? Absurd! He curbed

such thoughts—upon which he could have gluttoned—
became a Superintendent Medical Registrar again before
her very eyes.

CHAPTER TWENTY-TWO

As THE FIRST stab of sunlight pierced the room like a
burning spear Fiona awoke, looked quickly at the smooth
pillow alongside her own and sighed with bitterness and
frustration. He hadn't been near her for the fourth night
in succession. How long would her newly acquired husband
keep this up? How long could he keep it up? Wasn't he
normal or human like other men?

Who would believe that she—married four days ago—
was not yet a wife in the true sense of the word?

Fiona looked round the room resentfully. It was a
pleasant room and had been Zarek's until recently. It was
Zarek's bed she was lying in at the moment. It was a big
bed. The surgeon had urged her to accept it as a gift for
the wedding together with all the fine damask linen which
went with it. It was the only bed about the hospital big
enough for two, he had insisted with his usual charm, and
he would be very comfortable lodging with the Superintendent so she was not to worry on his account.

The new Mrs. Bellinger was not given to worrying on
anyone's account other than her own, however, though it
appeared lately that even her natural concern for herself
was being worked overtime. She had had a wedding, yes,
and Red had stood beside her in the main bungalow before
a makeshift altar and pledged to love, honor and keep her.
Student-doctor Ahmed and Nurse Ikote, both Christians,
had witnessed the ceremony: Sister Haifeh had contributed the ring which Fiona now twisted nervously on
her finger; it was a plain gold 'ear-ring and was intended
to serve until the real thing could be procured.

Fiona had been happy on her wedding day. She didn't
much care for going back on duty as though nothing had
happened, even seeing Red in his white coat once more,

calling her "Sister Bardale" without a quiver in his voice and asking for history sheets. But once they were off duty it all became wonderful. Zarek didn't join them at dinner and had arranged for them to have a *tête-à-tête* meal on their own veranda: they had melon, fried chicken with corn on the cob and iced peaches; there was champagne, too, and after the boy had cleared away they had each other, and that was all Fiona asked for at that moment.

She wasn't quite sure even now how the trouble had started. Red was saying foolish and tender things in her ear as she sprawled beside him on Zarek's silk-cushioned divan in the darkened living-room of the bungalow, and her heart felt warm and feather-light as her senses quickened to each urgent caress.

Out of the darkness had come his voice, startlingly clear.

"Fiona, honey, you might have a baby mighty quick now that you've gotten a husband who feels as I do! Had you thought of that?"

She recalled how she seemed to have to fall a long way down from some airy pinnacle of romance to appreciate fully the significance of his remark.

"Silly boy!" she said quickly. "I can't have a baby here."

"Why not?"

"Well—for obvious reasons, surely? We won't be here forever, then we'll see." She wound herself around him once more and pulled his head down towards her own.

"Where do you suppose we'll be, then?" he asked quietly.

"Oh, I don't know. Once Roy is back he can start looking for another doctor and somebody to take my place and we'll be free to go."

"Go where?"

"Don't be difficult, darling. I suppose we'll go to America, or/wherever it is you live. We'll call on our way to see my mother and be married again properly and then take our place with your family. After all, you're the eldest son and have your rights. You can mention babies then," she finished archly.

Red sat up suddenly and stiffly.

"Fiona, I'm sorry if I've married you under false pretences. Thank heaven it's gone no further than the ceremony!" he left her to switch on the light and stood fastening his tie very correctly.

"Don't tease me, Red," she said doubtfully. "You are teasing, aren't you?"

"No, I'm not teasing, Fiona. I don't know what you mean by 'then we'll be free to go.' Is marriage the short way out of another kinda contract for you? I don't live in America—as you call it—I live here. I work here. I cain't say I'm desperate for any change in my mode of living. It suits me. I'm goddam free of everything I don't like while I'm here in El Belada with sick folks trusting in me and the best damnedest superintendent a guy ever had to work under. I'm happy enough where I am. I wanted my wife here and—shucks!—I guess I wanted my kids here, too!"

"Red," Fiona approached him, looking white and shaken, "you do make me feel so angry at times! We've only been married a few hours and you're worrying about the future already."

"Because marriage is the beginning of the future, Fiona, or should be. Just anything could happen from this moment on, and you know it. Obviously you're not prepared to be my wife in the fullest sense, so it's just as well we're not 'married properly,' isn't it? After a few months, for obvious reasons, you can get an annulment. And now, good night!"

It was no use banging on that closed door, Fiona realized, the servants might hear and joke about her in their quarters. To be left alone on her wedding night! What an impossible state of affairs! Hadn't she a right to expect a settled state of living in a more suitable climate, like other women? Red was being unreasonable, demanding babies and making a serious issue out of her natural reluctance at this stage. But Red *was* unreasonable. Her mother wouldn't approve of him one bit.

"And I had to fall in love with him!" Fiona wailed miserably.

In the morning she was lying in wait for him, heavy-eyed and miserable.

"All right, Red," she told him in a kind of desperation, "you shall have your way about everything. If you want to force me to my knees you've succeeded, and it's quite impossible to consider an annulment. We'd look such fools."

"I'd rather look a fool than be one, honey," he smiled. "No, Fiona, I don't want you on your knees. I have no hard feelings towards you. I think perhaps we rushed into this thing and it may be as well to give it a little more thought. Let things ride, huh? I won't let you down in public, so don't worry on that score. This is just a difference of opinion as to the meaning of marriage between you and me. I never realized you were working to a nice little blue-print in that lovely head of yours."

Four days later he was still "letting it ride" and sleeping in his own room. What iron control the man had! Each night she prepared herself for the bridal with all the arts she knew, and each night he put her from him, kissed her chastely on the brow and left her. She didn't know he stood in a listening attitude on the other side of his room door, that he counted every sob and every sigh, treasuring them like so many jewels.

"I don't wanta break her," he told the stars one night. "I just wanta break even with her. Fiona's gotta learn to give without counting the cost to herself."

As to his iron control, this was in reality a myth. One night, unable to settle, he crept into the other room to look at her. She had cried herself to sleep, her eyelashes were still sticky with tears. Her hair was a dark veil over the pillow, one slender arm was thrown above her head. Her chest was bare and white in the moonlight, and a faint perfume rose to his nostrils as he stooped over her. In that moment it didn't seem important whether she looked upon him as a passport to the world outside El Belada or not. He wanted her. He lay atop the covers beside her, dallying pleasurably with the idea of awakening her and expressing his need in the language of a kiss. She would be off-guard, he knew, and succumb meekly to his desires. But in the morning she would realize his weakness and her own power: it wouldn't do. Fiona would be merciless when she wielded power. It was Fiona who must be humbled. He had given her his name. He wouldn't sacrifice his body until she was prepared to burn with him on the altar of love, putting all aside for him and not looking over his shoulder the while for the land of her heart's desire.

Fiona did not look up as Rajab knocked and, entering the bedroom, set a morning tea-tray on the table beside her.

"Very good morning, Sister," he volunteered, letting up the blinds. "Master Kingsland come back today, I think. The effendi Zarek sends compliments and these flowers."

He held out a bunch of scarlet canna lilies. Each day since the wedding Zarek had saluted the bride with a bouquet.

"Put them in water, please," Fiona said without interest.

Rajab silently left the room and hearing a sound in the adjoining bathroom Fiona slid out of bed, draped a négligé carelessly around her shoulders and crossed to the bathroom to fling open the door, assume an air of surprise at finding the room already occupied and then pose irresolutely in the doorway.

"I'm sorry, I didn't know you were here," she lied sweetly.

"Come in, wife," Red invited, regarding her through the mirror. He looked very masculine standing there shaving, naked to the waist, a towel draped round his middle. "Sleep well?" he asked.

"No." Her eyes fell before this apparently impregnable being. "I'm not sleeping at all. I was going to tell you."

"Remind me to give you two capsules of seconal tonight," he said through lips drawn tight to avoid the passage of the open razor.

"I don't want seconal, I want you!" Fiona told him throwing her arms around him in a desperation of frustration. She stood transfixed with horror as his blood dripped slowly and relentlessly from his chin into the white porcelain of the wash-bowl. "What have I done?" she quivered. "How bad is it? Come into the bedroom and let me see to you. Oh, Red, darling, do you feel faint?"

He was leaning on her unnecessarily, and trying to keep his mouth from twitching into a smile as she fussed over him and dressed what proved to be a very superficial wound at the corner of his mouth.

"Can you ever forgive me?" she pleaded, looking ruefully down at her stained nightdress.

"I'll try," Red decided, pulling her down beside him. "Oh, Fiona, we can't share the same bathroom without sharing everything else, can we?"

"I'm glad you're realizing that, darling. I'm not making any conditions. I simply ask—take me to be your wife and let me serve you. I've discovered I would rather be Red Bellinger's wife in El Belada than Fiona Bardale anywhere else in the world."

"You mean that?" he asked huskily.

"Yes, I do. Quite sincerely."

"Look, Fiona, so as nuthin' else can suddenly rear up between us I want us to have a long, cosy chat this evening after dinner. I'm not perfect and there's one or two things about Jefferson junior you oughta know now you're his wife. You get all your skeletons out too, honey, and let's bury 'em deep together so's we can concentrate on"—he lifted her chin up, his eyes growing suddenly sombre—"other things, shall we?"

"Whatever you say, Red."

As their lips brushed he murmured caressingly, "Don't let me down, Fiona, honey. A man's heart breaks so much more easily than his head. I was never helpless in a woman's hands before and it kinda scares me to think of it."

"Maybe it will be a precious bondage," Fiona told him. "I want to make you happy, Red. You must believe that. Now kiss me as though you meant it."

Rajab, arriving in the open door at that moment, turned tail suddenly as Doctor Bellinger proceeded to do as he was asked, and certainly looked as if he meant it.

*　　　*　　　*

At this time when Fiona was being given a chance to untangle the knots in the skein of her relationship with Red, Mac—innocently enough—was busily engaged upon making her own future with Roy more difficult.

In this early morning hour the Wadi Nahla party was striking camp; the tents were already down, folded and packed into the old lorry belonging to the hospital and purchased from the British when they had left the Sudan to look after its own affairs.

Mac paid a final visit to Safa and her baby, reminding the young mother that she was expected to bring the child, Hassan, to hospital for vaccination in three months' time and not to fail him. Her eyes met Roy's as he looked up from checking the drugs against a list he held in his hand, and they grew suddenly warm and soft with the wonder of all that had been revealed between them less than twenty-four hours ago.

"Here, let me read that and you check," she suggested eagerly, glad to be working alongside him.

"I've accounted for the cortisone. There. . . ."

"Penicillin . . . eight million units. . . ."

"Correct. Mac, I remembered something important when I woke up this morning. . . ."

"Yes?"

"I made several suggestions to you yesterday, and some of them would be considered highly improper unless they were preceded by a certain question which I omitted to ask."

"And what was that?" Mac asked, ticking off codeine and morphia as he paraded them before her eyes.

"I forgot to ask you to be my wife!"

"Oh!" Mac flushed and dropped the list she was holding from a suddenly nerveless hand. "Then ask me

136

later, Roy," she said hastily. "Let's make a real occasion out of it."

"Mac, I can't wait to see their faces, Red's and Zarek's when we tell them about us!"

"Don't tell them just yet, Roy."

"Why not, you funny girl? How else can I claim the right to make love to you? What have you against an immediate announcement?"

"Nothing really. It's just . . ."

"Is it Zarek you're concerned about?"

"No, I . . ." her eyes wavered and fell before his. He had actually hit the nail right on the head, though she didn't care to admit it. Already she felt she knew the young surgeon better than her companion did. Handled carefully and given time he might be brought to realize the futility of his pursuit of her. He also worshipped Roy Kingsland in a different way. If these two persons he held in his highest regard became obviously attached to one another to his exclusion, Zarek's love might be turned into a sullen resentment. Only Mac had seen Zarek when he was not playing the English gentleman: during those few minutes when she was alone with him in the lab she had seen a being capable of ruthless, primeval passions; a stranger, in fact. She did not fear for herself in announcing her engagement to the Superintendent: she feared for Roy and a possible repercussion on the hospital he had worked and slaved for all these years, the hospital which knew Zarek not only as its surgeon, but as a wealthy patron also. What an angry and bitter Zarek could do to El Belada and nearby El Arak didn't bear thinking about.

"I do think we should wait before telling anybody about us, Roy," Mac said uncertainly. "Red and Fiona will think we're stealing their thunder and with all this romance in the air the hospital might suffer. I feel light-headed myself. I would like at least to settle down into my routine again—tie up a few loose ends and so forth."

"This can't be a romantic time of day or something," Roy said quietly. "What happened to the girl with stars in her eyes?"

"She's still there," Mac said, looking up at him frankly. "Can't you trust me to have good reasons, Roy? It's going to be as difficult for me to keep this wonderful secret."

"Lovers are notoriously unreasonable, I'm discovering," he said grimly, then relented and told her: "All

137

right, a month to tie up your loose ends and dispose of surplus lovers. Fair enough?"

"Fair enough," she agreed, returning to the job in hand.

CHAPTER TWENTY-THREE

DOCTOR GARETH HENDON finished the letter home to his wife with his usual flourish, sat back in his chair and wondered how else he could pass the time. It had been a somewhat unfortunate sojourn for him at El Belada, and he had more than once regretted his decision to call here. He had announced himself as a friend of Doctor Hayes' and had been somewhat surprised at the reaction to his statement by two members of the hospital staff: Sister Bardale had looked very knowingly at him as though Mac had made a confidante of her, which he regretted if it was true for her sake more than his own; and the surgeon fellow—Zarek, or something—had obviously resented his intrusion from the outset. It didn't take Gareth long to realize that Zarek regarded any friend of Mac's as a rival for her affections, and her name had only to fall between them for the Sudani to grow almost openly hostile.

"The sooner Mac puts him wise the better," Doctor Hendon decided.

He took the news of Mac's absence philosophically. Wadi Nahla was quarantined so he couldn't go chasing after her, and as this was likely to be the last opportunity they would have of meeting there was nothing for it but to ask El Belada's hospitality and volunteer his professional services—if required—in return.

Red Bellinger immediately suggested Mac's job in the laboratory, but Zarek frowned his displeasure.

"Surely we don't need to trouble Doctor Hendon?" he demanded arrogantly. "I'm sure he was merely being polite when he made his offer. Ahmed will not enjoy a stranger walking into the lab and commanding him."

"I certainly don't wish to intrude . . ." Gareth said uncertainly.

Ahmed was by nature the most docile of creatures, who realized at this stage of his career that it paid him to do exactly as he was bidden, but Red gave a little shrug and looked at the newcomer somewhat apologetically.

"You're not intruding, Bud, but my colleague and I had better have a little chat about things first."

The result of that "chat" was that Doctor Hendon was given a room in the Superintendent's bungalow, a pile of *Medical Journals* and *Readers' Digests* and an old gramophone together with a selection of equally ancient records. He was called to join his hosts at mealtimes unless they were occupied, but otherwise it seemed to be tacitly agreed that they could manage very well without his professional help.

The situation wasn't helped by the fact that the Deputy Superintendent was emotionally involved with a lady at that time. The Reverend Mr. Watkyn had been called upon to perform a wedding ceremony before disappearing northwards in a Land Rover borrowed from the hospital, and one can't be newly embarked upon such a venture and worry about an unexpected guest's welfare at the same time. Gareth Hendon often felt he was forgotten during those first few days and had to resort to asking the servants for news of Doctor Hayes and her expected return.

This was the day she was to arrive, and Gareth felt almost excited in the prospect. It would be nice to see Mac again, observe what more than a year had done to her in her appearance, outlook and skill. He would never forget that dreadful night when he had told her of Claire's existence. Until that moment she had been something absurdly young and tender, a fawn gambolling through pastures of delight with him. Before his eyes, however, she had grown up; the flood of unhappiness washed the brightness from her eyes, the color from her cheeks, her lips even . . . and a woman's voice had spoken through the trembling mouth of a child:

"Garry, tell me once more that it's true, that you are married, and then we'll talk about it—about us——"

He had never known the woman he had created, but he often wondered about her and the man who would one day eventually fill the need in her heart. He couldn't take Zarek seriously in this role, but one never knew with a woman. Quite often the best of them cast their pearls before swine: maybe that's what he had been in Mac's

139

reckoning, a swine. He wanted reassurance from her that she was no worse for having known him; he wanted to see her beauty unimpaired by the ravages of tears she had shed over him, and then he could go his way in peace, content to work for Claire and the child and thankful for having been granted the best of what had at one time looked like being a bad job.

The boy brought his breakfast to his room, which meant that the love-birds were not up yet and the fellow Zarek obviously preferred his room to his company. Ah, well . . . he could move off again soon and leave them to it. Mac must be happy enough here to stick it.

It was a brave enough little hospital about a mile out of a somewhat grubby little town bearing the same name. He had run into town one day on some errand for the surgeon and been robbed of his spare tire and kit of tools. It was odd that when he called at a garage they should have an identical tire and tools he could have sworn were his. These items cost him the earth, too, as he hadn't learned to bargain successfully. He returned to the hospital somewhat rattled by the whole business.

It was also strange that Zarek should have said over dinner that evening, "I hear you had some trouble in town, my friend. You should leave the Sudan before you lose more things!"

"I will go when I have seen Doctor Hayes," he replied firmly, "providing nothing worse happens to my car to keep me here."

This had effectively silenced the Sudani for the time being.

Hendon strolled out on to the veranda as he heard a vehicle lumbering into the compound. He hardly thought it would be Mac returning already, so he was not particularly disappointed at seeing a horse-box drawn up at the gates. As the driver unlocked the doors a groom led two magnificent stallions down the ramp, beautiful beasts, both grain-fed, tails and necks arched to vouch for this, pawing the ground and rearing to go.

Zarek came briskly from the other side of the house, dashingly attired in breeches and boots and wearing a yellow silk shirt, lavender cravat and exquisitely cut hacking jacket.

"Ah, my friend Hendon!" he exclaimed expansively. "I realize that soon you must leave us and have had no entertainment. I am a terrible host, am I not? It is that I have been busy and there has been no time to give you tennis or squash or even a game of billiards. You will

140

understand that our friend Bellinger has been pleasurably occupied in other ways?" Zarek laughed wickedly. "I hope you will join me in a morning canter to show there are no ill feelings?"

Gareth looked uncertainly down at his bush shirt and shorts.

"I'd love to accompany you, dear sir, but unfortunately I have no togs."

"If you return to your room you will see a riding outfit laid out on your bed. Zarek thinks of everything."

"Well, thank you. . . ."

"Not at all. Not at all." The other waved him magnanimously indoors and strolled off whistling.

Gareth somewhat wryly regarded the jacket of hunting-pink laid out on his bed together with cream breeches and a peaked, black velveteen cap. Did the native imagine this was the Englishman's usual attire for a morning canter? He could hardly throw the fellow's kindness down his throat, however, when he was obviously extending the somewhat belated hand of friendship, so he donned the grotesque garments and went out into the compound feeling like a Master of Foxhounds in Sussex rather than a staid medico about to take a ride across the desert scrubland of the Lower Sudan.

"Bravo!" Zarek greeted him. "You ride well?"

"Only fair," Hendon admitted. "I hope the beast knows what he's about."

"I am in command of the situation, never fear," Zarek observed, a mocking smile in his dark eyes. "Follow me, my friend, and nothing can go wrong."

Following Zarek when he was out to elude, however, took some doing. At full gallop he always seemed to be disappearing over the horizon to Gareth, who—spur his mount on as he would—never seemed able quite to catch up. The hunting-pink became more than warm, but he dared not pause for a moment to discard it: after an hour's mad gallop under the now pitiless sun, Gareth Hendon began to doubt Zarek's pure motives in inviting him out. The most innocent of his intentions, it would appear, was to humiliate his imagined rival; but he could easily lose him altogether in this wilderness, and suddenly Gareth realized he *was* lost. There had been no sign of Zarek for fifteen minutes or more, and he was convinced that a patch of scrub coming up on the port side was not new to him, which meant he must have ridden a complete circle. He swallowed his momentary panic and decided he could think better if he was more comfortable. Therefore he dismounted and removed his jacket, revealing his shirt steaming and patchily dyed pink beneath it. Overhead vultures appeared suddenly, wheeling and gliding, screeching their peculiar cry of death, and as one planed down lower to investigate his condition, Gareth picked up a stone and shied it hard. Unfortunately the gesture caused the horse to rear and back away. Gareth realized he didn't even know its name, and the clucking sound he made with his lips didn't seem to mean a thing to a creature raised on pure Arabic. It was tired, thirsty and hot itself, and realizing it had been relieved of its burden it snuffed at the air and with a sense of direction denied to more intelligent human beings cantered away before his eyes.

Gareth watched the animal go with mixed feelings. It occurred to him, quite calmly in the first instance, that he was likely to die out here in the burning heat without water or shade. The thought rapidly became a conviction and he cried out once or twice in panic, then he controlled himself with an effort and tried to think clearly and constructively. He was really in the Sudani's hands: if Zarek didn't intend him mischief he would already be seeking him, but he would not be seeking a dismounted man. If the horse made its way back home it might be almost impossible for a searcher to find him. In this eventuality he would surely perish very quickly.

Would anybody really care if he was never heard of again?

Mac would care, he told himself fiercely, because she was a loyal and tender-hearted little soul: Claire would care too, he was necessary to her in some new relationship risen from the ashes of the old. But most of all he would care himself because he had a son who scarcely knew him as yet.

There is an urge in the most retiring of us which makes us see in the forgetfulness of our loved ones a worse fate than death itself. It was the thought of being anonymous to his living son which made Gareth Hendon spur himself on in the direction his horse had taken. To lie down and admit to being licked was even more intolerable than the ordeal facing him. He told himself that people could go without water for several days, and he hadn't even started yet, though his mouth was beginning to feel like sandpaper. If he took his bearings correctly and held a straight course he must arrive somewhere eventually, providing his legs didn't give out. After all, this was the

Sudan, not the middle of the Sahara desert, but it was also damned hot and he must take the wretched pink coat with him in case he was still lost by nightfall and needed its protection as a blanket.

*   *   *

Zarek, however, had never entertained the idea of actually disposing of his imagined rival. He was out for mischief, admittedly, and had restrained himself with difficulty from laughing out aloud at the somewhat ridiculous figure mounting Mabsut (the gay one) as he himself accepted a hand-up on to the broad back of the Black Devil, who had brought no mean credit to the name of Zarek on the race-tracks of his country.

Zarek had sent away to England for the hunting-pink when he had been young and foolishly trying to eliminate his father from his make-up. But a child is both his parents, he had discovered, and even by attempting to suppress a half of oneself one so readily becomes ridiculous in pretension. No English gentleman goes hacking in hunting-pink, and no self-respecting Sudani would be seen dead in it. The outfit had been preserved as a joke against his own immaturity; now it had come in useful in the effort to degrade another in a fair lady's eyes.

Zarek was crouching less than half a mile away from his riding companion on a rocky plateau which shielded the Well of Omar from the worst rays of the sun. The Black Devil had drunk his fill and was now cropping at the tough rye-grass growing in a jadwal, or irrigation ditch, dug by a wandering tribe which had camped here at some time or other. A colony of baboons was busily occupied higher up the plateau, the scouts warily watching Zarek and his mount for any intrusion upon their family life. But the Sudani was not out baboon-bating on this occasion. He had brought binoculars and delightedly focused the strawberry-roan Mabsut and his cherry-coated rider. He knew he was not visible to Hendon, and he also knew he had given the visiting doctor one hell of a run for his money. No horse on this continent could catch the Devil when he was given his head, though he must admit that old Mabsut had taken some shaking off. Now neither horse nor rider knew where they were. He watched as they cantered away in the wrong direction, and grinned as he saw the two accomplish a laborious circle and stop again uncertainly.

"I will let him sweat just a little," Zarek decided, and lay back and closed his eyes, dropping readily into the easy slumber of one who has always lived in the heat of the sun.

When Zarek awoke he felt immediately disturbed. He sensed his plan had gone wrong somewhere. Seeing two horses at the well confirmed his suspicions, for there was no sign of Hendon in the vicinity. With his binoculars he swept the arid plain below for the pink coat, but there was no sign of the Englishman. Zarek called at the top of his voice. The echo went rolling round the rocks like thunder, and the nearest of the baboons picked up a stone to fling should this madman's behavior threaten the colony.

Zarek panicked as he thought of that lone, rather pathetic figure walking around in circles in the baking heat. A man in a red coat on a red horse was a visible being, but dismounted any man would immediately divest himself of unwanted and hampering garments and was likely to crawl into a hole in the ground or under a patch of scrub, in fact anywhere to find relief from the worst heat of the day.

Zarek realized he was supposed to operate at two o'clock, but he dared not return to the hospital without Hendon. Why had the fellow allowed Mabsut to escape? He was a fool, obviously, but all the more reason to find him before he could bring himself to greater harm. Never once did Zarek regard himself as the villain of the piece. That his best-laid plans had gone somewhat agley was not his responsibility. Any deviation from a pattern was the point at which Allah himself took over. He and Roy argued much on these profundities without reaching conclusions agreeable to them both. But somehow Zarek didn't fancy the idea of presenting himself to Roy without Hendon on this occasion, be it by the will of Allah or not. He leapt up on to the Black Devil's back, wheeled him towards the plain and whistling Mabsut to follow, spurred his mount on, looking hopefully for the track of a man's trailing feet in the dry, sandy dust.

CHAPTER TWENTY-FOUR

As THE small convoy travelled through the dusty township Mac began to jump up and down in her seat like a small girl nearing the destination of a Sunday-school picnic.

"What's all that for?" Roy Kingsland asked indulgently.

"I'm just glad to be back, that's all. We're nearly home."

That "home" warmed the Superintendent to his heart. El Belada was "home" to him too. When he went away on leave he always experienced a thrill upon his return, though logically he could never account for this. All his dreams, his efforts and frustrations were encircled by the walls of the hospital compound. In his house he kept his favorite books and gramophone records; he had built himself a short-wave radio set from a blueprint and a host of spare parts; he had once made four unique chairs out of joghan fibre, the upholstery generously stuffed with kapok from the Indian cotton-tree; and another time, thinking he might one day have a daughter, he had made a dainty little doll out of camel-hide and named it Jane.

"I like the name Jane," he said aloud, and Mac—realizing his thoughts had been wandering—put her head on one side and pondered.

"So do I, and Elizabeth, too. I like boys to have names like John and Dick—except when they happen to have been christened Roy," she added with a smile.

Reaching out he put a hand sexlessly for a moment on her knee.

"You're a very understanding person, Mac, apart from this question of you and me. I think we ought to tell the world immediately that we're in love."

"And I demand my month's grace," she said firmly. "No, Roy, you must allow me this respite. I have to work something out to my satisfaction."

"Perhaps you don't feel sure . . . ?" he tortured himself.

"Rubbish! There's the hospital now. I remember the first time I saw it. I was so busy looking at you it hardly registered on that occasion."

Laughingly they stepped out of the white-painted ambulance which was pulled up neatly in its whitewashed square against the compound wall.

"They're apparently all too busy to come and say hallo," Mac observed.

"Then we had better go inside," Roy smiled.

They found Red in the men's ward with Fiona and Sister Haifeh attending him.

"Is Zarek with you?" Red asked hopefully.

"No. Should he be?"

"Well, we concluded he—they—had ridden out to meet you. Zarek took Doctor Hendon out riding this morning and they haven't returned. We had an amputation scheduled for 2 p.m. and it's now three. I don't suppose anything could have happened to them?"

"Who's Doctor Hendon?" Roy asked sharply.

"A friend of Mac's."

"A close friend of Mac's, I believe," Fiona contributed.

Roy turned to look at the girl by his side. Was it his imagination or had she really grown pale?

"Were you expecting this man?" he asked.

"Ye-es," Mac's voice actually trembled, "now that you mention it, I was."

"Now that I mention it?" his question was half an accusation.

"I meant I'd forgotten Gareth was coming, just as I forgot when it was Christmas."

"And he came all this way especially to see you, Mac," Fiona went on. "Shame on you!"

"The point is where can they have got to?" Roy said testily, then relented and observed, "I'm so sorry, Fiona. Congratulations on your marriage to this no-good character here! Congratulations, Red!"

"Thank you, sir."

Fiona looked suddenly self-conscious and lowered her eyes.

"It was a rather sudden decision, and I hope it doesn't inconvenience you at all?"

"Certainly not. Where are you living?"

"We're in number two bungalow, sir," Red replied. "Zarek has moved in with you and Hendon has been in your quarters, too."

"We'll have the place made into a real home for you as soon as it can be arranged. We bachelors can continue to live in together."

That "we bachelors" seemed to Mac bitterly significant when he had been discussing marriage with her such a short time ago. All of a sudden the whole atmosphere was pregnant with doubts and fears.

"Well"—Roy rubbed his hands together as though making an effort at concentration—"I had better have a look at this amputation case, hadn't I? If the matter's urgent I'll just have to tackle it myself."

Sister Haifeh had walked out on to the veranda. She turned to announce, "Here is Mr. Zarek now, sir!"

If there had been no committee of welcome for the Wadi Nahla party, Zarek certainly had no room to complain of lack of interest in his arrival. Five faces anxiously or accusingly peered out at him. He was riding the Black Devil and leading Mabsut alongside; Mac gasped as she realized that what appeared to be a bundle of rags draped over the latter must in reality be Gareth. She streaked across the compound, but even so Roy Kingsland beat her to it.

"Whatever has happened?" asked the Superintendent.

"Is he hurt—or dead?" Mac demanded shrilly.

"My dear Roy, Mac, how are you?" Zarek inquired genially, slipping to the ground. "How nice to see you both again! No, Doctor Hendon is not dead, just a very poor horseman." He tugged at one of the white-breeched legs. "Come along, now, Hendon, my good fellow! Look who is here to see you! It is Doctor Mac, herself. Oh, come now, make an effort! You walk so well when I find you, so why not now?"

Gareth was making inarticulate, apologetic little noises and suddenly slid off the saddle into a heap in the dust. He struggled to rise, still apologizing for the inconvenience he was causing, sadly hampered by the dirty pink coat which Zarek had insisted on fastening round him.

"I'm so sorry, Mac, sir"—he mumbled, finding his feet with difficulty as Roy gave him a hand—"I'm a little stiff and sore, you know. Not used to that sort of thing."

"That's quite all right, Doctor Hendon," Roy said quietly. "We'll have a chat when you've had a bath and feel a little better."

He motioned Rajab and Tia Kafi to help the visitor to his quarters and then looked in amazement down at Mac's face which was contorted with anger and pity as she

147

watched the grotesque and dirty figure shuffling across the compound between the two giant Nubas.

"He'll be all right," Roy said softly.

"I know, but . . ." she looked up at Zarek, who was smiling to himself, not a hair out of place, despite his day's adventures.

"What happened? Did you do this to Gareth?" she demanded.

"I don't know what you mean, dear Mac. This foolish friend of yours loses his horse for some reason and seems to prefer to walk. The English are keen—I think you say— on walking. The 'keep fit' and all that."

He turned blithely to command the groom lurking in the background to take charge of the horses.

"You don't know how happy I am to see you, dear Mac. And the worthy Superintendent also. . . ." He put a hand for a moment on Roy's shoulder. "I am late in theatre. May I be excused?"

He had taken two steps when Mac moved like lightning and whirled him round to face her.

"No, you may not be excused," she challenged, "not until I've got satisfaction from you!"

It was Roy who stared aghast at this apparently aggressive demand. He was thinking Mac was being altogether too emotional over Doctor Hendon and he hated public unpleasantness.

"Be reasonable, Mac," he advised gently.

She was as ready to turn on him, he discovered.

"Was it reasonable to make a fool of a friend of mine like that?"

"Zarek has explained what occurred. I think it all sounds very plausible."

"Do you?" Mac blazed.

"Just as I say"—insisted Zarek, but he was still smiling, which brought Mac almost to boiling-point—"he gets off his horse to have a scratch or something and gets lost. Did I not find him for you? I saved him from the vultures."

"After giving him to them in the first place, I shouldn't wonder!"

"I am a bad boy, then, and you may slap me, *ya habibti*," he invited, turning his smooth cheek to her. "Slap hard little one!"

Mac did so. Even Zarek was ruefully surprised by her strength and amused also. What a woman to have in one's house, he pondered delightedly, a woman who would fight on occasions like a cornered civet! What a creature both to tame and to master!

Roy said coldly, "I think you had better attend to your business, Mr. Zarek, and you, Doctor Hayes, go and lie down. You needn't worry about your friend any further. I'll see to him myself."

"But don't you see, Roy," she pleaded excitedly as Zarek strode off to change, "this is something I have been wanting you to know all along."

"I don't see anything but that you are obviously suffering some form of reaction and need to rest. Get up for dinner if you feel better."

"Oh!" Mac stamped her foot hard.

"Any further hysterical displays and I warn you I shall do something drastic," he said coolly.

There was nothing for it but to turn away and go to her quarters. She knew this being—so easily turned to granite—was quite capable of picking her up and dumping her there if she argued further. He didn't appear to understand what to her was so obvious, that Garry Hendon was to Zarek the symbol of something which possibly stood between himself and his desires, that whomsoever it had been Zarek was capable of utter cunning and ruthlessness frightening to contemplate. The young surgeon, in the role of lover, was quite prepared to eliminate any opposition.

"Roy's a fool, a fool!" Mac fretted, hurling herself on to her bed.

Sensing she was not alone she looked up suddenly. Roy, with a mask of a face, was standing tensely regarding her from the doorway.

"I thought I would come and see you settled," he said, as though with difficulty. "Doctor Hendon is feeling much better now, but do rest before you go and see him. I have persuaded him to stay on overnight."

"Thank you."

There was nothing to be gained in that moment by attempting to explain in the inadequacy of words a conviction she couldn't hope to prove. Men demanded facts in their dealings with one another.

Burying her face in the pillow Mac knew the exact moment he left her, and she also knew she had come a long way in those few minutes from the golden acacia grove sacred to the lovers of Wadi Nahla.

CHAPTER TWENTY-FIVE

GARETH HENDON was still apologetic when Mac joined him an hour later for tea in the Superintendent's bungalow.

"I'm sorry if I caused any trouble, Mac, honestly I am. You are all so frantically busy here, I realize I shouldn't have come."

"We have a right to entertain visitors," Mac said defensively. "I'm surprised they didn't ask you to buckle to and help."

"Well"—Gareth decided the least said the better—"I did half offer, but people are jealous of their positions, and I really wasn't needed. Sometimes a new bloke who doesn't know the ropes can throw all the rest out of gear. I quite understand how it was."

"Just how did Zarek get you into that filthy state?" Mac demanded, the light of battle still in her eye.

"Oh, come, my dear, one can't blame the strong for the waverings of the weak. My own damned vanity was at the bottom of it all, I suppose. I have only ridden a quiet old hack about half a dozen times in my life before, and this fellow, Zarek, managed to look so brave and dashing I fancied myself in such a part. But Zarek on a horse is Zarek. . . ." He shrugged and smiled ruefully. "I was never more relieved in all my life to see anyone, I can tell you, as that young man and his horses coming at full gallop towards me. I must have walked for more than five miles and I was just about all in."

"You seem to think Zarek saved you," Mac pondered.

"Of course I do. I would be an ungrateful blighter not to. I don't know how he hoisted me up into that saddle by himself. I couldn't help. He got something down my throat and I never recollected a think until I was back here in the compound. I must thank him properly when I get the chance."

Mac began to wonder if she had been unjust in her accusations, then her eyes narrowed again. Zarek need never have lost contact with Gareth in the first place unless he had intended doing so. He was both expert rider and coach: he must have realized from the moment they started that his companion was a raw amateur and should therefore be nursed, his mount kept under Zarek's —not the rider's—control. But Mac realized the futility of pressing this present charge against Zarek. Nobody else was interested, apparently, and as all had ended well and Gareth was proceeding south on the morrow it would be best forgotten.

The subject of her thoughts appeared suddenly in the doorway, and a cheerful voice assailed their ears.

"Have you a cup of tea for a tired surgeon, my dear Mac? I have just performed an operation; I amputated a foot for elephantiasis, Doctor Hendon. I don't suppose you see such things in U.K., eh? Now I come to be revived."

Mac poured without speaking, putting a slice of lemon in the teacup as she knew Zarek liked it.

"Thank you, little pussy-cat."

Still Mac didn't smile, and Zarek turned to Gareth.

"She is not a good one to marry, this Mac. Think again, my friend, if you are contemplating a union with her."

"He isn't," Mac said promptly.

"Oh?" Zarek looked kindly on the other man. "How are you now, Hendon? No ill effects, I hope?"

"None, thank you. My pride will never be the same again, of course. I'm not much of a horseman, as you will have discovered."

"It is the horse who finds this out, also," Zarek smiled. "Now take Mac, here. She was only so-so at first, but I tell her secrets and now she is best horsewoman in Sudan."

"You flatter me," Mac observed.

"Not at all. Now that we are all together again we must continue with our morning rides, dear Mac."

She stood up and carefully smoothed her dress.

"I'll never go riding with you again, Zarek. I should be terrified after what happened to Gareth."

"I do not understand you." The surgeon's usually smooth brow was in furrows. "Doctor Hendon and I became separated for awhile. But all is well now."

"Exactly. You might not be so lucky the next time and find me if we became separated." For the first time Mac felt herself to be in a position to do the smiling. "I would never have believed you, of all people, could lose anybody.

But since it has happened I'm certainly going to see to it that you don't lose me! Come along, Garry, I'll show you my lab and we'll have a look round the wards for half an hour. Good-bye for now, Mr. Zarek!"

For the first time she found herself looking up into the burning orbs of a very angry young man.

*   *   *

Roy Victor Kingsland, sitting behind several neat piles of papers on his desk, never looked more—or felt less—like a hospital superintendent. Though his qualifications were many and varied he was a G.P. at heart. He liked to poke about in everything connected with the job rather than to specialize, and his colleagues were inclined to forget that he had written his qualifying thesis on the subject of neurology, had taken a diploma in paediatrics, was a Master of Surgery and no mean virologist. The last time he had nipped up to Khartoum to press for more government aid for his hospital he had missed the once-weekly train back to Jebelein and had spent the seven lost days in Medical School with a class studying the physical and mental reactions to drug addiction. But now he was not thinking about drugs or antibiotics or nervous systems. He *was* thinking about Mac and himself.

Roy hadn't a deep understanding of the opposite sex; women were almost a closed book to him. He wasn't aware of the unassailable fact that a woman who loves cannot accept the role of friend to the man of her choice. She would much rather hate him than be asked to keep her emotions out of the relationship.

So when Roy found himself with Mac, whom he considered professionally necessary as his *aide* on the trip to Wadi Nahla, he sensed after a few days an urgent need in her for congenial companionship. Clumsily he had tried to fill this need. He tried to be Red, he tried to be Zarek—though compliments didn't sound nearly so graceful coming from his lips—and he even tried to be a father to her. In all these guises he had suffered rebuff, however, and when he had spoken for himself during that fateful Christmas dinner, he could hardly believe he had overcome apparently insurmountable barriers with her and discovered the warm and acceptable truth of the matter, that she wanted him as he was and as himself.

Mac responsive in his arms, Mac's mouth firm and rosy against his own, Mac's eyes soft and dewy with discovery and promise, the eyes of his dream-girl in fact, the girl

152

whom he, like all men, had cherished in imagination: then the image had become reality.

Why, then, if all this was true, was he sitting there at his desk in a black despair suddenly? What had happened to change things so completely?

He had stood in the compound as an onlooker while Mac seethed with fury over a wrong she imagined had been done to another man. Surely only one beloved could excite female passion to this extent? He had also heard—with ears loth to believe—Mac's voice decrying him as a fool. What could he read into such a display but a change of heart brought about by the reappearance of the old love?

Fiona had left him in no doubt that Hendon was the man who had colored Mac's past. She had told him, apparently playfully, to grant the two some time together in case they wanted to carry on where they had left off, which by her implication was well beyond the bounds of discretion: but as this was a broad-minded continent she didn't suppose any eyebrows would be raised unduly.

Roy could hardly bear the thought of Mac in Hendon's arms, yet hadn't she refused to tie herself down at Wadi Nahla? "Give me a month," she had insisted, but perhaps it wouldn't take a month to decide her preference. He had watched her go across to the bungalow and join Hendon about tea-time, had seen them deep in conversation in the comfortable lounge. In fact he hadn't done any work at all for watching the slow crumbling of his own happiness and peace of mind. It wouldn't do to go on like this. He couldn't exist a month in uncertainty such as this, his heart dying in his bosom a little more each hour.

He saw Mac lead Hendon out into the compound taking his arm in a gesture of familiarity. They were actually coming here!

Roy flicked hastily through a pile of history sheets and never read a word.

CHAPTER TWENTY-SIX

RED AND his wife had disappeared soon after dinner, and Mac was entertaining Hendon in the bungalow she now had to herself. Zarek was suffering some unknown malady which had caused him to take his meal in haughty silence, and he was now in the small room he had adopted which had previously been the Superintendent's study. As Roy fidgeted miserably through his gramophone records the surgeon appeared and stated he was driving into the town for the night.

"I hope you are well, Zarek?" Roy asked in Arabic.

"I am well, thanks be to God," the other replied coldly.

"An angry man is a sick man," Roy insisted. "Why are you angry, Zarek, and with whom?"

The Sudani drew himself erect.

"Sufficient that I am not angry with you, Roy effendi. There comes a time when a man must prove himself a man or retire to a harem. You nurse your own troubles and I will nurse mine."

"In other words mind my own business!" Roy decided bitterly as the other sped down the veranda steps and went across to the tarpaulin-draped line of vehicles where his sports model Lea-Francis was parked.

Roy felt he couldn't bear to be indoors once Zarek had roared away into the night. He lit his pipe and went out into the compound to smoke. There was no light from the Bellingers' quarters though it was scarcely ten-thirty.

"They appear to be happy in one another's company, at least," Roy pondered, and passed on, disturbing the fireflies in the tamarinds and ducking beneath the branches of the prickly-pear.

He came at length to Mac's bungalow, loth to admit that his footsteps had been impelled there from the very beginning. Here was a lighted window and two people in earnest conversation. Even as he watched he saw Hendon rise and stooping kiss the top of Mac's head, shining brightly under the lamp. Mac turned her face up and she was smiling. She rose also, put both her hands into the man's and then quite deliberately lifted her mouth to be kissed.

Roy closed his eyes and turned away. He heard Hendon say good night and crunch away across the compound. His heart was in a tumult. There must be an end to all this. He couldn't face a night not knowing where he stood with a woman who was treating his declared love as lightly as a toy.

"Well, hallo!" Mac greeted as he presented himself to her. "I didn't expect any more visitors tonight. I was going to bed."

"I won't keep you," Roy said more sharply than he realized. "Hendon is himself again, it would appear?"

"Yes. I'm sorry I behaved so badly this afternoon Roy. You didn't understand."

"I may understand only too well," he contradicted her. "I have some intelligence, you know. I want you to feel that you're quite free to act as you wish."

"Well, thanks. . . ." Mac said dubiously. "I think I realized that already, though."

"You may have fancied you were tied to me in some way by our emotional escapade in Wadi Nahla. Have no fear that I took you seriously, my dear girl. One has to take what is available on occasions when—chemically compounded as we are—we succumb to romantic urges. I have fortunately realized I was standing in for something or someone else, and it wouldn't really be good for discipline if we carried the pretence on into our life here, would it?"

Mac swallowed a lump in her throat which felt as big as an apple.

"Do you happen to know whom you were standing in for?" she asked quietly.

"Not at the time," he admitted, "but now it is rather more obvious."

"Oh. You have already impressed upon me the fact of your native intelligence. Forgive me if mine falls short, but I would like you to give a name to this romantic attachment of mine."

155

"I'm sure you must be joking," Roy said icily, "but the man who has just left you didn't do so exactly on a platonic note."

Mac looked at her toes peeping out of her white buckskin shoes and said slowly: "So it's Garry, is it? And you've been spying. May I please have blinds fitted in future?"

"You're deliberately trying to evade the issue," he said angrily. "I was walking round the compound and I innocently witnessed a somewhat indelicate and obvious scene. Couldn't you have turned the lights out?"

"We could," Mac said, breathing sharply, "if we had wanted things that way. What a mind you have, Roy Victor Kingsland, if you see in two people saying good-bye to each other all the cheap sensuality of a pair of lovers in the back row of a cinema!"

"I saw a girl volunteering a kiss," he said bitterly, "and I was humiliated to realize I had accepted the same tribute myself only yesterday. Zarek tomorrow, I suppose," he piled on.

"How dare you!" Mac flashed. "I understand you came here to release me from any imagined obligations I might feel towards you, not to insult me into the bargain. Have you anything else to say?"

He was pacing about like a caged animal. The girl refused to look guilty, even though he had caught her in a compromising situation.

"I came to say that if you want to go off with Hendon in the morning, El Belada will manage and—understand."

"Thank you!" Mac choked. "But though El Belada might understand I'm afraid Mrs. Hendon wouldn't."

"Oh. Is she important these days? I understand she didn't have much influence on your actions during your previous association."

Mac had grown pale and very tense.

"You know a damned lot, don't you?" she said with difficulty, and standing against the door indicated the blackness of the compound outside. "Will you go now, please?"

"Certainly." He bowed slightly and then stood arrogantly waiting, looking down at her.

"Well?" she demanded.

"Surely you are forgetting something?" he taunted. "Don't we all get kissed when we leave?"

"It wouldn't be good for discipline, would it?" Mac lashed him. "I don't know however I could have imagined you as anything but a diploma'd robot. You haven't a

156

heart like other people. I'm glad I found out before I—made a bigger fool of myself. Now, go please, or I must."

Without another word he left her.

It was an hour before he re-entered his bungalow and his face looked ravaged, like a man who hasn't slept for a long time. He was annoyed to find Hendon sitting reading in the living-room as though awaiting him.

"Good lord, man!" he said irritably. "I'd have seen you off in the morning. I'm a very early riser. I do all my reading between five and eight a.m. You should have been in your bed by this with a long journey facing you to-morrow."

"I wanted a few words with you, Kingsland. A few words I think we'd both sleep better for."

"I don't usually suffer from insomnia," Roy said coldly.

"Just the same I would appreciate your ear for a moment."

"Very well, Hendon. Go ahead." Roy laboriously lit his pipe once more. He wondered what had happened to the soothing properties of nicotine these past few hours.

"Earlier this evening I was with Doctor Hayes," Gareth Hendon ventured.

"I am aware of that."

"We were saying good-bye as I don't want to disturb her in the morning. I intend to push off for Malakal at first light. I missed my gold cigarette case when I got back here, so naturally I went back to Mac's place. . . ."

Roy Kingsland was growing tense and expectant.

". . . I couldn't help hearing you and Mac having a bit of a row."

"It's kind of you to put things so mildly," Roy said cynically. "I was in a filthy temper and probably advertising the fact."

"You were saying unforgivable things to a girl like Mac. I know her pretty well, and——"

"Need we discuss how well you know her?" Roy asked nastily.

"I think we do need to, since it was you dragged my name up at her. You were suggesting to Mac that she might care to leave with me tomorrow. Just what did you mean by that? I don't know what business it is of yours, Kingsland, but I was never Mac's lover. She isn't a girl like that. She didn't know I was married when we used to see each other. My wife and I were separated at the time. It was Mac who—patched us up."

There was a somewhat pregnant silence.

157

"I don't mind admitting I was in love with Mac," Hendon went on to say, "but what warm-blooded creature could resist her?"

Roy sighed suddenly.

"I was afraid I might have harmed her irreparably, and you don't know what a relief it was to find her so happy and unembittered by all that had occurred between us."

"Mac is remarkably resilient," Roy observed.

"No woman is as resilient as that," Hendon scoffed, "unless she is in love again. There's no love deader than the one before the last one."

"I am not so experienced in the ways of women as you appear to be, Hendon."

"Maybe you don't want to be," the other returned somewhat impatiently. "I don't know, and I don't particularly want to know since I'm pushing off out of your lives in a few hours, but I hope if Mac Hayes is in love that the man's worthy of her."

"I shall hope the same," Roy told him.

"Then—good night, Kingsland."

"Good night, and"—Roy held out his hand—"if I don't see you again before you go, good luck, Hendon!"

"It's you who need luck, I think. I've had two dips into the bucket, remember."

Roy lay pondering on that conversation far into the night. It was nothing but insane jealousy on his part which had distorted all the events of the day. Mac's guilty look upon mention of her old sweetheart's name when they had just arrived back at the hospital was probably due to a genuine lapse of memory about his intended visit. "No love is deader than the one before the last one"—as Hendon put it: Mac had been so engrossed with her love for him that she had forgotten all about Hendon. Yet he had hurled that same love back in her teeth and probably destroyed it forever.

He had never seen Mac so angry as when she had ordered him out of her house. What could he do or say that would remotely atone for the damage his cruel words had inflicted?

He slept eventually, but uneasily, and when he awoke the sun was brightly piercing the room and Hendon had gone on his way; lonely and unnoticed.

CHAPTER TWENTY-SEVEN

A WEEK dragged by with the serpent revelling in the Garden of Eden, his mischief well and truly accomplished. Mustafa Mohammed Zarek strode about the hospital like an offended monarch, only occasionally stooping to acknowledge those he could not very well ignore. Mac he shunned absolutely, but she was rather relieved about this on the whole. Roy wandered around like a lost soul trying to separate his professional occupation from his personal misery. He would never have believed a woman in one's life could affect one thus. He had tried to apologize, had tried to reach her to seek forgiveness and recapture that elusive joy to which only she had the key for him, but Mac was as one for whom all memory of the past had been suddenly wiped out. Her eyes were lack-lustre, even her spirit subdued. She did her work, took her meals and went off to her quarters like one in a dream. When he sought her out to try to tell her how much he still loved her and how badly he felt about everything which had passed between them that night, she merely sighed and said:

"I'm sorry, Roy. I have no feeling for anything. I just want to be left alone."

She wasn't even angry any more. She seemed to be burnt out.

Anger, love, pity and exhaustion had all combined to bring Immacula Hayes to the point at which a person must have respite from all forms of emotional demonstration or risk suffering a breakdown. She did not feel equal to diagnosing her ills, she simply knew that after that dreadful scene with Roy she must retire from the battle. Roy's visits of a personal nature upset her. She tried to make him understand this. She dared not investigate the dreadful wound she knew still to be gaping wide open from his verbal onslaught upon her. She shuddered away from the remembrance of things he had said or implied. No man had hurt her so much in all her life, and no man would ever hurt her so again. She must recoup her forces and make arrangements to leave El Belada at the earliest moment convenient to all.

Red and Fiona were suddenly two people in a world of their own, unmindful of the upheaval in the relationships of others. Fiona had grown soft-eyed and very lovely: there was an eagerness in her for any break in the routine which allowed her a few moments with her husband and the wonderful joy she was discovering in him. She was perhaps lovelier in that she was learning that happiness must be given before it can boomerang back to the giver. Red's softly drawled, "Honey!" was her nightly passport into the wonderful world it was his to give within the strong circle of his arms; his was her beauty and the miracle of the discovery that it was his to cherish or despoil. This knowledge created an unaccustomed kindness one towards the other and they began to merge in more ways than the physical and so accomplished more jauntily than they had anticipated those first steps along the road to connubial bliss. Roy, despite his own worries, watched them benevolently and decided to give a helping hand. He pointed out that Red was overdue for leave, and Fiona jumped at the idea.

"Red has been talking about motoring down to Juba and then flying on to Lake Chad for a honeymoon. He made it all sound so wonderful," she said excitedly. "Do you think you can really spare us, Roy?"

"I may be able to," he told her kindly. "I scanned through the mail at breakfast and there's a Government Commission coming here any day for a full report on the smallpox epidemic and our tackling of it. They also ask me if I can use three qualified Egyptians here: men with political pasts," he explained further. "We must have a chat, Red, and see what we can fix about time-tables."

"Thanks a lot," said Red, "if you're sure you can manage. I don't want to stand you up, but I could do with seeing my wife away from the hospital."

"My wife," Roy pondered as the pair went jubilantly off to start work. "What wonderful words those are! But I may never be able to use them, alas!"

He fingered the neat, plain envelope he had found on his desk bearing his name in Mac's clear, legible hand. He didn't dare to think why she should write him. She had been very quiet at breakfast time, apparently immersed in her own mail.

He pulled the envelope towards him resolutely and slit it open with a paper-knife. The stiff, white sheet he withdrew crackled as he opened it out.

"To the Superintendent Medical Officer,
El Belada Hospital.
"Dear Sir,
"Realizing I am still within the six-month trial period of my contract, during which time I understand this contract may be terminated by either party, I wish to advise you that I would appreciate my release from duty at the conclusion of six months if you cannot see your way to letting me go earlier. I would not wish, of course, to leave the hospital understaffed in any way, and am willing to wait for a replacement should this be required of me.
"Yours truly,
"Immacula M. Hayes."

So the blow had fallen at last.

"Mine own executioner!" Roy half sighed and half sobbed, crushing the offending sheet in his hand and hurling it into the waste-paper basket. "It appears there's to be no second dip into the bucket for me!"

*   *   *

Ahmed bumped into the surgeon and apologized volubly.

"Mr. Zarek . . . if you're not busy?"

"Ma'alak, Ahmed, what is it?"

"It is Doctor Immacula, effendi, she falls to the ground."

Zarek swallowed his bitter pride and hastened to the laboratory, the Assistant Pathologist at his heels.

Mac looked very slight lying there on the marbled floor, and the surgeon had a fleeting remembrance of his mother as pale as this before she died. He picked the girl up and to reassure Ahmed said, "She has only fainted. Where's your first-aid, boy? Sal volatile. Air. Loosen the clothing."

Ahmed approached uncertainly as Zarek placed the girl on the old examination couch under the window.

"No, I do it!" he said hastily. "The fairness of women is not yet for your young eyes, Ahmed. Back to your microbes!"

Mac sighed and put her hand up to her forehead.

"So hot!" she murmured.

Zarek loosened her white coat and her dress where it fastened over her chest. A warmth was slowly creeping back into his veins again. The little one had repulsed him twice. It must not happen again. He would go very gently this time and reach some conclusion with her.

She was looking up at him with eyes suddenly aware and watchful.

"It is all right, Mac. You fainted. Women do such things all the time."

"Not me, Zarek. I never did it before in all my life. But it was so hot suddenly."

"You are sad in the heart, my dear. I think you grieve for wounding your faithful one, perhaps?"

"Yes, I do," Mac agreed, thinking of Roy.

"Then you will forgive Zarek for loving you too much, eh?"

Mac swung her feet off the couch and sat up, self-consciously fastening buttons.

"There's nothing to forgive, Zarek. If I hurt your feelings it is I should ask forgiveness. I have been very tired one way and another; not myself at all."

"To work all the time is not for you, little one. You should lie on a divan with all to serve and one to worship you. I am happy we are—friends—again, Mac. Now I go to tell the Superintendent of your health."

"No! No!" Mac quickly protested. "Don't tell anybody else of my stupidity, Zarek, please; I'm quite all right again."

"How can I not do my duty?" he smilingly shrugged. "It is in Zarek's interests that you are well, dear Mac."

She realized he must have told when within half an hour she was summoned to the Superintendent's consulting-room. Sister Haifeh was waiting and smiling.

"What is this about you, Doctor Immacula? You have been looking unwell for some time now. You are to lie on the couch for an examination."

"But this is ridiculous, Sister! I'm perfectly well."

"Heat exhaustion, probably," suggested the other, whipping Mac's dress over her head and persuading her to lie down under a white sheet. "All ready for you, sir," she turned to say blithely as Roy entered the room and crossed the floor in two strides while adjusting his stethoscope.

She couldn't help looking up into the dark eyes as the stethoscope travelled over her chest and lingered under her breast.

"I can't find anything there to account for the trouble," he said at last. "Have you a cardiac history?"

"No," she told him. "I'm perfectly well."

He closed his eyes as though with pain as he whispered, "Oh, Mac, I was so worried about you!"

He stood looking out of the window as Sister Haifeh drew the screen while she dressed again. Only her hair remained a little disarranged as she emerged and confronted him.

"I'll go back to work now, if that's all, sir."

"No. Just a moment, please. You may leave us, Sister."

Mac wondered if she had developed cardiac symptoms as her heart did an incredible tumble in her chest.

"Sit down, please."

"I'd rather—not."

She sat, however, as his eyes besought her not to defy him.

"I got your letter," he said with some difficulty. "Is it for health reasons you wish to leave us?"

"No. Actually I heard today that a relative of mine has died——"

"I'm sorry," he murmured.

"——It's an aunt of my mother's. She was quite an old lady. I didn't realize she thought so much of me as to leave me all she had, but it does involve my return to England."

"I—I see," he said, rather at a loss. "Congratulations!"

There was an uncomfortable pause.

"I'll have to see about your being released from your contract," he went on, then his voice suddenly cracked and the cry became one of desperation from his heart, "Oh, Mac, don't leave me!"

She had risen, tense and alert for danger, not wishing to become emotionally involved in the scene.

She was easily ignited, however, and feeling flooded like pain through her being.

"It's not fair!" she said over and over again. "It's not fair! You have no right to rake it all up again! Let me go for God's sake!"

Such a desperate plea he could not ignore. His eyes hurt in their sockets as he watched her reach the door and hesitate.

"Have dinner with me this evening?" he asked. "If there's so little time . . . ?" She was still struggling to gain some sort of control and didn't answer. "The Bellingers are busily preparing for leave and have asked to be excused

163

a formal meal. Zarek is going home. He's having some alterations made to his house and has placed an architect in charge of things. He's always dashing off these days. So there'll just be you and me. It seems a pity to have one's meal alone when there are matters needing discussion. Such as your release," he added quickly.

"I want to go to bed early," she said, "but I'll join you for dinner at the usual time. Somebody told me you were planning to go to El Arak."

"I can't go now. The day is too advanced. I'll have to put it off until later in the week and then stay overnight at the colony."

As she left the room he felt a sudden upsurge of guilt. Everybody was expecting him to go to the leper colony, and because Mac had said she would dine alone with him his work and his duty had taken second place for the first time in his remembrance.

CHAPTER TWENTY-EIGHT

MAC GLANCED uncertainly round the now familiar room, looking somehow unfamiliar in the soft glow of candlelight. The table was laid with particular care on this occasion, yet the candelabra were dusty, as though brought on a sudden impulse from some place where they had lain neglected for a long time, perhaps since electrification had come to El Belada some years ago. There were also flowers on the table obviously arranged by a man, for no woman would have mixed pink roses with ramrod-straight, orange-tinted cannas in a top-heavy vase of purple lustre.

Mac smiled questioningly at the whole effort and forbade her heart to be thawed out by it.

She had not intended to dress up for the occasion, but the simple dinner-gown of *broderie-anglaise* she wore, which caressed bust, hips and waist before flaring out into fullness, looked as though it loved her. It complemented her eyes and her hair was rapidly regaining its normal satin sheen.

Roy was standing in the doorway observing her when she looked round. His eyes spoke the breathless, adoring words of any lover, and she promptly turned her back on him.

"I think I am a little early," she said as lightly as she could.

"No, it is I who am late. You must forgive me. The Bellingers are going away on leave tomorrow, so I had to acquaint myself with Red's special patients. He's very good on blood, you know. He can teach me quite a bit."

"I'm glad you can spare them for awhile," Mac said, as he stood behind her chair while she was seated, "I've been rather sorry for them since they married, carrying on with the daily round as though nothing was changed."

"I got the impression that they had already left us," Roy said somewhat cynically. "The patients haven't suffered, but I have felt almost transparent when in their company."

She didn't even smile, so he clapped his hands and Rajab appeared with a grin from ear to ear and a large dish in his hands.

"Habbash," Roy announced, studying her reactions. "I seem to remember you liked it the last time."

"Are wild turkeys plentiful round here?" she asked as he carved, her voice still toneless.

"No. But I told the boy to get one for tonight or never show his face again."

"Drastic," Mac granted. "You might have lost a very good boy."

"I'm in a drastic frame of mind."

The meal commenced in silence, then—as is the way—both spoke together.

"Mac——"

"Roy——!"

There was silence again.

"I was going to say"—Roy said firmly—"that things can't go on this way between us. It's an impossible state of affairs and you know it."

"Am I not doing my best to conclude it?" Mac asked simply. "I can do no more than go away out of your life."

"Out of my life?" he echoed numbly. "I can't believe you know what you're saying, Mac!" He came to kneel before her, seizing her hands and looking up imploringly into her troubled face. "What can I do to put it right again with us? Tell me what to do and I'll do it! I cannot love you more, Mac, my darling! I know I said unforgiveable and mad things, but I was jealous. My reactions to

165

seeing you with Hendon were new and overpowering. I have never been jealous before, you see: never really loved before to cause it. I have felt like a—a murderer, Mac, seeing you so stricken. Tell me I can have another chance to make you happy if you ever really did love me!"

She somehow thrust him away and went across to a dim corner of the room in her agitation, then she turned to face him.

"It's difficult to make anyone else understand, Roy. I came back with you from Wadi Nahla on an absolute peak of personal happiness. I never felt quite so happy before and"—she shrugged—"I don't suppose I ever will again. I said we would wait a month before declaring our intentions to the others: I should have given you my reasons for this, but in all good faith I thought them best kept to myself. I was afraid Zarek would hurt or harm you in some way if he knew we had fallen in love. He could harm you—this place—because in his own way he is very fond of me. I've told him no—and no again—but he still charmingly persists. He was after Garry's blood, I'm still convinced of that, and he would be after yours, make no mistake. I think I could have handled things, given time, but somehow Garry cropped up and got in the way and everything was distorted and—and horrible. You brought me crashing from my peak and—well, I don't really know what happened to me. I can't feel anything, Roy! I daren't feel anything!" A sob caught in her throat and he went to her, not as a lover but as a doctor who was suddenly concerned for the welfare of a patient. "It seems to me the way back to all the loveliness is through a sea of tears, and I'm not brave enough to plunge."

She crept into his arms as into a haven, and silently he gathered her to him and stroked her hair.

"I'm forgetting, Mac, my dear, that you've been weakened by fever and can't feel physically up to much yet. I should have put you on sick leave and not worked you like a cart-horse. I'm beginning to see why you didn't want me pestering you, darling. Forgive me? I shocked you, and these things take time for our patients to get over, so why not us? But please don't run away from me, Mac. Let your legacy wait until I've had a chance to undo the damage my insane jealousy accomplished in the first place. Even if you fall in love with someone else after all my pains. What do you say, dearest?"

"You'll be good to me, Roy?"

"I'll be so good to you, my Immacula. I won't ask what it isn't in you to give, but don't expect me to stop caring for you. I would be in El Arak at this moment if I didn't love you as I do. I'm also convinced I would follow you if you went away, so it would be a dreadful inconvenience all round."

She managed a wan smile and pressed an emotionless kiss on his mouth. She was glad he didn't misinterpret the gesture, but instead put his own lips to her brow.

Neither knew that there was an interested spectator to the scene in one Mustafa Mohammed Zarek, F.R.C.S. Zarek's car had suffered a puncture a mile beyond the hospital, and—not being mechanically minded himself—he had walked back to secure the services of a boy. He had called at the main bungalow to announce that he would, after all, be staying the night. Now, however, he turned away silently, his face strangely calm, his eyes smouldering. He viciously kicked the watchnight boy awake as he dozed by the line of vehicles drawn up neatly against the compound wall.

"Effendi!" wailed the boy fearfully. "Ley, effendi?"

"I take Land Rover. You tell Superintendent."

"*Aywa*, Zarek effendi. *Aywa*."

The Land Rover sent a spurt of dust up his nostrils as it shot away into the night, and the lad spat and settled down once more on his haunches, unaware of the drama being precipitated by his superiors.

The Hospital Commission arrived in great dignity early the next morning, having caught the weekly train from Khartoum. With the three-man commission were the three displaced Egyptians, curiously regarding the paradox of a hospital functioning apparently in the middle of nowhere, and the Superintendent's bungalow rang to the sound of El hamdu l'illahs and the clink of coffee cups as important discussions took place.

Fiona fidgeted with her straw hat as Red appeared from the direction of the hospital. She had been longing for this break more than anyone guessed, and she had an inexplicable but potent feeling that it was too good to be true, that something might yet go wrong.

"Do hurry, darling," she now urged. "Let's get on our way!"

"Aw, relax, honey! What's the rush? I'm not so sure we should push off yet. Zarek hasn't turned in and young Mac's by herself in there."

"Zarek will come," Fiona fretted. "Anyway, Roy said

167

we had to go. We're on leave and I want to make sure of it."

"You brazen hussy!" Red suddenly smiled. "You want to get me right away from all my friends and then try out your charms on me, eh?" She tried not to fidget as he caught her up in his arms and crushed her to him, newly pressed linen suit, hat, and all. "You know, beautiful, I didn't know you had it in you"—he winked—"whatever it is you have got in you. Did you notice how I've learned to say a very nice sorta 'you', like 'you' taught me to?"

"You're learning fast," she smiled. "Now will you hurry?"

"O.K. ma'am. Mebbe you could go get us a red-cross box from stores? It won't take you a minute."

"Very well. Be ready when I get back."

Red's car, their car, was already at the door, bright yellow and gleaming. The color made Fiona wince, but the American interior was certainly upholstered and insulated for comfort.

"I suppose I'm an American, now," she pondered jauntily.

Red, left alone, realized that though he had given Roy the Lake Chad address, he had added no details of their leisurely itinerary. Should he? Shouldn't he. . . . His sense of duty won and he hastily scribbled a note and gave it to Tia Kafi to pass on to the Superintendent.

CHAPTER TWENTY-NINE

ZAREK HAD been somewhat surprised to find his sister Fadia visiting his house.

"You don't look pleased to see me, Mohammed," she lightly accused him, offering her cheek to be kissed. "What is going on here? I find many changes in the house. One would conclude there is to be a marriage, perhaps?"

"Eskut, woman!"

"But surely there are rooms being prepared for a lady? Maybe a paramour, wicked brother?"

"You must never so call this lady, Fadia. Tell me what brings you on one of your all-too-rare visits? And is not Jamil with you?"

"No. Jamil could not be spared. I come to give you wonderful news. I think perhaps you will like to be an uncle?"

"Little Fadia!" Zarek swung her off her feet in sudden delight. "How our mother would have liked to hear of this!"

When he had set her down again the young woman said thoughtfully, "Always you speak of our mother, Mohammed. I do not remember her as you do. Perhaps you think of her too much?"

"Is it a fault, then, to think so? To remember our father's great happiness with her? But tell me, Fadia, how long do you intend to stay here?"

"I believe you want me to go!" she teased. "My! this boy is up to tricks, and no mistake! Am I not to know?"

"Soon enough you will know all, ya habibti. Now tell me when ibn Jamil is expected to arrive."

"Early in July, if it be God's will. I could keep the news from my beloved brother not a moment longer. Tomorrow I return to El Arak."

"Then come and give me your advice on my new guest-rooms, Fadia. Tell me as a woman what you think of them."

The two wandered through a Moorish archway into an elegant suite of rooms exquisitely furnished in maple with curtains and upholstery of pink damask.

"The pink carpet is wrong," Fadia decided. "You should have been more subdued over the carpet. Grey, perhaps?"

"I thought ladies liked pink?"

"But you will be sleeping here too, Mohammed?" Fadia asked, her tongue in her cheek.

"I shall consider it. Meanwhile I think a woman in your condition should go to bed, and not poke fun at her brother."

Fadia's laughter tinkled as he frowned playfully at her.

"Very well, Mohammed. I shall go to bed and leave you to your dreams of love. But we will have breakfast together before I leave your house?"

"Certainly. There is no haste for me to leave. I give myself a day off, perhaps."

Fadia nestled her head against him for a moment.

"I think that you are not yourself, Mohammed. I think that you perhaps love a little and it is a pain? Never

169

mind, when you have your woman in your arms it will be better."

He kissed the top of her raven head and turned away in the direction of his own apartments, leaving her wondering what could be amiss with him. Once these two had been all the world to each other, now they were strangers almost.

The following morning passed pleasantly enough in the Zarek residence. No one would have recognized in the Sudanese master interviewing his estate managers the anglicized surgeon who walked the corridors of El Belada.

Fadia enjoyed an hour's sheer luxury at the hands of the women of the establishment, allowing them to bath and pomade her to their hearts' content while they heard about the coming of the little one. All were delighted by the news. In every corner of the earth birth is always regarded as a miracle, but when it happens to one's social superiors it is as well to make even more of a miracle out of the event than usual. The women-servants smiled knowingly at one another and said confidently in their colloquial Arabic:

"It will surely be a son, this child."

"No matter," Fadia pouted prettily. "There will be more children in my house, please God."

Fadia's car and Nuba chauffeur were at the door, her woman-servant waiting obsequiously to ensure that various items of hand luggage were not overlooked, when the Superintendent's car arrived dust-bespattered from the journey, and Mac alighted, looking a little anxious.

"Doctor Immacula!" Fadia greeted gladly.

They had only met once, but had taken to one another on sight as is sometimes the way.

"Sister Azuri!" Mac smiled. "I hope your brother isn't ill?"

"Ill? He is never ill, that one. He says he takes a day off. Did he not tell you this himself?"

Zarek appeared in the dark arch of the doorway and Fadia saw his expression as he beheld the visitor and immediately knew the answer to her brother's sudden preference for pink upholstery and crystal baths.

"Salaam aleykum, and take care of yourself, Fadia," he hustled her almost eagerly into her car and waved the party away before turning those sombre eyes again upon the newcomer.

"You come to see Zarek?" he asked expressionlessly.

"Yes. I wondered what had happened to you. The hospital is positively crawling with people at the moment;

170

the Hospital Commission and three new doctors who are trying to make up their minds if they like what they see enough to want to see it every day. I was excused duty as from midday, I'm not supposed to be quite fit yet, so I asked if I could have Abdul and the car and here I am!"

"So nobody sent you?" Zarek asked, cheering up visibly as they went through into the cool courtyard behind.

"Nobody. Roy has wondered about your absence, of course. He says you have never let him down before. But he is too tied up to have done anything about it himself. What is the matter, Zarek? Why aren't you at work?"

"Perhaps I am tired of being nobody at El Belada when—as you so rightly pointed out—I am somebody elsewhere."

Sensing a mood in her companion, Mac looked up anxiously into his face.

"You couldn't be a nobody anywhere, Zarek. Roy and all of us fully appreciate you."

"It is sufficient that you perhaps like me a little?" he ventured.

"I 'like' you a lot, Zarek," she assured him, with emphasis upon the "like". Her play on the word might have been self-explanatory to an Englishman, but the surgeon didn't find it conducive to a purely platonic relationship. He now looked much happier, more like his normal self.

"Come, Mac, I show you how I make my house."

She viewed the alterations quizzically and with something approaching awe. The bath with its crystal mermaid holding a shell from which water cascaded continuously was something she hadn't expected to find out of the pages of the Arabian Nights, and when they reached the bedroom she gasped.

"What an absolute dream of a room!"

"You like it, Mac?" Zarek almost chuckled. "Perhaps the carpet should be grey, you think?"

"It's quite perfect as it is. I wouldn't change a thing."

"Then nothing shall be changed," he told her, in a way which made her quickly avert her eyes.

She fingered the quilt on the exquisite bed, which had a motif of cherubs and rosebuds richly embroidered in white on the pale cherry of the silk. She positively jumped as Zarek touched her arm. She must get away from this particular setting; it was too suggestive a background to share with the wrong man.

"You wish we should swim, Mac?" he said with some difficulty.

"But aren't you going to the hospital at all today?" she asked him. "Supposing an emergency is admitted?"

"Pooh!" he dismissed this trifle. "Our Superintendent is a Master of Surgery, is he not? For once he can do my work. I am in a sulk with Roy today."

"What has he done?" Mac demanded.

Zarek looked at her, liking the blue of her eyes and the corn-silk of her hair better than ever before.

"This——" he said, and put trembling lips to her brow.

Mac lowered her eyes self-consciously.

"How do you know?" she asked.

"I see him—last night. I do not like seeing Roy—anyone—do that to you."

"But, Zarek. . . ." With a sinking at her heart she realized she would have to tell him all there was to be told. He must not dwell in a fool's paradise any longer. "I want to talk to you very seriously, Zarek. Would you like to swim first?"

"Yes, we will swim. I, also, have serious things to say to you, Mac, but they are best said when the head is cool and only the heart burns."

As the girl Amna beckoned her away to change, Mac felt an overpowering wave of sadness engulf her. She, too, thought of the pink bedroom and Zarek's delight in her approval, and suddenly realized it had all been intended for her.

CHAPTER THIRTY

MAC THOUGHT the Sudani was never going to break a silence grown oppressive with emotion. She heard clearly every plip-plop of water splashing into the fountain behind her.

Zarek's sigh, when it came, quivered through his heavy frame.

"Try not to hate us," Mac implored. "I couldn't bear that."

He had to force his eyes from his inward shock and pain back to her face, uncomprehending for a moment.

"You will marry Roy effendi?" he asked conversationally.

"I can't answer that yet. I want time to think. But I wanted you to know. . . ."

"That you can never marry me?" he asked with a twisted smile. "The little one is so sure of herself on that point. All life can be confusion for her, but standing out so clearly is the fact that Zarek is not to be considered as a husband at any price. How could I have been such a fool, I wonder!"

Mac stood up, breathing hard.

"This is awful! I can't help my feelings, Zarek, any more than you can. Let us be adult about it!"

"We will be adult, as you say," Zarek agreed with sudden calm. "I forget you are my guest and embarrass you. Spare alms for the beggar, dear lady, and grant me one last request."

"I will do what I can," Mac promised sincerely.

"Then one final ride together before I take you back to the hospital. Fadia's clothes will fit you."

"Isn't it rather late?" Mac demurred.

"She closes her purse to the beggar!" Zarek said contemptuously.

"No. I'll go," Mac said, not liking the idea of leaving him alone in his strange mood.

"You are not afraid Zarek will perhaps lose you as he lost your friend Hendon?"

"I'm not afraid," Mac told him.

He began to laugh appreciatively, but it was laughter without the ring of mirth about it.

"You are such a one after my own heart," he said with a sharp sigh as he turned away from her.

The magnificent Ibrahim and a smaller chestnut, Koko, were saddled and ready in the stable-yard when Mac arrived some minutes later wearing Fadia's jodhpurs and a blouse. Zarek was in his robes and turban. He looked like a character out of a film as Ibrahim reared and pawed the ground beneath him to the shouted encouragement of the stable-boys. Suddenly the animal appeared to rear out of control over where Mac was standing: she saw Zarek's excited, triumphant face taunting her as she lifted her arms to ward off what looked like certain death for her, then a strong arm swept her off her feet. She could still hear the excited shouts of the grooms and the galloping of hoofs, but it was some moments

173

before she realized she was drawn up in front of Zarek on the great white stallion, and that Ibrahim was not bolting but being given his head to carry them both away as fast as the wind towards the black cloud of the approaching tropical night.

Mac had more sense than to struggle and perhaps cause an accident, but her heart was thumping like a hammer within her chest. What was Zarek's game? Was he merely trying to frighten her? When she looked up at him he grinned and shouted into the wind.

"All is decided for us. The horse has gone mad."

"So has the man," Mac feared.

The terrain became more rocky and washed up in terraces towards the distant Nuba Mountains: sure-footedly, however, Ibrahim negotiated the rocks with his double burden, and just before the sun dipped he stopped by a long stretch of water, palm-rimmed. Built into the nearby rocks was a cave-like dwelling with iron grilles protecting door and windows.

"My father's hunting-lodge," Zarek explained as he dismounted and set Mac down stiffly upon her feet. "We stay here tonight, I think."

Mac had difficulty in restraining herself from questioning his words. She had determined not to play up to his already outraged ego with displays of feminine tears and protestations. They would serve no practical purpose and merely exhaust her. She felt she would need all her strength before this night was over.

She crouched down by the water and bathed the dust from her face while Zarek made a great show of unlocking the building behind them.

As she did not move from the stone upon which she had decided to sit, Zarek eventually came to squat beside her. He offered her a Turkish cigarette, which she refused, and as fragrant smoke curled gently in the cooling night air a semicircle of red eyes gathered to watch unwinkingly from the far side of the water.

"Jackals," Zarek explained. "With luck Mister Lion may come to drink. If he does, Ibrahim will tell us. I will not let anything harm my little Mac."

"At this moment I'm not afraid of lions, Zarek."

"Ya habibti!" he crooned into her ear, his lips hungry and impatient.

"Zarek!" She jumped up suddenly. "What's that? Over there. . . ."

As he peered into the darkness she slid quietly into the deep, surprisingly cold water and struck out for the

174

far bank. There was no light, and in a few moments she was lost to him.

"Mac!" his voice appealed sharply. "Mac, come here! Animals . . . predators are about. This is their drinking-hole."

Still she made little sound. On the far bank she dragged herself out of the water and lay for a few moments regaining her breath, then she stumbled towards those watching eyes, driving them back before her.

Zarek had wasted no time in creating light. He had matches in the lodge and there were lamps. He came in pursuit carrying a burning brand and muttering Arabic imprecations against all women in his anger and anxiety. She gave him a good run for his money, however, and when at last he caught up with her she was just about all in. She had fallen several times, had cut her knee and torn Fadia's jodhpurs in several places. Mud, blood and all, he carried her back to the lodge, locked the door firmly behind him and laid her on the silken bed.

"You shall not escape me now!" he roared at her, arrogant and masterful. "What are you but a chit to defy Zarek so! I offer to marry you. I do you great honor. You insult me by your preference for another. I do not tolerate this. I take you and I do not marry you. This is my revenge against Roy effendi. He will not want you to-morrow, little gazelle. I know, because with her knowledge of the ways of Europeans my mother tells my father this thing and it proves so. Now take off your wet things and wear this."

He tossed her a silken dressing-robe and turned his back. When he looked again she was still clothed as before, but was toying with a dagger-like knife he remembered seeing on the table by a bowl intended for fruit.

"Now you kill Zarek, eh?" he asked in some amusement.

"No. It's for me if you come any nearer."

Anger and consternation flashed across the proud countenance.

"You are so small to be such a nuisance," he decided, keeping his distance. "If I say you don't mean this thing I cannot be sure in case you do. What to do with such a creature? She prefers death by drowning, tooth and claw, night exposure and a dagger in her heart to Zarek's love. Tck! Tck! I give in. Put the knife down, Mac."

She never knew why she obeyed, but she did so without argument, and as he picked up the knife and her last defence against him was gone, she crept willingly into his arms and opened the flood-gates of her tears against his breast.

A new tenderness stirred within him, and with it a new strength. His mother would be glad he had kept his word, like an Englishman. When this night was over this girl could go back to the man of her choice without hatred and bitterness against him, and perhaps she would always remember him kindly for it. He stroked the bright hair as he had seen Roy do, and though his heart ached a little he would never let it show again to anyone.

*   *   *

Roy Kingsland never wanted to live through such a day as this had been ever again.

Normally life at the hospital, though busy, was quiet. The outside world rarely intruded, but the place might have been Mecca on this January morning with waves of visitors milling through the compound gates. The Hospital Commission he had, of course, been expecting, but the three Egyptians were more of an embarrassment than otherwise. There was the question of salaries, the hospital being by no means wealthy, and the last thing the officials seemed to want to discuss was finance. Doctor Ali fadal was a family man with a wife and three children at present staying in an hotel in Khartoum: he was already worrying about housing for his family and raising the question of a school, but obviously he would get around to the subject of suitable reimbursement later. Young Doctor Wazili didn't appear to consider El Belada much of a place socially. He was not much of a one for tennis and such games, he confided, as he saw the court Zarek had provided for the staff's recreation, he preferred to dance in the evening. The third member of the party was perhaps the most difficult of all. He was a highly qualified surgeon, but he had spent so many years in prison and been subjected to such torments and privations that he had lost his nerve, and was all but a physical wreck. He was, however, eager to work, which impressed Roy more than a little.

"You give me a chance to show you how I can help in any way," he pleaded. "I take no money. Some day I will be good again at my job and God will reward you, Doctor Kingsland."

"Start now," Roy said impulsively. "The hospital seems to be running itself at the moment."

It was Mac who reminded him that Zarek was still not on the premises. She looked pale and somewhat strained, darting from ward to ward, her own work neglected for the moment. Roy told her to go off duty and stay off for the rest of the day as Doctor Osman was anxious to get his hand in and might as well take over relief duty at a time when relief was most needed.

"Are you feeling all right yourself, sir?" Mac asked him, and though he dismissed this airily enough, he began from that moment to wonder what he had eaten which was causing the mounting pain in his abdomen.

"Zarek had better turn up in case I need him," he joked. "You go off and relax, Mac. I don't want you to overdo things again."

That was what had decided Mac's afternoon for her. She determined to find out why Zarek should let down the man he professed to hold in such high regard. If there was a simple explanation of his absence, she was quite prepared to enjoy his hospitality for a pleasant hour or two. Roy entertained his visitors to a luncheon that he himself could hardly touch. He was feeling more sick and miserable every moment.

Red and Fiona were relaxing blissfully in the rest-house, only a short run from El Belada, that marked their first stop on their journey. Red's heavy drinking was a thing of the past now; he could take it or he could leave it alone; still, it was nice to think that this evening he could legitimately enjoy a sundowner without the fear that any emergency would call for him to be fully alert.

He was saying as much to his wife when he saw Tia Kafi standing before him, a sweat-stained envelope in his hand. Red recognized the writing as Roy's.

"*Dear Red* (Roy had written) *I can't apologize enough for cutting in on your leave, but could you get back here just for twelve hours? I'm stuck with all these people and the most awful gripes in my interior. I'm clearly in for an attack of dysentery. Zarek hasn't turned in, Mac has gone off somewhere and there are several cases that want watching. If you could just tide us through the night, the others should be able to cope tomorrow. Tell Fiona I'm truly sorry.*"

Red got to his feet, tossing the letter across to Fiona. He knew only too well what it was like to go down with dysentery and feel you had to stagger about your business because there wasn't anyone to take your place. Probably Roy was much more seriously ill than he had admitted. . . .

He turned to Fiona, automatically bracing himself for a tearful scene. To his surprise, she was serenely getting ready to accompany him. Red smiled to himself. Fiona had become a "giver" after all.

Back at the hospital, Red found Roy folded double in his office, Sister Haifeh fussing a little over him.

"Where's the circus?" Red asked.

"Gone to El Arak," the other said thankfully. "I never had a belly-ache like this before, Red."

"He also vomits and has a temperature, Doctor," said Sister.

"Let's have a look at you."

"Not just now," Roy said, standing up with difficulty. "I want to finish all my business and get to my bed. Thank you, Sister. . . ." Sister Haifeh shrugged and left the two men together. "Now, Red, the things that must be seen to this evening——"

He had got about half-way through the list when he collapsed.

CHAPTER THIRTY-ONE

"OUR TEARS have mingled at last, little one," Zarek said almost happily, rubbing a finger over his own damp eyelashes. "Where does all this water come from? My shirt is soaked."

"I feel so much better for it," sighed Mac, drawing long, quivering breaths. "I remember a poem which says:

" 'There's a joy to waking and a joy to sleeping,
    But nought is akin to the joy of weeping. . . .'

"I've proved it in a jolly good cry. I feel alive again and—and I'm hungry."

"She is hungry now," Zarek shrugged helplessly. "How could one be romantic with such a creature! Fortunately for you that Doctor Bellinger had impressed upon me the unique qualities of canned foods. Here in this cupboard I have supplies of Bellinger's sun-baked beans; Bellinger's grass-green peas; Bellinger's crisp corn-on-the-cob and Bellinger's flavorful fruit cup."

"No ham?" Mac asked hopefully as she stood behind a make-shift screen and changed her wet clothes for a spare shirt and breeches kept at the lodge for Zarek's use in emergency.

"Infidel!" he lashed her. "A good thing I find you out in time! You would have my servants cook filthy pig for you?"

"Never the twain shall meet——" Mac pondered, coming round the screen and smiling at him. "Zarek, how did your father and mother overcome the religious question?"

He shrugged.

"My father became a somewhat confused Christian for the duration of my mother's life. But I was thrust into the arms of Islam at birth as a sort of belated penance for his defection. I think perhaps I am not as brave as my father. I could not do this thing even for you, Mac. It is well you hate me."

"I don't hate you. I might have done if . . ." she paled and then looked up at him as he opened a tin of beans with the dagger. "I love you as Fadia does, Zarek. You're the brother I always wanted and never had. I have only just realized it."

"This brother is going far away from such blue eyes," the man told her firmly, handing her a small dish of cold beans. "I never felt so for Fadia, so I cannot return the compliment."

"I wish you didn't have to leave El Belada."

"It will be better so. I could not bear to see Roy effendi loving you. Even the thought makes me hate him."

Zarek's eyes grew hard again and Mac quickly remarked on the quality of the beans.

"I perhaps visit my house in Khartoum for some little time. I will look up the daughter of Amir Said Abdullah, who is my Professor of Surgery in university. Always he speaks of the little Halyma, who is twelve years old at that time." He did some mental arithmetic. "She will be eighteen years by this. Yes, I will visit Khartoum."

"And she won't ask for filthy pig," Mac said, her tongue in her cheek.

"You laugh at me?"

"No, Zarek. I want you to be happy. Halyma sounds nice."

He came and squatted in front of her.

"Can you hurry yourself out of my heart, little one?"

"I would try—if I knew how."

"I believe you. Such things heal in time, they say. Hark! Ibrahim calls from his stall! It must be Mister Lion approaching!"

Mac felt her hair pricking against her scalp as they stole out into the night together. A fire burned low and Zarek kicked it into a blaze again which lit up the whole area of the water-hole. A few dik-dik were on the far bank, watchful at the sudden brightness, but there was no lion.

"The moon is rising," Zarek told her, looking towards the east. "I will take you back to the hospital as soon as it is bright enough to venture. Eskut, Ibrahim!"

The stallion had whinnied again.

Mac turned her head.

"Maybe I'm imagining things, but I'm sure I can hear another horse approaching!"

Zarek listened attentively.

"You are right. I will go and get my gun."

"Are there bandits hereabouts?" Mac whispered.

"It is doubtful. Many thieves flourish, but they are not usually armed. Nevertheless, a gun in one's hand is not amiss when one is in doubt of another's intentions."

"I must remember that in future," Mac said drily.

The sound of horse's hoofs slithering on rock came clearly to their ears as Zarek returned to crouch beside her.

"It is a brave rider who travels in the dark," the man decided; then the moon broke over the distant mountains lighting up a white-robed figure on a dark horse.

"That is Koko!" Zarek exclaimed. "*Leish es-sabab el safariya, Mahmoud?*"

They exchanged a few words.

Mac, straining to follow the Arabic with her limited knowledge of the language, caught the name of Kingsland and now leapt in with:

"What is wrong with Roy? Tell me, Zarek!"

"I do not know," he said with deliberate and cruel calm. "The boy says he is sick."

"I knew it!" Mac said as though to herself. "He looked awful this morning. I should never have left him."

Zarek questioned the boy further and then announced, "We will return to my house and you can go to your beloved in his need. By all accounts that need is dire. Doctor Bellinger has sent word that the Superintendent has a perforated appendix. How jolly! And a new surgeon who suffers from an ague and cannot hold his hands still. Ho! Ho! A pity I will not witness this night's work!

Maybe you will have to operate on your darling yourself, Doctor Mac!"

She looked up as though not recognizing him:

"You mean that you are not going to help? That you would let Roy die?"

"I had a grandfather who used to fight the British. He would say one more or less didn't matter as there would always be plenty British to annoy the rest of the world. I say leave things to Fate, dear Mac. That is the Moslem way."

"Then it's a good thing for Fadia that Roy isn't a Moslem!" Mac said angrily. "Take me back at once, please, and we'll do the best we can for Roy without you!"

Zarek was silent and offended again as he took Mac up in front of him and set Ibrahim in motion to follow Koko as pathfinder.

"My evening has been ruined in every possible way," he sulked. "I shall be glad to go up to Khartoum and forget you."

"I hope your conscience will let you, because if anything happens to Roy I'll track you down and haunt you! Or don't Moslems suffer from either conscience or ghosts?"

"Eskut, woman! I am having great difficulty hardening my heart after what you say about Fadia. Roy effendi did give Fadia her life, and now she is giving life, bearing a child. All this is only possible because of Roy effendi. . . . A pity he chooses to love the woman I want. There! Already my heart is hard again."

"I wouldn't trust you with him," Mac said scornfully. "It's too easy to have an accident when you hate somebody.'

Zarek jerked the reins a little too tightly and Ibrahim all but put one leg down a small crevice between the rocks.

"Do you say I would deliberately . . . ?"

"If you would deliberately abandon somebody you would as casually do the other thing," Mac said relentlessly.

"I am best surgeon in Sudan," Zarek expostulated.

"That is only your opinion. The best surgeon would put a patient before pique."

"I should have left you to Mister Lion, I think," Zarek decided.

"His company would have been preferable," Mac retorted.

*   *   *

"We're going to have to act soon," Red Bellinger said worriedly. "Why is there no word from either Zarek or Mac? They are together, I presume?"

No one really knew. Mac had gone off in the Superintendent's car with Abdul, the chauffeur-mechanic. Nobody had returned to the hospital.

"I sent Tia Kafi with a message," Red went on, "and how *he's* missing. Hell! Osman, d'you think you could direct me if I make a start on him?"

"I think we must try, Doctor Bellinger, at least. Nothing is improving inside there the longer we wait."

"Then I'll scrub up. Fiona, honey, your husband's practising for his F.R.C.S. at long last. Tell Ahmed he qualified today and is going to give the anæsthetic. Not that poor old Roy knows much about anything at this moment."

Red's obvious efforts to make light of the task ahead of him were a mask to his true feelings. He felt that poor old Roy had "had it" in a big way. Like all professional healers he had neglected to recognize his own symptoms soon enough, and the trouble had got out of hand very quickly.

The El Arak party were obviously benighted at a rest-house somewhere along the route, for the radio had failed to contact them.

If a physician had to operate, Red decided it was better to be himself than a stranger. No stranger would take kindly to an almost certain fatality for his introduction to El Belada, the patient being the Superintendent, of all people.

Sister Haifeh stood tensed and ready under the strong lights, frowning over her mask. Doctor Osman lifted the sheet flap and indicated where the incision should be made.

"If you are a Christian, Doctor Bellinger, pray," he said surprisingly.

"I am and I have," Red replied. "You pray to yours. That way we ought to contact someone influential. Well—I guess here goes!"

"Wait a moment, sir," said Sister. "I hear voices!"

"They can'ta heard up there already," Red said reverently.

The theatre doors swung open and Mac was revealed wearing the oddest of clothes, a man's huge shirt tucked into a pair of breeches.

"Are we too late?" she inquired.

Behind her stood Zarek, his natural arrogance over-ridden by anxiety.

"Help me scrub up for the love of God!" he pleaded.

CHAPTER THIRTY-TWO

An ODD thought crossed Mac Hayes' mind as she stood, an onlooker at that complicated operation on the man she realized she loved more than life itself. She found herself wondering if the hospital outside the theatre was still functioning. It seemed to her the whole world of events and possibilities was there in that rather small space—Zarek's province—not in any way resembling the vast theatres where Mac had done her training, but adequate and shiningly neat and clean.

Only Fiona was missing from the band of the Super-intendent's usual associates: she was probably buckling to and keeping the normal troubles of hospital night-life away from the drama taking place here.

There were far too many people in such a small theatre, of course, but who would want to be dismissed and fret outside somewhere, fearing the worst so much more readily, as one does when one relies upon one's imagination?

The patient had been on oxygen for a long time: occasionally Zarek paused and watched the big bag swelling to the rate of Roy's scarcely discernible breathing, then back he would go to his job, asking Doctor Osman's views on this or that as the Egyptian leaned across from the other side, envying the younger man's steel nerves and physical control.

Mac wondered if Zarek was finding it difficult to work on a man who he considered had robbed him of his chances of happiness, but at the moment he looked intense in occupation, grave and not a little worried.

She remembered how she had feared abduction for a second time when Zarek had insisted she accompany him back to the hospital in his car. The drive had been accom-plished in silence as the miles raced by. Only when they reached the hospital had Zarek spoken in a tight, rather high-pitched voice.

"I will do this thing not for you, Mac, but for all my countrymen whom Roy effendi has served so well. I do it a little for myself, too. I cannot hate him enough because so long I have loved him. God be with us!"

Mac opened her eyes from thinking another prayer and caught the surgeon's eye.

"Is it very bad?" was torn from her.

"Bad, yes. But not the end. I will soon have finished."

There was a final swabbing, then the arteries were joined and the operation entered its final stages.

Somehow a small ward had been prepared in readiness and Ahmed was waiting and ready with the blood transfusion apparatus. Mac accompanied the stretcher-trolley along to the ward and saw Roy gently transferred to the bed. He looked ashen after the long ordeal. Red inserted the transfusion needle and suggested that Mac should stay with the patient for the first vital hour or two.

"All night," Mac insisted. "Let me stay all night."

Red had begun to be wise about these two. Recently he had been so wrapped up in his own affairs he hadn't noticed the obvious, that other lovers existed within his orbit.

"How is he, Red?" Mac pleaded. "I don't seem to be able to decide for myself. I might not be a doctor at this moment."

"I know, Mac, honey. When anything hits home we can't think quite as straight. He lost a lotta blood and his pulse is weak. But I've never known Roy ail much and he must have a lotta resistance stored up somewheres."

An hour later Zarek came in, his face weary, his eyes very bright.

"Thank you, even if . . ." Mac gulped.

"Do not thank me for anything," the surgeon forbade her. "I will never forgive myself if the effendi dies. He should not have wanted for attention in his direst hour after the years he has sacrificed himself for others. I have seen myself through your eyes, little one, and I am a small man compared with Roy effendi. You chose rightly, and God grant he lives to give you the happiness you both deserve. Oh, Mac, when I remember you with that knife in your hand . . . !" he fell forward on to his knees, his head in his hands.

"Don't think about it," Mac said gently. "Let's concentrate all our thoughts on Roy. I think his pulse is a little stronger," she told him.

Zarek put his finger on the limp wrist.

"It is still like a bird which may take flight at any moment. Oh, why does he not show us some sign!"

"Go and rest," Mac said kindly. "I will let you know the instant there is any change."

"It is strange you are calmer than I," Zarek pondered. "To you his pulse is stronger when to me it is not. Have you some secret knowledge denied to me?"

"Perhaps I have," Mac smiled mistily. "A woman's intuition, perhaps, but I suddenly know Roy isn't going to die. He couldn't die with us all as one for him. When we were divided it was all so wrong, but it came right in time and you'll see, Zarek. You'll see."

"I would wish to share your confidence," sighed the other, comforted nevertheless, and wandered away from the scene with hands deep in his pockets.

*   *   *

As though at least one had injected the life-force into his consciousness, the Superintendent showed the first signs of rallying during the early hours of the morning. He lightly fingered the hand holding his, and Mac's heart rose in her throat, as she saw a flickering of the eyelids and heard a breath quickly caught in the surprise of pain.

"Roy?" she questioned him softly.

He made another effort and opened eyes stupid with drugs, then he slid back into semi-consciousness. He held on to the hand, though, as at a life-line.

Thereafter life became interesting to him again from the viewpoint of a patient. Long before he could enter into conversation he studied the effects of the pain-killing drugs his nurses injected into him. They really did nullify discomfort, he was gratified to note, and when the sleeping-drug was added in the evening there were moments of near-bliss before the mind entered the dark cavern of enforced unconsciousness. Struggling up to the surface again in the early hours of the morning was not nearly so pleasant: sometimes sensation awoke before all else, and one became disembodied pain seeking for a means of expression. Roy decided this was caused by inner cells of the brain stirring into activity before the whole, and wondered if he had discovered a subject worthy of investigation.

He also learned from experience that a patient needs more than efficient attention in his worst hour: he needs affection. The softness in the voice, the warmth in the eyes of the person bending over you mean more in that moment than all the diplomas in the world. Roy had been more conscious of one voice and one pair of eyes than any other: he learned to listen for the one and to make the effort of raising leaden lids to regard the other. In this one person he found encouragement and a sympathy which went beyond his comprehension. During those first days following the operation he didn't recognize an individual, merely a physical anodyne, but as the link with life grew stronger he learned to anticipate Mac's visits with a welling of pleasure he hadn't known since his boyhood.

Rapid physical improvement meant that he saw less of her, however. The work of the hospital had to go on as it was without its Superintendent, and a food-poisoning epidemic meant that Mac's department was fully occupied both with the cause of the sickness and its effects.

Roy was subjected to the normal hospital routine and not allowed visitors after seven o'clock in the evening. He would fretfully lie thinking of the staff taking their dinner without him, wondering what they talked about and how they occupied themselves thereafter.

It was the twelfth day after the operation before Zarek decided to remove the stitches from Roy's wound and allow him to sit up a little. There was a carefree air about the staff dinner-table that evening. It had been mail-day, and if there was not much conversation it was because all were thinking about their own personal friends and the news from "home". Mac pondered upon the news of Barney's impending marriage and was glad for him: his letter ran rather like an itinerary, as though falling in love, getting engaged and married was a matter of dates rather than emotions. Barney sounded so solid about it all, so heavy-footedly earth-bound that she could not but feel a little sorry for the girl who would irrevocably be tied to him.

Fiona was happily thinking of the letter her in-laws had sent her, welcoming her into the family circle with a thousand-dollar cheque.

What a present indeed!

"Send it back, Fi," Red had told her immediately, "tell 'em you cain't be bought any more'n I can."

At first she had looked at him in amazement, then her voice came quietly and obediently:

"Very well, Red."

That was not quite the end of the matter, though: Fiona sat through dinner remembering Red's sudden swoop on her, his lips in her hair, her ear, blotchily on her mouth, and his words ringing, "You're a real wife, Fi! A real wife! You didn't jib. You just did it because I said. Oh, honey, I'll take you on the best damnedest honeymoon a girl ever had when we can get away from here. . . ."

When! she thought ruefully.

". . . the States . . . I'll show you off to the family. They'll see what a prize I got for a wife. An' we'll call on your mom on the way back and play cricket with your upstage cousins. . . ."

Fiona laughed aloud during the fish course, and then apologized hastily.

Zarek frowned, wondering if Sister was a thought-reader and found his private meditations amusing. He had written to the Professor of Surgery who had been his tutor, and this day had received a reply to his letter. The girl Halyma was still unattached, well formed, unblemished and comely according to her father. It was difficult to dispose of educated daughters, he complained, and the girl had just recently returned from a finishing school in Cairo where she had learned a great deal of unnecessary foolishness. If Zarek was interested in the girl he had better act quickly and come to Khartoum at the earliest. In the meanwhile perhaps he could send pictures of himself for the girl's eyes. Modern girls were inclined to the belief that they could choose their own husbands, but so far Halyma had not met anybody who interested her among their social equals. Zarek had been picturing himself in this pose and that when Fiona had laughed suddenly. He knew the Superintendent was an expert photographer, and he would ask him—in secret—to take pictures of him; on horseback in his robes (Zarek had once seen an old film of Valentino in *The Sheikh*, and didn't think he had much to fear if women liked that sort of thing!) in his white coat in front of the hospital; in British bush-shirt and shorts, to show off his admirable calves to advantage, and in full evening dress, for if Halyma was "finished" she was obviously capable of doing some entertaining.

Red pondered on the hospital's business, wondering how he could break it to the Superintendent that the Government Commission had now sent a copy of their report, an excellent document in testimonial, but unfortunately declining regretfully to increase financial support for El Belada.

"A good thing for us Ali fadal and Wazili decided their

lot was not with us," Red pondered. "As it is, I'm sure Roy is standing Osman's salary out of his own pocket."

It was one of the best things Roy had ever done when he decided to employ the shattered Osman. Here, again, he had made a friend for life. Osman didn't mind how menial the task allotted to him provided he was trusted to do it. Sometimes he acted as orderly when one of these worthies was absent. Then he came in close contact with Sister Haifeh, dwelling on the bright, black eyes and the pale coffee of her face with an increasing interest in living. Osman was an old-young man: prison had turned his days into weeks, his months into years, and at thirty-two his hair was grizzled and failing, his skin wrinkled and his nerves shot to bits. But the young man in him could still be recalled in the soft glance from a woman's eyes, and even Sister Haifeh was discovering a certain pleasure outside of antiseptic bathrooms and well-scrubbed patients.

Osman's eyes lit up therefore as he saw Sister high-stepping across the compound towards the party on the veranda. He was invited to take coffee with her in her room at nine o'clock and hoped she wasn't coming to cancel the appointment. She did not look at him, however, as she went up to the Deputy Superintendent.

"Doctor Bellinger, I can't get off duty for the Superintendent. He's being very annoying. He won't take his capsules; he won't get into bed; and he is full of complaints. Will you come and speak to him?"

"He's obviously getting better," Red grinned, "but he must be restrained a little longer for his own sake."

"Of course he must," Mac agreed, rather too vehemently.

Red's tongue was in his cheek as he asked her, "How are you fixed for time, Mac? I have a bit of correspondence to attend to. If you can settle that man down for Sister—"

"I'll certainly settle him," she promised grimly, folding her napkin, and marched off once more towards the hospital.

"He's in the right hands now," Red observed with a deep sigh of satisfaction.

The obstreperous patient was surprisingly docile, however, when he beheld his visitor, her eyes gleaming with purpose.

"Good night, Sister!" she called o·er·her shoulder. "I'll see to Doctor Kingsland." She closed the door. "Now, into bed with you at once! How dare you keep Sister on duty after hours? You're going to take your capsules and go to sleep."

"Yes, Doctor." He slid into bed looking somehow very boyish. "I'm sorry to be such a nuisance. May I have some lemonade, please? There's a bottle in my locker."

Mac felt for the bottle and drew it out, still trying to look severe.

"There! Anything else?"

"Yes," he said in a most un-docile voice and pulled her down on to the bed. "You can keep your capsules from now on. I want a good night kiss, instead!"

"My! You *are* better!" she smiled with a sudden flush, remembering the last time they had kissed. "I don't think I should encourage you in these temperature-raising pursuits, not without permission."

"Grrrrr! I' ve had enough of hospitals and doctors from this end, my girl. I want you in a purely unprofessional capacity from now on. You came in today with Zarek and looked at me like a—a pathologist. How dare you!"

"If Nurse Meryam comes in I'm going to look a little too unprofessional, don't you think?"

"Nurse Meryam knows better than to interrupt us. You are the victim of a deep, dark plot, my girl: this is the spider's hideout and you are the sacrificial fly."

"You mean you planned I should come here?"

"I did. I told Red earlier that I was going to find it difficult to settle down tonight, and that *he* needn't bother coming to rock me. Do you know the moon's at full?"

"But we can't see the moon in here!"

"I know. But my diary says it's full moon, and that's the time a man ought to be with his girl."

Mac lowered her eyes, then looked up uncertainly.

"Are you sure you're comfortable with me like this?"

"I'm quite comfortable." His eyes were warm and dark above her. "How about you, Mac? Can you ever feel as we did at Wadi Nahla again?"

"I can and do, Roy."

"Without a swim in the sea of tears?"

"I took that plunge while you were ill. I nearly lost you, don't forget. I don't want to go through that again."

"I couldn't have died happily without you, Mac. But I got a shock too when I wanted you and you weren't around that night. Where were you?"

"I was with—Zarek," she told him, lowering her eyes for a moment. "It's all right, Roy. He knows and he has accepted us."

"Splendid. The padre came to see me today."

"Yes, I know. We had a little service of thanksgiving for your recovery, Moslems and Christians together."

189

"He's coming back tomorrow in case we need him."

His voice was almost casual now, as is the case when something of tremendous importance has to be said.

"How 'need' him, Roy?" she asked innocently, then her face suddenly suffused and she slid forward against his chest while a glory of possession flooded through his being.

"I can't bear not to have you around ever again, Mac. You'll have to marry me, I'm afraid, and get the bungalow ready for your husband's return in a day or two. You're not raising any objections, are you?"

"None," came in muffled tones from his heart.

"Good! Now kiss me, and to hell with the pathologist for a moment!"

Nurse Meryam opened the door quietly and observed:
"Doctor Immacula, I think you should go now!"

Nobody heard her, however, and with an indulgent smile the girl hurried away, carrying the happiness she had just witnessed along with her into the night which lay ahead.

THE END

Romance is Beautiful

Get to the HEART of HARLEQUIN

HARLEQUIN READER SERVICE is your passport to the Heart of Harlequin ...

if You...

♥ enjoy the mystery and adventure of the world's leading romantic-fiction publisher.

♥ want to keep up-to-date on all of our new monthly releases — eight original Romances and four Harlequin Presents.

♥ are interested in valuable reissues of bestselling back titles

♥ are intrigued by exciting, money-saving jumbo volumes

♥ would like to enjoy North America's unique monthly Harlequin Magazine — available **ONLY** through Harlequin Reader Service

♥ are excited by **anything new** under the Harlequin sun

· MORE DETAILS ▶

then Don't Miss...

any of the exciting details offered by the Harlequin Reader Service's INFORMATION PLEASE. It costs you nothing to receive our news bulletins and intriguing brochures. Highlighted in each information package are the services offered, the publications available and a host of other things that could mean a great deal more reading pleasure for you. It's simple to find out all about us — without any obligation, of course. All you have to do is send us your name and address on the coupon below, and we'll be happy to tell you all about some of the things we do for Harlequin readers.

Get to the Heart of Harlequin, today!